PAUL MICOU

THE LAST WORD

BANTAM PRESS

LONDON · NEW YORK · TORONTO · SYDNEY · AUCKLAND

TRANSWORLD PUBLISHERS LTD
61–63 Uxbridge Road, London W5 5SA

TRANSWORLD PUBLISHERS (AUSTRALIA) PTY LTD
15–25 Helles Avenue, Moorebank, NSW 2170

TRANSWORLD PUBLISHERS (NZ) LTD
3 William Pickering Drive, Albany, Auckland

Published 1993 by Bantam Press
a division of Transworld Publishers Ltd
Copyright © Paul Micou 1993

The right of Paul Micou to be identified
as the author of this work has been asserted in accordance
with sections 77 and 78 of the Copyright Designs and Patents
Act 1988.

All of the characters in this book
are fictitious, and any resemblance
to actual persons, living or dead,
is purely coincidental.

A catalogue record for this book is available from the
British Library

ISBN 0–593–026802

Typeset in 11½ on 14pt Bembo by
Chippendale Type Ltd, Otley, West Yorkshire.
Printed in Great Britain by
Mackays of Chatham, PLC, Chatham, Kent.

For Anna U

1

A few years ago, in the summer, I was summoned back to my home town. The message that finally reached me was a curious one, from my sister Jean. It expressed a vague concern, a need for assistance, and it mentioned in passing the ill health of my Uncle Ian. It was nothing new to be worried about Uncle Ian, but it was a departure for anyone to take action. I am afraid to say that my sister had some difficulty in tracking me down; my so-called career required me to travel frequently, and randomly. I found that I was flattered to have been judged a competent enough member of the Richmond clan to help out, and quite happy to go home for the first time in three or four years.

I come from the pretty, New England seaside town of Gaw-passat. Our jealous neighbours say, 'Go pàst it.' The name Gawpassat means 'Don't lie down and fall asleep on the slimy rocks by the water, lest the tides come in and carry you away.' Our town is wealthy, thanks to the men and women in suits who drive down the three hillsides to the train station and go into the city each morning, bringing money home in briefcases at night. Those who do not commute benefit indirectly from the suited ones: Gawpassat's schools are excellent, its works and services modern, and its ten policemen equipped with the latest weapons. Gawpassatans are liberal-minded and tolerant, in part because they have so few problems of their own. There are twelve thousand of them, and they are pleased with themselves.

Gawpassat has a Yacht Club, of course, and one popular harbour-side restaurant. It keeps the tourists away by not having a proper public beach. The climate is extreme, always. There exists the usual small-town proportion of gossips and busybodies. Some people, as everywhere, are richer than others (in a couple of cases far, far richer). We have our cranks and our crazies, our lovable old ladies, and our delightfully privileged young.

I spent selfish years pretending to disdain my home town, but soon after I moved away I realized how much I had taken Gawpassat for granted. It is just possible, I now see, that Gawpassat was the most pleasant, democratic, secure and prosperous small community in the world. The town was practically unimprovable. It did not even lack for scandal and spice: several years ago the town was rocked with amusement by a transvestite named Rick; and, of course, they've always had my Uncle Ian.

2

I was greeted at the airport by a limousine and my least favourite weather: oven hot and jungle humid. I had not been expecting a chauffeur to meet me, and I assumed he was one of Uncle Ian's. The young driver said his name was Francesco, but I didn't quite believe him. He tried to talk to me from the front seat, which I hate. I told him to close the partition. Even the limousine's powerful air conditioner couldn't entirely cut the heat and humidity. It was one of the Gawpassatan's pleasures to know that there was no cooler place on the coast than where he lived, but in that kind of muggy, oppressive heat it wasn't much of a consolation.

Home was exactly one hour's drive from the airport; it was not a pretty journey. During that hour there was no sense in looking up from one's work, from a newspaper, from the limousine's television. The scenery did not become remotely appetizing until one hundred yards after leaving the freeway for Gawpassat, an exit ramp shared with two other, larger towns. There, a canopy of leaves welcomed those lucky enough to have business or residence in the area. Suddenly, the road smoothed out. Big clapboard houses hove into view. A fine sand lined the streets and gathered against stone walls. In the summer, the smell of freshly mown grass mingled with the perennial essence of brine. It was so quiet and so rich, back home in Gawpassat. My little town amazed me.

I asked my driver, the one who called himself Francesco, to take me on a nostalgic tour. All was as sleepy as I had fondly remembered. A new batch of youths sulked in the same places we used to: outside the liquor store; on the short length of sea wall near the Yacht Club; on the banks of the mighty Gawpassat River itself (actually a two-foot-wide trickle, in summer). Young mothers fed their children ice cream in the park. Old Mr Casinove sat outside his hardware store in the shade of a picnic umbrella. Only a short stretch of shops was new, and even that, thanks to the strictest imaginable zoning regulations, seemed authentic enough to trigger childhood memories I could not possibly have had.

We have a Minuteman statue in our town centre. Our Minuteman takes a lot of abuse from marauding vandals. He is sometimes discovered wearing funny hats or pumpkins on his head, as well as dark glasses and fluorescent paint. For some reason the hooligans across town lines think they are desecrating a symbol of Gawpassat alone, rather than a monument to our shared Revolution.

3

On Lincoln Street, a mile from my parents' house, we drove past a girl I assumed was hitchhiking back into town, although she wasn't holding out her thumb. I told Francesco to turn around and pick her up. I had the most vivid memory of myself, at exactly that spot, wearing a baseball uniform, trying to hitch a ride to the High School field. I remember my cleats sinking into the melting asphalt. I remember cursing the two or three cars that drove past me without stopping. I even remember the smell of the plastic upholstery of Mrs Hackney's new station wagon when I finally got a lift.

Francesco asked me if I was sure I wanted to stop for the girl, as if he suspected the probity of my motives. I told him of course I wanted to stop – I'd said so, hadn't I? – and he did. It isn't easy to turn a stretch limousine around in Lincoln Street. When Francesco finally succeeded and we wound back down the hill, the girl was still there. She looked about twelve years old. She wore beach clothes and carried a beach bag. She was freckled and pretty, the way hillside Gawpassatan girls invariably were, and I could sense that Francesco really did think I was an ungentlemanly pervert for wanting to pick her up. I suppose I have to admit that the sight of a long black limousine with smoked windows picking up a little blonde girl on a leafy hillside street might have struck some as out of the ordinary. At the time my thoughts were so nostalgic and pure that this sinister tableau never occurred to me. It had, however, occurred to the girl. She refused to get into the car. Francesco gave me an 'I told you so' look over his shoulder. I said a few words to the girl, trying to change her mind and to defend my honour, which only left me sounding more like a sociopath.

'Look,' I finally said, leaning out into the heat. 'I'm Matthew Richmond. I live at the top of the hill. You know me, don't you?'

'You don't live there,' said the girl.

She was quite right, of course. I hadn't lived there permanently since before the girl was born.

'My parents do, is what I meant,' I said. 'I've come home to visit.'

'Good,' said the girl. 'Anyway, I don't want a ride. I'm not hitchhiking.'

'What are you doing, then?'

'None of your business.'

She sounded awfully tough for such a young girl. I suppose I should have been proud of her and her parents for such a pre-emptive attitude towards strangers, but it saddened me. Gawpassat really was the kind of place where you wouldn't mind your children hitchhiking, and not a lot of towns could say that.

'Back up the hill,' I told Francesco. 'Let's try going home again.'

We had to drive all the way in to the centre of town to turn around. When we came back up the hill the girl was still standing in the same spot. She gave the car a mean, squinty look as we oozed past her.

4

Gawpassat is built on three hills: Black Hill, White Hill and Gray Hill. I was told they got their names from the way they looked at dawn in late autumn, probably to colour-blind people. My parents lived on Gray Hill, right up at the top. From my old bedroom – and from most of the other bedrooms, for that matter – we had a terrific view of the ocean. The house itself was one of those brick, ivy-covered quasi-mansions with crenellated walls and turrets here and there. Its grounds fell away steeply towards rocky cliffs and the water. In winter we could toboggan four hundred yards straight down from the main porch, all the way to the trees over the cliffs. In summer, my father and I used to hit golf balls up the same hill, never endangering the house. Also on the grounds were a swimming pool and a couple of reasonably good clay tennis courts.

We were not quite so rich as we looked. Few people knew that the Gray Hill house actually belonged to Uncle Ian. No-one in town could believe that my father was a mere cartographer. It wasn't just our house, it was the way he dressed. He wore dark, heavy, double-breasted suits and a walrus moustache. He walked with a cane that was not entirely justified by the stroke he had suffered. I wouldn't say that he was in the least eccentric; these were just the clothes and the attitude he had inherited from my grandfather, the manners of an antique family.

My mother looked just as patrician, if not more so, by which I mean she knew how to wear pearls. She chose to exercise her modern right to employment, as a university professor, which confused her colleagues no end when they were invited over for tennis or swimming or cucumber sandwiches. She taught economics, and the others in her department reckoned she must have solved a few key problems in her field to live the way she did.

That wasn't the case at all. My mother's younger sister, Charlotte, had married Uncle Ian; Uncle Ian owned the Gray Hill house, the White Hill house and the Black Hill house – all three. No-one in our family thought this arrangement was entirely fair until Uncle Ian said he would like to lend the Gray Hill house to my parents, when I was two years old. Evidently he never needed the house after that, or forgot that he ever owned it. He loaned the White Hill house as well, to his only, older sister. That is the only really huge house in Gawpassat, which Uncle Ian and his sister used as a research institute: the White Hill house was where people teased the meaning out of my Uncle Ian's Word.

5

At the top of Lincoln Street there is an unostentatious wrought-iron gate surrounded by giant rhododendrons. These were in full bloom as Francesco guided the car into the asphalt drive. I thought I heard Francesco whistle as my parents' house rose into sight. The place seems to have quite a majestic façade, until the first-time visitor realizes that the front door is only a few dozen yards away. At a mile, it would have been a splendid house indeed.

There were no other cars in the drive, nor any visible in the three open garages. I could hear the distant buzz of a mower: the size of our lawn was such that it kept a rota of teenagers busy daily, throughout the summer growing months. I asked Francesco to leave my bag at the front door, and enquired about the arrangements he had made for his payment. He paused just long enough before replying that I knew he was on Uncle Ian's regular account, so I merely tipped him as I sent him on his way.

I walked round to the back of the house to the spot where

my family had kept a spare key since the day they moved in thirty years before: in a flowerpot next to the back door, the first place any self-respecting burglar would look. We had never been robbed (Gawpassat just wasn't that kind of town). I retrieved the key and wiped off rusty, wet soil with my fingertips. It was so hot that I regretted not having taken off my jacket, fine linen though it was. Before unlocking the door I loosened my tie and shook some hot air down the neck of my shirt. It was as I did so that I noticed a shape on the lawn through the usual moogly summer mist.

It was another girl. This one was about the same age as the hitchhiker – it was hard to tell exactly from fifty yards away – but not dressed for the beach. She wore what I associated with English Victorian summer dress: white and frilly, long-sleeved, high necked. The only reason I had the impression that she was a young girl, not a woman, was that her feet were disproportionately large. She stood there in the heat paying no attention to me. I knew she wasn't a statue because she twirled an open parasol on one shoulder. I thought she must be a niece or cousin of mine; I had been out of touch, after all. My relatives had a way of putting on poses every now and then, like my father with his unnecessary cane. You have to do *something*, if you live in a large house.

6

There was no-one inside the house, unless they were hiding. I went to the front door, retrieved my bag, and took it to the bottom of the main staircase. I removed my jacket and draped it over my bag. I went to the kitchen and filled a glass with tap water. I took my drink out to the main enclosed verandah, and opened the French windows. I kept the outer screens closed against insects. I stood still for a minute or more trying to be nostalgic, then sat down in a wicker chair and took a sip of water. In dripping heat like that, one is made conscious of nature's rationale for eyebrows.

The lawn, patchier and browner than I remembered, fell away towards the water. The heat seemed to have silenced all the usual birds and insects, leaving only a vague fizz in the air of nature slowly exhaling and inhaling. A boy riding our ancient mower rounded a corner, wearing white shorts and sneakers, sitting in the shade of a beach umbrella affixed to the machine. The smells of grass and sea and my own sweat were utterly familiar to me: the smells of my home town, Gawpassat, in summertime. I wondered where everyone had gone.

I heard the decrescendo of the mower engine being extinguished. A minute later the youth who had been driving it appeared in front of me, on the other side of the screen. I offered him a glass of water, and opened the screen to let him in. He looked about sixteen, was already almost my height, and had grass cuttings stuck to his sweaty chest and legs. I went and got him a glass of water, as well as a towel. He was polite, as Gawpassatans tend to be, and thanked me in the proper way. He sipped his water slowly, like a trained athlete. Each of us remarked once on the terrific heat. I could see by his expression – he could almost not look at me, in fact – what he would ask next.

'You're Matthew Richmond,' he said. 'Aren't you?'

I nodded.

'Wow,' said the boy. 'They show us the film in school every year. There's a picture of you in the entrance and everything.'

'I've seen it.'

'There's a display case, a map, more pictures, a model—'

'I've seen those, too.'

The boy wiped his face with the towel, then his head and his shoulders and his chest.

'Wow,' he said again. 'You're famous.'

'I wouldn't say that. Down at the High School, maybe. What's your name?'

'Don. Tell me what it was really like.'

'It wasn't as hot as here, for one thing,' I said.

What I had done that got so much attention down at the

14

High School wasn't really all that interesting. I had made a decision, right out of college, to attempt something ever so slightly out of the ordinary, and to try to make a good job of it. I looked around me to see what it was that I was good at, and landed on only one outstanding talent: I was good at walking uphill. I had proved this over and over again, walking briskly home, uphill, from school. I had also climbed great big mountains, and been taken along on an unsuccessful but educational McKinley expedition by my climbing mentor from a neighbouring town. So, I said to myself, what is a reasonably sophisticated ambition for a young man who feels that he knows a thing or two about walking uphill? Mount Everest, was the obvious answer. You could get tougher, but you couldn't get higher. Objectively, Everest remained tops. The expedition took three years: two and three-quarters to get there, a quarter to climb to the summit.

Climbing Everest was like most things in life: first one had to get the money together. Uncle Ian was an obvious financing target, but I knew Everest would not be his favoured type of project. He might have sent me on a quest for the Holy Grail at three times the cost, but Everest, for Uncle Ian, was too secular, too physical. I had to go the usual sponsorship route, through equipment manufacturers, magazines, television producers and so on. The trouble was, Everest had been climbed in so many ways, by children and the elderly, blindfolded and one-legged, that it strained the imagination to devise an original angle. New routes were out of the question – I wanted adventure, not adversity. I took what my friends thought was a cynical way out, which was to pander to my country's great enthusiasm for things racial, and offer to bring along the first man or woman of African extraction to reach the summit. I had a partner in mind, of course. He was a former classmate and one-time ice-climbing partner of mine named Marcus Field, whom I did not particularly like. Luckily I knew from experience that whoever spent a few weeks alone with me in the cold would end up as a lifelong enemy anyway. What did it matter if we started off disliking each other?

Marcus was an ambitious man, and at first he didn't take to the idea of wasting a couple of years to climb no matter how high a mountain. Still, I was able to make him see the potential of his successful assault on Everest. He sighed, he thought it over, he sighed some more. He called me conniving, greedy, racist and unscrupulous, but he thanked me for thinking of him first. He said he'd just wrap up some paperwork – turning down the eighteen law schools that had accepted him, telling the Rhodes Scholar guys that it was all off for now, begging the business schools to stop sending him their junk mail – and he would be right with me.

It isn't going too far to say that there was a mutual antagonism between me and Marcus. At the very least we had a sort of indifference towards one another. I thought he was arrogant, and that most of his supposed talents were overrated. I'm willing to admit to certain prejudices, and one of them is against fellows who wear white scarves. Marcus wore white scarves in college; that seemed to me patently wrong. Why he took against me in those early days, I'm not sure; an accusation of standoffishness would probably not have been misplaced. Certainly, I was envious.

None of that mattered after Marcus accepted my invitation. He proved to be a businesslike and often charismatic fund raiser. One minute we were vague acquaintances speaking on the telephone, the next we shared an office in my parents' house talking to Vortex and West Wind and Foremost, sounding like seasoned mountaineers and eyeing each other nervously to see who would laugh first.

The rest of the story is so tedious it merits only a summary. We trained – unnecessarily, as it turned out. We tried to cut down on our smoking. We piled up money and gloated. We sweated out visas. Marcus worked part-time at a computer company in the city. I taught sailing and tennis down at the Club. We flew out to where the mountains are. We hiked to the base camp where our supplies awaited us. We climbed Everest, just like that: one foot in front of the other. We enjoyed perfect weather. We photographed each other on the summit. We walked back down and out again. It all happened quickly – so quickly that we almost panicked during the descent when we realized that nothing newsworthy had occurred. Marcus offered to throw me down a crevasse, which would really have turned a profit for him. We wrote a book.

7

Don, the lawnmower boy, finished his water and went away. I wondered when a family member would show up, and which one it would be. I had an angry sister and a kind sister, respectively two and five years older. Melissa was the kind one. Jean was the angry one. Jean chose angry fields of work. She had danced angrily as a girl, she had photographed angrily as a young woman; angrily, of late, she had bred angry dogs. Melissa, the kind one, seemed incapable of impure thought. God knows how her brain was organized in order to work the way it did. Ever since she was about fifteen years old everyone wanted her to have a large number of children so that they might benefit from her saint-like patience. She did not disappoint, but waited like a well-brought-up girl until she was twenty-one before marrying and conceiving on the same day.

Like any good family, there lurked in our history one Great Unspoken Tragedy: another sister, no longer with us. Claire died in a yachting accident at thirteen – not the usual boom to the back of the head, but the far rarer strangulation by main sheet, falling overboard and being dragged out to the open ocean by the neck. As must always be the case when a child dies, Claire was soon deified by the rest of the family. She was alluded to so reverently by my mother – but never directly nor by name – that there was no doubt in our minds that Claire would have been the brightest, the most beautiful, the most talented Richmond of all time. We bought this line, I think. In any case, Claire's legend grew with every dishonour of her survivors.

For years, my angry sister Jean and my kind sister Melissa and I used to fantasize morbidly, based on the expanding aura of our departed sister, about what Claire might be doing had she lived.

'By now she would be an environmental epidemiologist,' Jean suggested, when Claire would have been only twenty-three years old.

'No doubt,' I agreed. 'Having given up on the crassness and materialism of being a Hollywood starlet.'

'Please,' my kind sister Melissa might say, covering her ears, 'how *can* you be sarcastic about her?'

Claire's death lent a certain glamour to me and my sisters. Gawpassatans were unaccustomed – and therefore attracted – to grief. There were other deaths in town, almost always by automobile, but none could compete with Claire's grisly and rather mythological end. Boys at school used to speculate, within my hearing, about whether or not the ocean had stripped my dead sister of her clothes, or even her flesh; or whether the family had concocted the whole story to cover up some unmentionable lapse of morality on my sister's part.

8

Someone had come inside the house, through the front door. Too hot and sticky to stand up, I stayed where I was on the verandah. I heard the person walk across the main hall to the kitchen, and drop what sounded like two full grocery bags on the counter. I wondered lazily if I could tell the footfalls of my sisters apart, and decided that I could. Jean's would be quick and loud, Melissa's slower and muted. I listened carefully when the person walked back through the hall, and decided Melissa had come home.

Like all perfect children, Melissa had not moved far away; she lived halfway up White Hill. She had married a bland but well-meaning lawyer named Reed. She had at least eight or nine, possibly even ten children, though she was still just thirty-seven years old. She would probably have a few more, then begin adopting. It follows from all of her frantic procreating that Melissa was an optimist. Certainly, she was distracted by her endless labours from the alarms of the wider world.

I remained on the verandah, in the heat. I had reached an impossible social impasse, something Gawpassatans hate: to get up now and greet my sister, whom I had not seen for more than three years, would suggest that I hadn't been impatient to lay eyes on her; to wait longer might imply some long-held grudge or inexplicable bad temper. I thought this over, and decided to pretend to be asleep. I sank in my chair and slumped my shoulders. I turned my head to face the entrance to the verandah, and half closed my eyes. If Melissa had noticed my bag and jacket at the bottom of the staircase, she would already have called out my name. She thought she was alone. I heard her go into the downstairs bathroom. After she had washed her hands she came back out again. She sighed. She went back into the kitchen and began to unpack groceries. She hummed a nursery rhyme.

I didn't like the bind I found myself in. If I tried to get up and cross the front hall and burst through the swinging door into the kitchen, I would scare the life out of my sister. I thought and I thought, and I came up with a solution I was proud of. I got up, I went outside, I circled all the way round the house to the front, and rang the doorbell: a noise Melissa would be comfortable with. She met me at the door, I gave her three years' worth of hug, and she never seemed to notice – at least she never mentioned – that my bag and jacket had preceded me.

9

'I can't believe it's you,' said Melissa, holding me by the elbows at arm's length. 'What are you doing here, out of the blue?'

'Out of the blue? But I was summoned. Jean asked me to come. Didn't she tell you?'

'She certainly didn't. What is this all about?'

I replied that I had very little idea, but that Jean's tone – and the mention of Uncle Ian's health – had made me feel that my fraternal duty lay in Gawpassat. I thought I had done the right thing, by not asking too many questions.

'Where have you come from?' Melissa asked me.

'From Dublin. Well, from London, actually, but I had to stop for a couple of days in Dublin.'

'What on earth were you doing in Dublin?'

'It's all too boring. Wow, you look terrific, Mel. I keep expecting you to get big and mom-like. Look at you – so thin.'

Melissa was slightly built; at twelve she had looked exactly like the girl who had so rudely turned down my offer of a ride on Lincoln Street. She had started her family so early that I didn't really have a clear memory of her as a young woman. She was so thin that when pregnant – which she appeared not to be at the moment, at least not heavily so – she looked like an egg on legs. Now she wore flat-soled shoes and baggy clothes, as if to ease the transition to her next pregnancy.

It was Melissa's turn to appraise me.

'It can't be that sunny in Dublin,' she said.

'No.'

'I meant your tan.'

'A round or two of golf,' I said.

'Come on, come inside,' my sister said, as if it weren't equally my house. We went back to the verandah where I had spoken to the lawnmower boy. Melissa looked surprisingly cheerful for someone with so many chores to do, and for someone who had no idea why her younger brother had flown the Atlantic to be there with her. Also, Melissa didn't sweat.

I asked her about the girl in the white dress on the lawn. She said it couldn't have been one of hers, they were all accounted for. She had the night off from the family, and had brought over some groceries to have dinner with Jean on neutral ground. Jean hadn't mentioned me at all. The parents were in California for a week, looking at primitive arts and crafts to donate to the elementary school. They would return in two days.

'I bought enough food for all of us,' Melissa said.

'Oh, fine.'

'Fresh artichokes.'

'Good.'

'And little minute steaks and new potatoes—'

'Marvellous—'

'—and ice cream.'

'Great.'

'You're hungry, I hope?'

'I didn't eat on the plane. I'll be starved. Whenever it is we're eating, that is. How are the children?'

Melissa seemed not to have heard my question, which was just as well. I couldn't remember more than two or three of the children's names. One of them was named Matthew, after me. I asked Melissa if she wanted something to drink, saying that I was going to get myself a refill of water.

'Oh, I'm sorry,' said Melissa, as if she were my hostess. 'I'll be right back.'

I sat there listening to the crickets, watching the sky go all gaudy, feeling the temperature drop by the second. The air was so still that not a single one of our millions of green leaves was disturbed.

Melissa returned with my water and sat down. I repeated my question about her children, my nieces and nephews; again she ignored or did not hear me. She certainly looked far away, sitting upright, her hands folded stiffly in the baggy cotton of her lap, her face turned out to sea. She blinked about three times more often than I thought necessary, and she had the makings of a spiritual smile at the corners of her lips.

'Did you have a chance', she asked, still not looking at me, 'to see the lobster-pot museum?'

'I beg your pardon?'

'The new museum, in the new library annexe. It's only temporary, of course.'

'An exhibition?'

'Yes, of lobster pots.'

'Sort of the . . . the *history* of lobster pots?'

21

'Exactly.' She turned to look at me, now that we had communicated so thoroughly.

'Have lobster pots, I mean, lobster pots can't have changed all that much.'

'You're right, they haven't. We all found that very interesting.'

'You and the children?'

'Yes.'

'Well, no, I didn't have a chance to see it. I came almost straight here, after a quick tour of the centre. Nothing seems to have changed.'

'Except for the lobster-pot museum.'

'Right.'

I had never been very close to Melissa.

10

With so few running costs – thanks to the generosity or forgetfulness of my Uncle Ian – my parents had begun to spend more of their time and money playing at philanthropy. The trip to California Melissa had mentioned was a perfect example of their recently monomaniacal dedication to the improvement of Gawpassat's already stellar institutions. They would return laden with southwestern souvenirs, and organize an unveiling in front of the elementary school faculty and student body. They would appear wealthier than they were or had a right to be, but I never believed that was their aim. They thought primitive arts and crafts really were a valuable addition to the Gawpassat school system's decor.

I thought then – and I am still partial to the theory – that they embarked on such enterprises to excuse themselves from Uncle Ian's company. He had always tended to overwhelm my insular parents, and to demand somewhat more than was the prescribed due of former in-laws (Uncle Ian had divorced my Aunt Charlotte; she had died twenty years later). Everyone else in the community at large would have given anything to dine with the Great Man, but my parents weren't as welcoming of his constant attention. For people living in one of his houses there was no way to avoid him short of leaving the area altogether.

I know that in-laws often come as a shock, but I simply cannot imagine what it must have been like for my maternal grandparents when Aunt Charlotte married Uncle Ian. I suppose it was just a giant wave of revulsion followed by awed surprise when Uncle Ian started buying huge houses in beautiful Gawpassat.

My mother and her sister Charlotte were English, which many saw as a possible explanation for the latter's decision to marry Uncle Ian (who was then simply Ian Victor Armstrong): they assumed that as a foreigner she could not really have known how controversial a character she had chosen as a mate. It pains me to think what the folks in the Old Country thought of their two girls marrying first Uncle Ian, then my father. I don't suppose my father would have been all that intolerable to my mother's English family, because native Gawpassatans are for some reason required to be Anglophile well beyond the point of aping English clothes and mannerisms, and they emulate the accent as best they can. Uncle Ian, who was not a native Gawpassatan, would have seemed rougher hewn to the English lot. I have heard stories about his first trip to England with Charlotte, forty years ago or more when, I gather, Americans were actually liked over there.

Uncle Ian had never been to London before, nor, I'm sure, had my grandparents ever been exposed to someone who so thoroughly lived up to the American reputation for innocent optimism. Ian Armstrong was then a young Virginia lawyer with overt political ambitions. From a penniless family, of somewhat gangly and awkward appearance, he must have brought Abraham Lincoln to mind. He had met Charlotte in New York, where she had gone to experience the New World. He was there to hobnob with big-league politicians. One thing I'm certain of is that Ian Armstrong would have been irresistibly charming to an English girl in those days. London must have been awfully unromantic, what with so many men removed from the eligibility scene by death or serious injury or a pressing need to be alone. Ian Armstrong would have seemed so energetic, so positive and so hopeful; old photographs show him to have possessed a cheerful and welcoming smile. The war had left him not just unscathed, but at a peak of physical fitness that would last him well into his forties.

I don't know if people slept together premaritally in those days, but Ian and Charlotte sailed for England together only a few weeks later to announce their betrothal to Charlotte's stunned parents. My mother's strongest recollection of the event is what she called the 'scent of American male' she detected in the bathroom Ian shared with the two girls. They had never had a *man* sleep under their roof before. Perhaps she liked the scent of American male, for it was only months later, on her first visit to her sister and brother-in-law, that my mother met and became engaged to my father.

11

My conversation with Melissa stumbled along, and I soon decided there was something different and strange about her. It wasn't just that eerie half-smile and the non-meeting of the eyes, nor the sudden wide-eyed stares with which she randomly punctuated her sentences – no, the thing that struck me most memorably was her posture. We Richmonds are not supposed to have good posture. We are tall, we have long necks, and we slouch and droop as much as we want to; yet here sat Melissa with a broomstick spine, her hands still folded in her lap as if glued together, and her feet flat on the floor. It was a position I could not have maintained for five minutes, even at gunpoint.

The things she talked about were somewhat odd as well. The lobster-pot museum was only the first in a series of what struck me as far-fetched or irrelevant topics of discussion. She used the words 'marvellous' and 'delightful' over and over again, when 'adequate' or 'better than expected' might have been more apposite. 'Reed planted a marvellous Japanese maple in the churchyard, just delightful. We had a marvellous crowd at the ceremony, all the delightful children's faces, just marvellous.' All of this she uttered in a queer monotone, not looking at me. And then, with a snappy turn of the head and a wide-eyed *stare*, 'Isn't that delightful, Matthew?'

She had never called me Matthew before. My nicknames were 'Top' and 'Matt'; nine times out of ten I was called 'Top', a nickname I earned early on for my fondness for spinning around in circles on the marble floor of the main hall of our house. My parents called me 'Matt' when I had done something wrong, reserving 'Matthew' for the day when I would commit arson or murder.

'That is delightful, *Melissa*,' I said. Her nicknames were 'Mel' and 'Miss'. When she failed to reply, I softened my voice and said, 'Come on, Mel. I missed you. I want to catch up.'

'Oh, look at the time,' she suddenly said, looking at the time on her wrist. 'The show will be starting in a minute. Come on, you can watch with me in the kitchen while I unpack the food.'

We were about to see Uncle Ian's television programme. I followed Melissa into the kitchen, and observed that her bearing remained militarily rigid when she walked. There was a small television on the kitchen counter, which Melissa switched on with a remote control. It offended me that Melissa preferred watching Uncle Ian's television show to grilling her younger brother about his life, and I was not at all curious to see the programme. I knew what it would be like. Someone with too much hair would explain to the viewers that their money would be put to much better use in Uncle Ian's pocket than their own, so much so that something like eternal damnation awaited those who held on to their cash or spent it on anything else.

12

Uncle Ian was in the religion trade. He had capitalized on a phenomenon that he was by no means the first man to detect, i.e. that no-one anywhere in the world had the first clue as to why all of this 'life' or 'existence' business ought to be going on. As a consequence of this universal confusion there was a huge and permanent demand for answers, the simpler the better. Uncle Ian had provided one of these.

Uncle Ian had first hung out his religious-leader shingle before he married my Aunt Charlotte. He still lived in Virginia then, where his law practice had hit hard times, and where no-one's congressional seat looked up for grabs. I honestly think Uncle Ian believed that the founding of a new religion might ease his path into politics, but it didn't work out that way. All that happened, after his first oracular book hit the stands, was that people started throwing money at him. Embarrassed, but gratified nonetheless, Uncle Ian laid plans to take on the rest of the world. For this he needed a headquarters, and he chose the lovely home town of his future brother-in-law up north.

Uncle Ian's book really was a model of the genre. It was entitled *The First Word* and, like all good, seminal religious texts, it claimed divine co-authorship. Founders of religions usually disappear into the mountains or the wilderness before unbosoming themselves of the Truth, and to this rule Uncle Ian was no exception. He wrote his book in a cabin next to a trout stream in the Rockies, or so the story goes, looping his line out over beaver dams between bouts of inspiration. It is a tantalizingly ambiguous text, to be sure, but its lessons are simple enough to be understood by a five-year-old. For the most part Uncle Ian's Twenty Laws follow the more widely known Ten Commandments, having to do with what can and what cannot be considered decent behaviour towards one's fellow man; these are common sense. Where his Laws departed from the Commandments, they sounded like a lot more fun. They had the advantage of being written in modern, not to say vulgar English. His stroke of genius, and prescience, was to suggest to a not yet entirely obese America that to follow his Twenty Laws was not only to gain salvation, but to *lose weight*. This would create yet another fortune for him in years to come.

26

In modern times the founder of religions is well-advised to inject a scientific ingredient into his teachings. In Uncle Ian's case this made calling the White Hill house his Institute of the Word, and having bespectacled men and women in white lab coats walk the grounds toting clipboards and jotting down their observations of the universe from that lovely vantage point. Expensively bound policy statements emerged from the Institute for the perusal of a heathen press. Experts in fields as diverse as poltergeists and marine biology were invited to stay at the Institute for purposes of cogitation: no area of human study was irrelevant to the Word.

The next step for the modern religious leader was to cloak himself in mystery and reclusiveness. At this, my Uncle Ian excelled. Walled up as he was inside the Black Hill house, Uncle Ian was in the perfect position to project an image of secrecy and portent. Like any self-respecting multi-millionaire, he travelled in his own helicopter, so that his Gawpassatan followers could look heavenward as their leader came and went. His helicopter, canary yellow and sporting the crest of the Institute of the Word, had a rather military look to it and was rumoured to be heavily armed. When he came home from the airport he did so from the sea, low over the water, at terrific speed, right over the Yacht Club towards Black Hill; with an aerobatic swerve, he would beat it up the hill and disappear over the treetops into the grounds of his mansion. The people in town would say, 'The Great Man is home.'

13

I wasn't at all sure that I wanted to see Uncle Ian's programme, but Melissa had finished unpacking the food and sat close to the television on a stool she had pulled over from the kitchen table. I stood behind her, next to the sink, and refilled my glass of water from the tap. I almost laughed out loud when I heard the show's theme music, saw the homey set, heard the announcer's voice. This sort of programme normally gave me the creeps, but it was an additional shock to see the sweeping graphics trace out the name of a man I had known all my life, who lived on the next hill, who was related to me by ex-marriage. Uncle Ian's show was nothing like the regular fare of television evangelism, most of which, one had to assume, amounted to unsophisticated self-parody. Uncle Ian's presenters did not go in for histrionics or healing or volcanic eruptions of scripture. They promised nothing. The onus of self-improvement was on the viewer. Perfect people were displayed, and they explained that the Word had at least contributed to, if not caused, their state of emotional quietude and physical repair.

Uncle Ian would not appear on the show in person, of course: he was far too well established as a recluse. His main spokesman was as I imagined he would be – a thick helmet of salt-and-pepper hair over a wide smile of abundant teeth. This fellow, whose name was Frank, told us that we were going to meet two new surprise recruits to Uncle Ian's religion, a man-and-woman, husband-and-wife team of untold celebrity.

I wasn't going to take much more of this. A man in a tracksuit would tell us about the route to salvation through sustained periods of physical exercise and calorie-counting. A long-range presidential candidate would be endorsed. An almost threatening tone would be employed to solicit funds so that this information, and solicitation, could continue to be brought to us. The international news would be interpreted for us by a middle-aged woman with sympathetic eyes and a phenomenal knack for seeing mind-boggling connections in what the uninitiated took to be unrelated events. I shuddered to think of the reading level of most of my fellow viewers.

'Really, Mel,' I said, after perhaps eight minutes of Uncle Ian's programme. 'Mel? Don't you think we've seen about enough of this? Mel? Miss?'

I leaned away from the counter so that I could see her face and attract her attention. I felt the hair stand up on my forearms when I saw her expression. My sister was mesmerized.

14

Gawpassat suffered a second young death while I was growing up, other than my sister Claire's. When I was fifteen years old and theatrically oriented, a girl was killed on the stage of our beautiful High School theatre (Ian Victor Armstrong Hall, actually). Dorothy was her name, and I was in love with her at the time. At fourteen, she was the loveliest and most talented girl in our school: a natural to play Peter Pan.

Our theatrical director, Raymond Furness, outdid himself with the design of Peter Pan's flying machine. The Gawpassat school system had lots of time and money for culture, and no expense was spared on the black-wire trapeze worn by my little Dorothy. There was only one scene in which she had to fly dramatically back and forth across the stage, singing and thrusting out her dainty bosom. Her wire was hung from a point directly above the centre of the stage, and she simply let go of a platform thirty feet high stage left, swooped circumferentially stage right, and alighted briefly on another steel platform. Opening night was a triumph. Dorothy sang her heart out, and flew with confidence and grace. On the second night, all did not go well. Two small errors combined to end Dorothy's life: someone had shifted the focal point of Dorothy's trapeze five feet stage right to make room for a new prop; and for the same reason someone had moved Dorothy's landing platform the same distance in the opposite direction. With a high-pitched cry of delight, Dorothy flew from her perch, crossed the stage, and had her neck neatly broken by the steel edge of the ng platform. I was backstage at the time, but I heard the screams. Friends told me it was strange to watch her swing back and forth like a pendulum, that it took ages to find a ladder to get her down, that she still looked sexy and Dorothy-like, but limp. Dorothy made national news.

My close friends and I profited from Dorothy's death, socially speaking. We got to stand at her graveside. I, especially, was revered for having been so close to both of Gawpassat's deceased girls. We planted a tree in a courtyard at school and I recited Dylan Thomas in quaking voice. We basked in the aura of death and shared tragedy. Even years later, we felt special. Some of us used the story of our loss in college application essays.

15

I left Melissa in front of the television and went upstairs with my jacket and bag. On the first landing I stopped to squint out of a dirty, lead-mullioned window that gave on to the patch of lawn where I had seen the girl in the white dress. It was still light enough outside to see that she was no longer there. I climbed the stairs to the top landing and went down the corridor to my old bedroom, wondering who the girl was and where she had gone.

An unpleasant surprise greeted me in what I still thought of as my room. Someone had put up one of Uncle Ian's posters, the one that shows him shaking hands with an astronaut and sports the calligraphic caption, 'The Word Will Take You to the Highest Places'. Evidently the astronaut, made ontologically queasy by his extraterrestrial travels, had taken up Uncle Ian's Word as his personal philosophy. He spent much of his time lecturing, spreading the message, reaping considerable financial reward for having been one of the earliest converts to Uncle Ian's eccentric creed.

On another wall was a framed newspaper column written long ago by one of Uncle Ian's critics. The writer had taken objection to Uncle Ian's style of living, and pointed to what he saw as hypocritical discrepancies between the teachings of the Word and Uncle Ian's practical arrangements at home. 'Prophet and profit may not mean the same thing,' the columnist had written, 'but they sure do sound the same to Ian Armstrong.' Uncle Ian got a lot of comic mileage out of that sentence over the years. He called himself a 'propheteer'. I can remember when I was about seven years old, seeing him screw up his face into the expression of a dim-witted journalist angrily typing '*but they sure do sound the same to Ian Armstrong.*'

Uncle Ian had always been vulnerable to such criticism, although it was often more cogently expressed. Ever since his first success, with *The First Word* and various immediate spin-offs, he lived extraordinarily well. He began to devote himself to what he considered to be man's three great pleasures: women, moderate but perpetual drunkenness and the acquisition of power. He looked at a map of his fabulous country to choose a place to live. He selected Gawpassat sight unseen, because of its reputation for stuffiness and exclusivity: Uncle Ian liked a challenge. When he first laid eyes on the town, he fell in love.

His subsequent real estate purchases on all three hills, over a period of several years, provided him with the physical and social outlook of a feudal lord. He had been prepared for his new town's disapproval and thinly veiled jealousy, but what he could not understand, as a trained lawyer, was everyone's objection to his tax-free status. Was he, or was he not, a religious leader? Was his Word, or was it not, the basis of a religion? Well, then, Uncle Ian said, only a fool or a truly un-American type would fail to take advantage of so striking a law as the one that exempted churches from taxation. What kind of idiot would throw in his lot with a religious leader who did not seize such a boon by the horns?

16

I was in the shower when my sister Jean arrived. I could hear her impatient footfalls as soon as I turned off the tap. I stepped out of the shower room with a towel around my waist. I had seen Jean more recently than Melissa, but still eighteen long months had elapsed. I hugged her loosely, so as not to get her wet. She looked dissipated and attractive, as always, if slightly thinner than I remembered. She and I were the dark ones in the family, Melissa and the late Claire the fair ones.

'Did you see Mel?' I asked.

'I saw her, yes. She's downstairs, just gaping at Ian's show.'

We called him Ian behind his back, Uncle Ian in the family, and Mr Armstrong at all other times. In town, people called him the Great Man.

I crossed the corridor to my room, and Jean followed me. Jean sat on my bed. She had always been an intense-looking woman, with dark, narrow, concentrated eyes. I remember a friend once remarking that she looked so thin and severe that she could cut you if you danced with her. She had been one of the most popular and, I am proud to say, selectively promiscuous girls at Gawpassat High School.

'Thanks for coming,' she said. 'You're probably very busy. Aren't you?'

'Yes. But you caught me at a pretty good time.'

'You were just in Tel Aviv.'

'Is that what Mel told you?'

'Yes, just now.'

'She misunderstood me. I was in London and Ireland, for the most part.'

What worried me was that I actually *had* just been in Tel Aviv. I had lied to Melissa about London and Dublin – but there was no way in the world she could have known that, and I was an expert white-liar. I thought about this as I stepped modestly behind Jean's back and drew on my underwear. I dried my hair and tried to look innocent. I put on shirt and trousers and socks, as Jean complained in her typically blunt way about the nincompoops and incompetents who made her every day a trial.

'I'm getting out of dogs,' she said, which was no surprise. She had inherited the dog-breeding business from a boyfriend who had fled the country – and her ire – leaving instructions that she ought to carry on and good luck to her. She lived ten miles away from Gawpassat in a marshy area not necess- arily suited to huskies and the other highly furred animals she bred, but they loved it in winter. Jean didn't like dogs, and it showed in her dogs' demeanour. Customers seemed less interested than they had been when Jean's dog-loving boyfriend had been in charge.

'I'm selling out to one of the Periman kids and moving back to Gawpassat.'

'Is that why you need my help?'

'No, no,' said Jean. 'We'll talk about important stuff in a while. I'm just glad you're here.'

It made me feel good to hear Jean say that.

'We shouldn't leave Mel alone downstairs,' I said. 'Ian's show must be over by now.'

'All right, but we'll talk alone later, OK?'

'Sure.'

We went downstairs together, and found Melissa happily washing the new potatoes.

'The thought of the day,' she said, 'is "Togetherness means what it says." Don't you think that's apt, for our little reunion?'

Jean and I gave her identical blank looks, aided by a strong physical resemblance. No-one in my nuclear family had ever come under Uncle Ian's spell, not for a moment. The more famous he got, the more fun it was to think of him as a lovable uncle with bizarre ideas and the best swimming pool in town. It was for others – the masses, as Gawpassatans thought of them, bored and overfed – to take notice of and trade in Uncle Ian's thought.

'Say, Jean,' I said, to change the subject. 'I was asking Mel earlier. There was a girl on the lawn here when I first arrived. A young girl in a white dress. Mel says it wasn't one of hers.'

Jean gave me a very sudden shake of her head, like a twitch. Melissa had her back to us, busy over the sink. 'I don't have any idea,' said Jean, twitching at me again, making it clear that this was one of the things she wished to discuss with me later on. 'Any wine, Mel?'

Melissa looked at her watch. 'I suppose so,' she said, going to the refrigerator to fetch a bottle.

From then on it was slightly easier to keep the conversation moving, although I felt the verbal equivalent of kicks in the shin every time I said something about Uncle Ian and Jean had to interrupt me. Melissa talked about the lobster-pot museum, about togetherness, about her children, one by one. After what I had seen, I was not surprised to learn that her children were growing up the Uncle Ian way, stoked up with vitamins and, until recently, allowed to watch television for as long as they could keep their eyes open. Uncle Ian's theory had been that children would rebel against what they were encouraged to do – but television was one of the few cases where Uncle Ian and his people had been forced to retract a policy statement. Quite recently his religion had become a proscriptive one, like most of the others.

We ate dinner out on the verandah in the warm, breezeless night; the candle flames burned straight and still. A yellow moon rose through the trees at the bottom of the lawn. I was quizzed about my recent activities, but I teased my sisters by revealing nothing but tantalizing half-truths. This mystery made it seem that I had been up to something interesting, which was far from the case. My most recent assignment had been to accompany a computer to Israel – it sat next to me on the plane – ensuring that it went to its rightful destination. There had been no real need to conceal this pedestrian errand from my sisters, but I lived in a transparent fantasy world that required their curiosity about my life. How Melissa could have known or guessed about Tel Aviv, I still had no idea. Evidently spies were everywhere.

We struggled through the remainder of our catching up, until we were stirring melted ice cream in our bowls. Predictably, Melissa excused herself first. She had to return to her enormous family. As she left, she gave us Uncle Ian's Word Sign: tips of thumbs and fingers of each hand touching their opposites in a steeple-like shape, and *pressing*, plus intense eye contact. I tried not to laugh as Jean and I returned the Word Sign and said good night.

17

Jean and I strolled slowly down a dead-quiet Lincoln Street, talking in the lowest of voices. A heavy ceiling of leaves arched over the narrow road. Jean smoked, while I kept my hands in my pockets. We spoke of old times in our town, the long summer and the sudden autumn, the brutal winter and the scented spring. Jean was less rhapsodic than I; part of her personality was never to be contented, even in retrospect.

The unlined road had recently been resurfaced. We were good at that sort of thing in Gawpassat, along with being litter-free, impeccably groomed, and almost self-consciously *just so* in our town's quaint appointments. The Congregational Church never lacked for a fresh coat of white paint. Our Minuteman was cleaned and polished within hours of each attack. Our residents' cars, by some unspoken agreement, never aged beyond three years. Our Yacht Club never failed to reach its charity fund-raising targets. The town produced one criminal youth every year, who was almost invariably killed in a drunken car crash on the ugly road to the city.

I asked Jean about Curtis, her new boyfriend, a native, dyed-in-the-wool Gawpassatan. It was unusual for Jean to date someone from our town – it went against her self-perception as a rebel. I had known him, of course; he was a member of that Olympian group of boys five or ten years older, boys whose names had echoed through the school's corridors for a few years before being replaced by our own.

'Curtis has gone to work for Ian,' was the first thing Jean had to say. 'Like everybody else, it seems. And he isn't really my boyfriend, not yet.'

'Does he work at the Institute?'

'Almost,' she said. 'He works just down from there on White,' (meaning White Hill), 'with his own staff. He's on the network, doing computer stuff.' Ian's network was a simple computer billboard that united anyone with the equipment, a few dollars for telephone bills, and a desire to download the Word. 'He manages part of the network, and hopes to oversee the whole thing one day.'

'The whole thing? My God, the *heir*?'

'No, no. Of course not. He would kill for that, but for now just the computer department, which will grow and grow. The heir is another matter entirely. You haven't kept up, have you.'

I had pretty thoroughly ignored the tenets of the Word, but the last information I had was that Uncle Ian would appoint some sort of successor to take over the family religion business after his death. Naturally, the religion business makes for a tricky leadership transition, what with all the mystical signs that have to be in evidence, and the martyrdom. Because Uncle Ian had no children of his own (*The Second Word* blamed this condition on my Aunt Charlotte, which was unfair), an heir had to be selected from the population at large. Uncle Ian, who let this information leak out of the Institute when he was in his late forties, suddenly found that a lot of local young men really, truly believed in the Word. There was also a preordained Date, the date of Uncle Ian's death, but at that moment I don't think I remembered just how close at hand it was.

'I always thought the thing would fall naturally to Barbara.' Barbara was Uncle Ian's older sister, a spinster with a wonderful flair for accounting.

'It's complicated, but the Word has it that an heir will announce himself – it is assumed that the heir will be a man – or will be revealed, as it were. I think people like Curtis are wasting their time kissing up to Ian, when his choice will obviously have to be someone independent, precisely someone who *wasn't* waiting in the wings with a big smile on his face.'

'I thought Curtis had done the Bad Thing.' The Bad Thing, to lazier Gawpassatans, was to commute to the city, to a financial or legal job.

'He did do the Bad Thing, for a while. He hated it. Sort of like you, he lasted only a short while, then he quit.'

I don't know if I appreciated Jean's reference to my dishonourable exit from conventional working life.

'Are you saying Curtis actually found the Word?'

Jean coughed. 'Are you kidding? He saw an opportunity to earn the same money without leaving home, except to surf.'

'Curtis surfs? In Gawpassat? We don't *surf* in Gawpassat, for heaven's sake.'

'Only every now and then, to be seen to be surfing. It's a statement, really. It's a statement about his individuality and his independence.'

'Why do you like this man, this Curtis, this *surfer*?'

'You remember him, don't you? You've seen him.'

'My own sister, exploiting a man's tender young flesh.'

'We have had fun together, you know. I'm not claiming to be as profound as you are, Top.' This was a fairly stinging reference to my continuing failure to live up to my claims of romanticism. Only recently had I admitted a real fondness for someone. 'We have a pretty . . . informal relationship, you'll be glad to know. Also, I like the tales he has to tell about Ian and the Institute. I don't think you realize how powerful the organization has become. You've been away too long.'

'I've read the occasional article, but they're usually so sarcastic I can't tell where the truth lies. To be honest, I haven't really wanted to know.'

I wasn't alone in being embarrassed by Uncle Ian's huge following, though most other members of my family, including Jean, took it with more equanimity than I did.

'You've seen Melissa,' Jean said. 'Isn't that something?'

'She's not serious about it, surely?'

'If not, then she's putting on a pretty good act. That's why I didn't want you to talk about the girl in the dress at dinner.'

'So that *was* one of Melissa's? One of our nieces?'

'No, not at all. This is going to take some explaining. Uncle Ian has got a new idea. He's taking these girls, all from Gawpassat, all about ten to twelve years old, and he's posing them around town.'

'Posing?'

'Yes, in little costumes.'

'The girl I saw this afternoon was wearing an old-fashioned white dress, with a parasol over her shoulder.'

'That's just one example, probably a summer theme. Anyway, all of the costumes are supposed to connote a certain moral attitude.'

'Virginity?'

'Exactly. The girls are supposed to be symbols of Ian's values – all wholesomeness and purity. They are the angelic foot-soldiers of the Word.'

'Since when has Ian been wholesome and pure?'

Uncle Ian was anything but. He had brutally divorced my Aunt Charlotte when I was a little boy, perhaps still hoping for an heir, and followed this treachery by several years of fantastically overt fornication before marrying his second wife, Agnes Rush. His philandering was said to have continued unabated, but at least he seemed to have decided that marriage vows meant committing adultery discreetly rather than on board his yacht in full view of the Trainer's Restaurant clientele. Agnes put up with this, the way some women will, because she lived for material possessions and decor. Uncle Ian's wealth was, in other words, a good enough reason for Agnes not to make any kind of principled stand against him.

'I know it sounds strange, but Ian has been tinkering with the Word for so many years, he's finally decided to go vaguely moral on us. It's eerie, the way you come upon these girls propped all over the place. Even at night. You'll find them on the pier, on the baseball diamond, just standing by the side of the road. Creepy. It's all supposed to be a build-up to the Date.'

Jean shivered. She had mentioned the Date.

'Does he pay them?'

'Top dollar,' said Jean. 'Seriously, he does. Every little girl in town who qualifies takes the job. Two of Melissa's girls do it.'

'How do they qualify?'

'They have to know the Junior Word inside out. But then they all do anyway.' Uncle Ian's Word was taught at the local school; it was a voluntary course, but everyone seemed to take it. 'And they mustn't be overweight.'

'Of course not.'

18

The connection between faith and weight-loss was Uncle Ian's great intellectual triumph, and the one that made him the wealthiest man in a very wealthy town. In the quirky way of the majority of the Word's precepts, a case for thinness through spiritual enlightenment was argued with marvellously convincing illogic. Ascetics, Uncle Ian pointed out, tended to be thin; the more devotedly spiritual they were, the thinner they tended to be. He offered a few obvious examples of these people, most of them living either in prison, or in impoverished lands, or in societies where suicidal overeating was not the norm, and back-breaking outdoor labour was. So why not dip a toe into mysticism and spirituality, he concluded, when such a step seemed guaranteed to set off an automatic shedding of unwanted fat?

Uncle Ian eschewed the usual before-and-after marketing technique for his discovery, preferring to rely on his tried-and-tested celebrity endorsements. Celebrities, who on the whole were thinner and more interested in the spiritual avant-garde than the average man or woman, and who were anything but rigorous in their analysis of the unexplained, appeared on Uncle Ian's behalf displayed to their best ectomorphic advantage in figure-hugging clothes, claiming to have kept fit through paying close attention to the Word. Because it all had to do with religion, the celebrities donated their time and sponsorship. One can only speculate as to why they thought this in any way an admirable or necessary gesture, when it simply meant that Uncle Ian's profits would be all the larger.

Teleologically speaking, Uncle Ian's view was that the forces of creation had intended human beings to be thin. His argument was not Darwinian, it was economic: thin people, he said, made more money than less-thin people – at least in America and Europe. By adopting the tenets of the Word, an individual could allay any fears about the pointlessness of existence; lose weight and harvest the many corollary advantages of that condition; and make money.

19

Jean and I had reached the second of the two bends in Lincoln Street, after which the road straightened and flattened out along the coast. In that night's weather there was hardly a sound to be heard from the sea except the sucking noise of water emptying from the rocks as the tide went out. Jean was on her second cigarette, and still wanted to talk about Uncle Ian and his little girls. She walked and talked quickly, flicking ash at the side of the road. She wore two slender brass bangles that clinked with every step and every flick.

'You're going to think I'm crazy,' she said, 'but there are some things about Ian and these girls that are sort of disturbing.'

'Uh oh.'

'No, nothing like that, don't worry.'

'A scandal of that nature would put some holes in his credibility, I would have thought.'

'Shush. Of course it's not that. Listen, I might as well just tell you. It's been bothering me for years, you know. I never said anything before because I just didn't want to find out for sure myself.'

'Go ahead, Jean. I won't think you're crazy.'

'Do you remember, about twelve years ago, when Ian opened the sailing school?'

'Of course I do.' Uncle Ian had donated a dozen small sailboats to the Gawpassat Yacht Club, and hired a squad of instructors – including me. He had surprised everyone in my family by dedicating the school to the memory of my sister Claire, she of the death at sea. He had already rechristened his favourite yacht the *Claire*.

'Do you remember how strange and let down we all felt after the ceremony? The way you and Mel and I were so uncomfortable with the whole thing?'

'I remember wishing the *Claire* was our boat rather than his.'

'Seriously, Top. We were offended.'

'I suppose so.'

'But since then, I've started having the most paranoid thoughts about that day, and some other signs afterwards. Oh, you'll say I'm crazy.'

'No, I won't say you're crazy. Go ahead, Jean.'

'The more time has gone by, the more it seems to fit together.'

'What does?'

'The idea that Ian was, or at the very least thought he was, or could be, Claire's real father.'

Jean's idea appeared to be that our mother had cheated on her husband and her sister, then given birth to Ian's child.

'You're crazy,' I said.

20

I didn't really think Jean was crazy. I thought she was stating the obvious. For years I had lived with the same secret suspicion, and with a strong belief that something like that ought not to be talked or even thought very much about. Now I regretted my stoicism. I suppose I had always thought that it only added to the small-town drama of a sister's death to discover that a sordid affair lay behind her existence – especially an affair with the Great Man. Spice is immensely important to a Gawpassat family, bland as most of them are.

As Jean made her confession, I thought back to the times I had scrutinized our few photographs of Claire, comparing them with the thousands of photographs of Uncle Ian we had lying around the house. Depending on my mood, they looked either like long-lost twins or like members of entirely different species. Quickly, though, and unlike Jean, I managed put the matter out of my mind. I was not the sort to worry in any fundamental way about people's indiscretions, even my mother's. It also had to be kept in mind that we based our conclusion only on Uncle Ian's behaviour at the time of Claire's death; who was to say it wasn't just wishful thinking on his part? Claire was, at the very least, Uncle Ian's niece; as a man without issue, he might well have thought of her as a daughter even if he hadn't been secretly involved with my mother. I thought I could understand how frustrating it would be to have enough money to buy anything at all in the world, and yet to be denied what one wanted most.

21

'What I'm also telling you,' said Jean, as we strolled along the sea wall in the moonlight, 'is that Uncle Ian's little girls aren't just the angelic foot-soldiers of the Word.'

'No?'

'I believe he intends them to be symbols – incarnations, if you will – of Claire, frozen at the age she died.'

'Morbid.'

'Yes. There's no official word on this from the Institute, but it seems kind of obvious to me that that's what Ian is up to.'

'What does he hope to gain?' I had never known Uncle Ian to do anything for frivolous reasons, for any reason other than direct or deferred profit, or self-aggrandizement.

'I've been wondering the same thing. Could it be that he's actually flipped? He's not all that well, you know. Rumour has it he's polishing *The Last Word*. The Date is at hand.'

The Last Word, Uncle Ian's long-awaited testament, was rumoured to be a summing up of his life's work. Word-watchers said that it was likely to state the conditions under which his heir would reveal himself, a supposedly messianic figure who was fated to carry on as chairman and head prophet. *The Last Word*, released to his followers only at the moment of his death, would contain descriptions of what he expected to find thereafter. Uncle Ian was said not to be in the best of health; tension reigned at the Institute, and at Uncle Ian's eager publishers in the city.

Uncle Ian's reclusiveness had grown so obsessive that it extended to his own family. Jean and I compared dates, and decided we hadn't seen him in the flesh for nearly five years. Only my parents and a few other close confidants saw him socially. He conducted his business by telephone. His highest-placed employees were sworn to secrecy, and did not mingle with other Gawpassatans. Sightings of him were reported from all over the world, especially just before natural disasters – or so the Institute of the Word would have us know.

I remembered the last time I had laid eyes on Uncle Ian in public. It was the day I returned from Everest with Marcus. There was a ceremony in our honour, in pouring rain, down at the football field. Marcus, who had never been terribly comfortable in Gawpassat, let me bask in my homecoming and the numerous summer liaisons it generated. He was fascinated by the idea of my Uncle Ian, and was the first to spot him, disguised, in the crowd. It wasn't much of a disguise, considering Uncle Ian's resources. He wore a baseball cap with some sort of redneck logo on it, a blue bandana around his neck, and a quite attractive fake grey beard. Marcus was shrewd enough not to raise the alarm, but simply to sidle ever closer to the man until they were practically arm in arm under the same umbrella.

At some point during the proceedings – perhaps during the unveiling of our summit photograph – Marcus leaned over and whispered, 'Nice to see you, Mr Armstrong.' Uncle Ian hated to be found out this way, but I don't suppose he was nearly so surprised by Marcus's greeting as Marcus was to be grabbed tightly from behind by both elbows and pushed forward into the crowd. When he had brushed off Uncle Ian's thugs, he turned around to see that the disguised figure had vanished. Marcus made his way over to me, where I was blushing under an enlarged and rain-spattered summit photograph of myself, and whispered that his brush with the Great Man had not gone exactly as he had hoped it might.

22

'I suppose *The Last Word* will be worth waiting for,' I said to Jean, as we neared Trainer's Restaurant.

'The amazing thing is, no-one has leaked a single syllable of the thing. You'd think with all his ghost writers and re-searchers, we'd have heard something. Not a peep.'

'It does exist, though?'

'I hope so for our sake, Top. You don't think he'd leave us out of his will, do you?'

'Prophets are *so* unpredictable, Jean. I wouldn't count on anything.'

'I really want to inherit some of that ridiculous money.'

'Me too. What would you do, first thing?'

'No sense fantasizing. The money's the thing, just to have in case it comes in handy. Do you know what you'd do?'

'I'd get me a woman,' I said, in a southern accent. I wanted to prompt Jean into asking me about Laurie, whom I had nearly persuaded to be my permanent girlfriend. She was unpopular with my family, and they seemed not to want to know about her.

Jean said nothing. We had reached Trainer's Restaurant, after what I thought had been a rather scatter-shot conversation. We had covered some ground, but Jean had still not quite brought herself to tell me whether there was some specific reason why she had asked me to come home.

'We aren't going in, are we?' I asked. I didn't have a lot of friends left in Gawpassat. I was still well known from the various tributes to my Everest expedition, and I didn't like being recognized or asked about what it was like. If I was in a good mood I would tell them a bit about the sky and the ice and the occasional steepness; in a bad mood I would instruct them to read my book, which they could find in the Gawpassat Public Library.

'I think we should go in,' said Jean, who was by far the heaviest drinker in my family. 'I'm a single woman, after all. Curtis is in Atlanta. I'll get me a man.'

Trainer's Restaurant had always been crowded on summer nights. Jean and I entered and squeezed past what I took to be a queue for the Ladies', but which turned out to be just one of several gossiping outposts. I felt old.

We didn't make it to the bar before running into people we both knew. 'Yo, Matt,' 'Hey, Jean,' 'Say, Matt.' I have a terrible memory for names. Some of these fellows had been friends of mine. One of them I remembered, though. He had considered himself my best friend when we were fifteen or so, then we drifted apart. We even climbed together, but he wasn't at all serious. His name was Noel, and Noel had become just as famous locally as I had, if for different reasons. Noel was a rapist. Noel had raped someone. Everyone knew this, and it would have been difficult for Noel to keep his crime a secret because he was that rare creature, a *convicted* rapist. Noel had done time.

'Hey, Noel,' I said.

'Yo, Matt.'

Here was Noel in his Gawpassat uniform: baggy white cotton button-down shirt, khaki trousers belted with jib-sheet, no socks, sailor shoes. He was clean-shaven, and his sun-bleached hair fell thickly over his tanned brow.

'How's it going, Noel?'

'Not too bad, Matt. You?'

'Not too bad. You know my sister Jean?'

I was introducing my sister to a rapist.

'Sure, you know, well, seen her around. Hi there, Jean.'

They shook hands. The rapist smiled wolfishly. Jean, who knew all about Noel, let go of his hand and announced that she would buy us drinks while Noel and I caught up on old times.

I hadn't seen Noel since his trial: I was a witness. I had been at the scene. It was a party at the Perimans' house, where there were always lots of girls because Mr Periman owned at least one television network. This was during my Everest fund-raising period, and Marcus had come along with me to meet some locals. Noel did the strangest thing. He simply grabbed a girl and dragged her, right past his friends and her friends, into a bedroom. We could hear her pleading with him to stop fooling around, that he was hurting her. There was plenty of noise in the house, so we heard nothing more when the bedroom door slammed. I cannot believe we simply stood there, boys and girls with drinks in our hands, and did nothing. Someone, possibly me, might have made a wry comment or two. Minutes went by. Our conversation dwindled to nothing. Finally Marcus, who as the outsider probably felt less socially inhibited about interfering in the private affairs of our good friend Noel, started banging on the door. 'I'm coming, I'm coming,' we heard Noel say. We probably laughed at that.

Well, Noel had raped the girl. It was quite puzzling to those of us who had either intuited or been firmly taught that rape was wrong, that Noel showed not the slightest remorse, and in fact displayed incredulity when informed that he would face criminal charges for what he had done. In the end we only barely got a conviction because the unfortunate girl, who was seventeen, had a *past*. Noel got four years, served eighteen months. Most Gawpassatans liked to say that they hoped he suffered in prison. On the other hand, most Gawpassatans seemed to welcome him back to town as if he had been away on a successful archaeological dig up the White Nile.

'What are you up to, Noel?' I found myself asking the loathsome monster.

Noel sucked at the rim of a tall, ice-filled glass of something dark. 'Things are great,' he said. 'I suppose you've heard.'

'Actually, I haven't.'

'The Great Man? You didn't know? I'm what you'd call an assistant to the Policy Director, Section D.'

If I'd had a mouthful of anything I would have spat it out.

'You're working under Sohlman?'

23

Dr Max Sohlman, supreme egghead of the Institute, the only man whose telephone messages Uncle Ian always returned. Dr Max Sohlman, just hitting his stride as a Swedish professor of psychology, had discovered the Word during a sabbatical at a California university. He made his pilgrimage to Gawpassat, asked around, was interviewed at the Institute, and given a lowly post with the other clipboard-toting savants on the lawns of the White Hill Institute. His rise to prominence took only two or three years, and there were those uncharitable enough to suggest that his appearance and accent were the catalysts of his promotion. The encephalitic shape of his head suggested supernatural powers of intellect; his clipped, not wholly Swedish accent (he had been educated in Switzerland) intimidated all who heard it. His large, thick glasses, stuck under the ledge of his protruding brow, magnified his intense blue eyes and prohibited disagreement. Dr Sohlman ran Section D – D for Death.

No religion is complete without an ornate and clouded description of the great beyond. To this end, Uncle Ian assembled the best minds in such various fields as parapsychology, cosmology, ontology, mythology, theology, biology and economics. Dr Sohlman, who had made his name studying incest in Lübeck, had exhibited strengths in each of these areas. His rare pronouncements were awaited by his colleagues and *Last Word* stalwarts as if they had the imprimatur at least of the Great Man, perhaps of God.

I had met Dr Sohlman on several formal occasions, never socially. He didn't get around Gawpassat much – you would never find him at Trainer's, for example. It is safe to say I have never known anyone else quite like Dr Sohlman, nor would I want to. My impression was that he had never said anything frivolous in his adult life: every word spat between his tight Scandinavian lips was intended to carry the greatest weight. A conversational gambit pertaining to the weather might elicit a carefully phrased paragraph, sounding like an excerpt from a doctoral thesis, on photosynthesis or circadian rhythm. No-one knew how old Dr Sohlman was – he had that kind of face, creaseless and bland; his head, though bald, looked as if it had never sprouted any hair in the first place. I gather he played a bad-cop role around the Institute, and his employees lived in constant fear of his power. He had been known to sack people for failure to shave, for sweating too much and, in one case Jean told me about, for 'emitting high-frequency radio waves.'

Dr Sohlman's slowly evolving theory of death and the after-life (there had, of course, to be an afterlife), had been distilled into language thought fit for national and foreign consumption: death, it turned out, was a bit like television. Dr Sohlman's analogy – rubber stamped by Uncle Ian, of course – was one of the most popular aspects of the Word. In death, so the theory went, the individual would spend his time doing pretty much what he had done in life, that is to say watching a big colourful screen of continuing events on earth, with the ability to switch back and forth between an infinite number of channels. At the same time, the deceased would star on a channel of his own, within reach of his loved-ones and other surviving mortals, if only they could tap into the proper fre-quency. By extension, followers of the Word were encouraged to believe that their favourite television personalities might very well be long-lost relatives or ancestors, reincarnated on a cathode ray tube. Dr Sohlman's theory relied on the well-tested philosophical view that belief alone makes subjective truth: if a man somewhere honestly believes that his best-loved film star is the reincarnation of his Polish great-grandfather, any opinion to the contrary is irrelevant. Dr Sohlman gave people a view of the afterlife with which they could easily identify, along with a handy excuse to watch television with a clean conscience.

24

'I can't believe it,' I said to Noel, the rapist. 'No offence, of course,' I added, to a character who made Judeo-Christian Hell worth believing in. 'It's just that I thought his people were more . . . academic.' Noel's rape conviction had permanently interrupted his education on the last lap of a turbulent few years at a sub-par college out west somewhere.

'What do you think I do up on White?' Noel said, nodding in the direction of White Hill. 'Look at dead people's brains through a microscope? Come on, Matt. I'm Sohlman's *driver*, for God's sake.'

That was even more peculiar. Noel's father was something huge in brokerage. For his thirty-two-year-old son to be working as a chauffeur seemed a step in the wrong direction, disgraced rapist or not.

Jean returned with our drinks, and made a point of standing with me between her and Noel. I assumed he was used to that sort of treatment from women, but I was pretty sure he didn't care.

'It's a great job,' said Noel, after I had explained to Jean what it was he did for a living. 'Sohlman hardly ever goes anywhere.'

'No?'

'He's happy just thinking, up there on White. He's a genius. I mean, he's been interviewed in national magazines. His ideas are just so . . . so fundamental,' said the rapist. '*Very* strong.'

Looking over Noel's shoulder, I noticed a young girl sitting alone at a table by the window, looking out over the moonlit sea. I pointed her out to Jean, who nodded solemnly. It was another of Uncle Ian's angels.

Jean shook her head. 'How can he put one here, in the smoke and booze? That's one of our nieces, by the way,' she added.

Hearing this, Noel turned around to take a look. 'Little Lizzie? Reed and Melissa's girl?' he said. '*Cute.*'

Jean and I winced, but Noel took no notice. The girl, evidently my niece, wore a plaid skirt and bobby socks and brown penny loafers. She looked bored, but I reminded myself that she was being well paid to sit quietly. I asked Jean if we ought to go say hello, being blood relatives, but she insisted that it was against the rules for the foot-soldiers of the Word to speak on duty.

My presence in Trainer's had not gone unnoticed. Several people dropped by to say hello. These were not close friends of mine from the old days, who tended to have gone on to greater things; I quickly gathered that almost all of those from my generation who had stayed behind now worked, like Noel, in lowly capacities for Uncle Ian's organization. I learned that satellite businesses had sprung up in Gawpassat, specifically geared to the Institute's needs: among these were a caterer, a dental clinic, a new garage, an electronics supply business, a computer consultancy, a health club and a sporting goods store. With Jean at my side, I met representatives of all these enterprises. Jean and I agreed, when we had a chance to whisper a word in private, that it felt odd to be worshipped just because of our relationship to the Great Man. Men crowded around Jean. Women flirted with me. I was offered addresses and telephone numbers, which I declined. One woman, whom I dimly remembered as a fifteen-year-old delinquent, asked if it weren't time for me to get married, and, while I was at it, to get married to her.

Noel, the odious rapist, hovered around as if he were our closest confidant, making introductions and generally implying intimacy. At one point, he put his arm around Jean's shoulder. 'Don't do that, Noel,' I said quietly. 'Don't touch my sister.' Noel desisted with his usual look of obliviousness to other people's codes of conduct.

I made it clear to Jean that I wanted to leave Trainer's as soon as possible. I couldn't imagine why she had thought it a good idea to go there, unless she felt a kind of *noblesse oblige* about my making an appearance on my first night in town. People did seem fascinated, I have to say, especially the young men and women I'd never met before. They wanted to know about Everest, of course, and about whatever happened to my partner, Marcus Field, the most famous African-American mountaineer in history – and certainly the most handsome. I told them the tedious truth, which was that Marcus had gone on from the heights of Everest to the depths of corporate law. And what about me, they wanted to know. I told them my business was a secret, and Jean was able to back up that claim.

The little girl, my niece, went unremarked upon. I spied on her as much as I could without being obvious. There was a pitcher of ice water and a glass on the table in front of her. I liked the idea of Melissa's children, and wanted to talk to this one. I tried to catch her eye, but she was well trained. Only once did she move that I saw, when she leaned forward and rested her elbow on the table and put her chin in her hand, still gazing out on the black, silent sea.

I felt Jean tugging at my sleeve.

'Don't stare,' she said. 'You aren't supposed to stare.'

'The town goes along with this? Don't we have child labour laws?'

'I don't know if you'd call that labour. There's some matching-funds charity scheme involved.'

'I can't begin to guess what charity.'

'Right you are, straight back up the hill to Ian.'

'It all seems so peculiar.'

There were plenty of peculiar things I wanted to ask Jean about, but could not raise in public. One thing I had just noticed, for example, was a woman seated near my niece, also alone, also staring out to sea. I had to look twice, three times to be sure. Once again Jean tugged at my sleeve.

'I said don't stare.'

'Can that really be the same person?'

'It can.'

'Right here, with *him* in the room?'

'There's no accounting for taste,' said Jean.

So I was right. The woman across the way, emulating the pose of my angel niece, was Noel's rape victim's younger sister.

'She looks sad,' I whispered to Jean, as an unwelcome, champagne-laden tray was brought to me, care of well-wishers. I tried to smile as I spoke, so that no-one would think something had upset me.

'I'd be sad, too,' Jean whispered back. 'If I were engaged to Noel.'

'You can't possibly be serious,' I said, hearing myself raise my voice, seeing five people, including Noel, raising expectant faces to be let in on the news.

A glass was poured for me. The music was louder than it had been. I could see people pouring their own glasses, raising them, and I could hear their toasts: 'Welcome home, Matt!' 'Atta boy, Matt!'

I didn't know most of these people. What had I done to deserve such a welcome? I put this question to Jean, when I had a chance, and when some thug didn't have his lips in her ear.

'What's going on?' I asked her. 'Who am I, all of a sudden?'

'Think about it,' said Jean, smiling tipsily, poking at a man's ribcage with her elbow.

'I'm thinking,' I said, 'but I still don't get it.'

Jean was laughing now, being spun around and begged for a dance by one of the thugs, possibly even Noel, who all now worked for my uncle. She released herself from the man's grasp, lurched towards me, put her hands around my neck. I bowed my head slightly so that I could hear her, and detected the pleasant smell of scotch and cigarettes on her breath.

'You know more than you're letting on,' she said. 'Don't you?'

'Not at all. What's going on?'

'The town,' she said, 'has been waiting for a sign.'

'Oh?'

'The ill health of the Great Man? The necessity of an heir? The Date?'

'But surely *he* wasn't the one who . . . You were the one who sent for me, Jean.'

'That's right, I did.'

I must have been tired from my flight, from our reunion, from learning all I had learned in one evening, from the heat. I'm sure it took Jean five more minutes, before she was finally swept away to the outdoor dance floor, to get her point across. I was part of some scheme. She had played politics with the Word. A leak here, a leak there, a brother full of mystery. These beaming Gawpassatans thought they had found their Heir.

25

Everyone enjoys a bit of celebrity, but to be swarmed around by strangers in good old Trainer's Restaurant felt odd and smothering. I shook hands with the men and hugged and kissed the women, and I tried to keep my distance from Noel. Just after midnight a man in a chauffeur's uniform entered the bar, took my niece by the hand, and escorted her into the night. When I could escape politely from my well-wishers, I went in search of Jean. I found her necking with one of the men who had asked her to dance, who must have been ten years her junior, against the wooden railing that surrounded the dance floor. The dance floor was built out over the water, so it was pleasantly cool there. Jean had the man's sweater around her shoulders, and seemed engrossed. A couple of girls had followed me outside, but I told them I merely wanted to have a word with my sister. Jean heard this, and looked away from her necking for a moment.

'I have a ride,' she said, so I left her alone.

I walked briskly back up Gray Hill, eager to give Laurie a call. There is only one really steep section of Lincoln Street, which I tried to take at double time. Ever since those last few steps at twenty-nine thousand feet, I hadn't climbed so much as a flight of stairs with any enthusiasm. Now I felt even Gray Hill in my legs. I was weary from my journey – Tel Aviv to Nice, Nice to London, London home – and somewhat bewildered by what I had seen since my return. By the time I reached my parents' driveway I was winded and drenched in sweat.

Once inside the house, and fairly certain there was no-one around – not even one of Uncle Ian's angels – I stripped to my boxer shorts, got a glass of ice water, and took a telephone out on to the verandah. I switched on an overhead light and sat down in the big wicker chair. Outside, not the slightest wheeze of fresh air disturbed the fat blanket of Gawpassat heat. I took a few deep, damp breaths and tried to compose my thoughts. Laurie was thousands of miles away, not yet awake. I wanted to hear her voice, and to tell her I had arrived safely in Gawpassat.

I had known Laurie for two years. My plan was to organize some money and a fixed address, then decide whether to ask her if she felt at all like marrying me. I held out a great deal of hope for her wanting to do so, unless she thought the hostility of my family outweighed her steadily improving feelings for me. I had often asked myself how it was possible for my parents, whose very mission in life seemed to have been to foster tolerance and goodwill, to have turned so nasty when those traits were required closer to home. There were few things that Laurie could have been or done that would have set my parents against her to the point of making their antipathy obvious. Had she been a non-English-speaking, raw-seal-eating Eskimo, they would have learned the Inuit language and accepted her with open arms. A Brazilian transsexual? Welcome to the family, dear. A South-Dakotan wing-walker with a criminal record and bolts through her ears? These things could be sorted out in the privacy of a strong and loving relationship.

Laurie was divorced. That was all. She had been married for three years to a failed musician – a sad and defeated character, from the sound of him. My parents had a horror of divorce and divorced people. When Uncle Ian had divorced my mother's sister, I thought we were going to have to abandon Gawpassat and all the fruits of our closeness to the Great Man. They thought divorced people lacked character, will, good sense and application. They brooked no argument on the subject, and cut off long-term friendships – even *doubles partners* – who went their separate ways after having taken matrimonial vows. I had withheld the news of Laurie's perfectly amicable divorce, and she had been welcomed into our home in the way an energetic, amusing, well-educated, pretty, helpful potential daughter-in-law deserved to be. They probably couldn't believe their luck, in fact, given some of the potential wife material they had felt duty-bound to entertain in the past. I broke the news of her divorce from the musician as casually as I could, while Laurie bathed upstairs before dinner. The chill that descended on our household must have frozen Laurie's bath water.

My parents expressed a disingenuous fascination with Laurie's ex-husband, first grilling me about him, then actually raising the subject at the dinner table that same night. I had never seen them behave that way – on the contrary, I had seen them defuse arguments between Gawpassat anti-Semites and unsuspecting, indignant Jews who had been trapped together over the same sixth bottle of wine. I had seen them smooth over political, religious and moral differences with good humour and deftly applied devil's advocacy. And yet, there they sat, stony and supercilious, taking turns patronizing dear Laurie with such questions as, 'A *bass* player? How marvellous. I suppose today that would be an *electric* bass. A lot of *stuff* to carry around. And did you *accompany* him, to his . . . his *concerts*, when you were *married*? Eh?'

Laurie had weathered this unsubtle and unexpected onslaught, only to burst into tears later on and sob on my chest for three hours before falling asleep. I was only grateful that she didn't appear to blame me. The next morning, Laurie steeled herself and marched down the stairs as if nothing had happened. She had taken the view, optimistically encouraged by me, that my parents had been drunk; taken by surprise; emotionally unbalanced by the sheer beauty of the sight of a son in love; quite justifiably wary of a woman who had made a mistake, and might very well harm their only boy; well-meaning, liberal-minded but repressed people who simply wanted to get an obvious matter for concern out into the open.

'Do you eat breakfast, Laurie?' my mother had asked, first thing. 'I suppose the musician's life is all steak and eggs in the afternoon. Or am I wrong?'

It struck me at that moment that what I had witnessed was not a symptom of pre-senile dementia, not a long-repressed resentment of Uncle Ian's treatment of Aunt Charlotte, not a misunderstanding between generations, but a wilful, calculated effort to drive Laurie from my parents' house and out of my life. It was medieval. I threw a tantrum. Laurie fled down the lawn, down the path to the rocks by the sea. I spent a few minutes trying to shame my parents by mimicking their remarks and their tone of voice, then raced to Laurie's side. I pretended my parents had apologized. I promised I would do whatever the reverse of disowning children was. I held her in my arms and pleaded with her to be brave and to consider my parents insane, pretending that I had always done so.

That was Laurie's first and last visit to Gawpassat. I saw my parents only a few times afterwards myself, each time to be stung by a familiar and volatile mixture of Gawpassatan and English sarcasm. 'Where is that *nice* girl who visited?' my mother might say. 'Laura, wasn't it? Yes, she seemed *awfully* nice, didn't she Elliot?' My father would look up insouciantly from what he was doing, perhaps cutting the rind off a piece of salami with his cartographer's precision. '*Very* nice. A pretty little thing, too, as I recall. Married to a cellist, isn't she?'

26

Out on the verandah, in the heat, I shook my head at the memory of my parents' behaviour. The moon had disappeared over the city, and it was so dark and so still beyond the screens that I could have been sitting in a walled room. I dialled Laurie's number slowly, pausing on the last digit, imagining her asleep, in silence, her eyes lightly closed. I blinked at the thought of the connection I was about to make with the simple depression of a plastic button, for all I knew shooting a signal into space, working through terrestrial lines at inconceivable speed, racing to Laurie's bedroom to bleat softly by her ear.

I cleared my throat and pushed the last button. Technology worked its magic. In the London bedroom of a friend of mine, where I had arranged for Laurie to stay, the telephone rang once, twice, three times. Between the third and fourth rings I had the opportunity, like a skydiver whose reserve parachute has failed, to let an infinite number of unpleasant images wash over my consciousness: Laurie in God-knows-whose arms, free from me at last, in someone's house in the country, or being driven home from an all-night party, or high over Europe in someone's plane *en route* to someone's yacht . . .

'Hello?' Laurie said.

'It's me.'

Laurie sighed. I could hear her settling back into the pillows. 'Where are you?'

'Gawpassat.' I was almost whispering, but it was so quiet on the verandah that I thought my voice could probably be heard at the bottom of the lawn.

Laurie exhaled into the telephone, as if she were falling back to sleep.

'Laurie? I just wanted you to know I got here all right. I'm so sorry I couldn't stay over in London to see you.'

'I'm here,' she said. 'Waking up.'

'Don't, if you don't want to. I'll speak to you later.'

'Matt?'

'Yes?'

'I'm waking up. I want to talk to you.'

'I miss you.'

'Thanks.'

There followed two or three minutes of somewhat one-sided endearments and declarations of love, as Laurie slowly surfaced from slumber.

'I'm sitting up now,' she said. 'It's already light outside. I can hear birds.'

'You wouldn't believe Gawpassat, Laurie,' I said. 'It's beautiful. It's unchanged, mostly. It's hot as hell. Jean seems fine – you know how Jean is. We went to Trainer's and she left with a local boy. Can you believe her?'

'Mmm, yes.'

'There's a real buzz in town about—' I had to pause, because I'd heard a noise somewhere. Inside or outside, I couldn't tell.

'A real buzz? Matt?'

'Sorry, yes, about Uncle Ian. The whole town seems to have turned itself over to him.'

'Oh?'

'Yes, everything from the gang at Trainer's – they all seem to work for him now – to my very own eldest sister Melissa. You should have seen her this evening, she was—'

There was another noise, this time almost certainly outside. The light from the verandah illuminated only a thin strip of lawn beyond the screen. I thought it could be a deer, or a fox, or an escaped mass-murderer.

'Matt?'

'Sorry, Laurie. I lost my train of thought. Yes, Melissa, glued to Uncle Ian's television show. Did I tell you he had a television show?'

'I think so, yes. Televangelism?'

'Not really. His own intimidating brand of direct fund-raising, with some macho frontier-politics thrown in. I'm terrified he'll run for president. Melissa found it riveting. Jean has maintained her scepticism.'

'I like Jean.'

'Me too.'

There was someone outside. I was sure of that now. The sound I heard was that of a human being taking extreme care not to make any noise while approaching me step by

58

slow step on a freshly mown but very dry lawn. Whoever it was had been betrayed by twigs and dried leaves. Whoever it was would have known that I couldn't see anything beyond the sticky enclosure of the verandah.

'I'm glad you woke me up,' said Laurie, yawning. 'I can't believe what I have to do today. There's an awful man I have to see about a book that's supposed to exist that tells all about a very important part of my thesis.'

'The book is in London?' I was trying to keep my voice under control. There was someone watching me, probably only a few feet away.

'That's what I'm told. I just reckon an obscure source is worth a lot. The book was self-published, badly, by a Scot, sixty years ago. The awful man thinks he knows another awful man who knows where I can get my hands on the awful book. Am I boring you?'

'Never.' I could see a shape now, against a slit of sky between the silhouettes of two distant trees. It was a tall figure wearing a baseball cap.

'The rest of my education is going to cost me a fortune, the way I have to jet around laying my hands on unlikely material.'

Laurie had been trying to complete her doctorate for six or seven years – far longer than I had known her, at any rate. Her original thesis had been a thing of great beauty and simplicity, and had disintegrated over the years into a complex web of international thought and persiflage: she had set out to discover why men were so cruel to one another, citing specific historical examples, when little of value ever seemed to spring from the suffering they caused. When she complained that all these years had elapsed without her being able to nail down an explanation, I tried to help by pointing out that we would all go to our graves without illumination, and that she ought to savour any stimulation gained from the futile exercise itself. Her thesis had descended from the general to the specific, so that poor Laurie had become one of the world's experts on individual methods of *torture*.

'Just try to enjoy it,' I said. 'Have some fun.'

59

'It's great of you to have found me this place to stay, Matt.'

'No problem. Christopher's an old friend. He doesn't burst in on you, or anything?'

'No. He gets a lot of phone calls from breathless young men, though.'

'Good for him.'

27

Whoever it was outside was scaring the hell out of me. I was reminded of the time I was the most frightened I had ever been in my life. After Everest, I had been forced by default into making my living, such as it was, by going to out-of-the-way places and suffering greater or lesser amounts of discomfort so that I could write or lecture about it back home.

Once I was sent out to the God-damned Brazilian rain forest, ostensibly to talk to picturesque and persecuted indigenous people. The Amazon river itself gave me the creeps, so I set out by jeep. The gestalt of such enterprises requires the explorer to eschew all luxuries – no matter that he might be able to afford them – and for him to court danger at every turn in the hope that something so horrible will happen that an audience might be entertained. Never mind that the people I ended up photographing and interviewing could have been reached by telephone – and that on my arrival I had to queue up behind squads of journalists and tourists come from a dozen countries for the same purpose. My great achievement was to get lost in the jungle on my way out. Whenever I get lost, I take a nap. I threw down my authentic explorer's safari jacket and napped on a hillside in the shade, thirty feet from my jeep. My plan was to follow my tracks back to the persecuted indigenous people, ask them directions, and quit the explorer business.

That is exactly what I did – at high speed. When I opened my eyes on that jungle slope, it was to a darkening sky and the distinct impression that someone or something was snoring in my ear. What it was, was a jaguar – the animal, not the car.

I suppose the jaguar was purring, if jaguars purr. It was not a comforting sound. In fact, it was so unpleasant that, on the spot, I proved the basis in fact of the expression 'to have the shit scared out of one'. I readily admitted this to friends and colleagues later on, self-confident as I am of my nerve *vis-à-vis* the next man. I voided my bowels, or I suppose it is more accurate to say that they voided themselves for me. This had an interesting effect on the jaguar, who flared his or her nostrils and circled upwind. His or her nearly black face bore the expression of an animal who scared the shit out of people all the time, and found it distasteful. When I try to put myself in the jaguar's position, I can readily imagine how frustrating it would be to wander around trying to make friends with the only other big mammals around, only to see them blanch and shit themselves and run screaming into the undergrowth. Which is not what I did. As with any brush with death, the whole thing is tormentingly vivid: I spoke English to the Brazilian jaguar. 'Good kitty,' I said, to an animal that probably weighed three hundred pounds. Humans are foolish. That kitty could have torn out my evacuated bowels with a single exploratory snatch of his or her left front paw, and I put out a hand, saying 'Good kitty.' The jaguar visibly winced. I sat up, squatted, tried at first to pretend to be minding my own business. I recalled a friend's remark that no-one, ever in history, had survived an unarmed encounter with a Bengal tiger, and wondered what the jaguar's record was. Pretty favourable, I would have thought.

'Good kitty,' I kept saying, standing up and brushing the poisonous insects from my clothes. I began to walk towards my jeep, head high, hideously befouled and disgraced before nature, not looking back. When I reached the car I lunged at the door handle and opened the door and threw myself into the passenger seat. I looked out the window and saw the jaguar pawing at the jacket I had left behind. The jacket with my keys in it.

Night fell suddenly. I suppose it was no longer a night than some of the nights on Everest, with Marcus thrashing away in his sleep or waking up with a start, shrieking 'Caroline! No!', as he tended to do. At daybreak, with no sign of the jaguar, I simply made a pact with fate, flung open the car door, sprinted to the jacket, snatched it off the ground, and sprinted back to the car. I got myself cleaned up at the indigenous people's village, and entered law school six weeks later.

28

'You sound strange, Matt.'

'Do I? I suppose I've been awake for a couple of days.' I shifted in the wicker chair, which creaked into the night. Whoever was watching me stood stock still in the darkness, and was definitely too tall to be one of Uncle Ian's angels.

'How long will you be in Gawpassat?'

'It's impossible to say. I want to see my parents.'

'I'm sure you do,' Laurie said, sarcastically.

'They are my parents, and I apologize for the hundredth time. They should be home in a couple of days, if Mel is to be believed. They're out west buying some more Indian garbage for the elementary school.'

Maintaining my calm had become something of a meditative exercise. I had spied on people in my day, and I knew how hard it was to act naturally when one was aware of being observed. I scratched myself and sat in an unladylike position. The person beyond the screen seemed to be inching forward. It was almost certainly a man. If he moved any closer I would be able to see his shoes, at the very least.

'Well, give them my love, won't you?'

'Of course I will, Laurie.'

'"And how *is* her husband?" they'll say.'

'Probably.'

'It's a class thing, I know it is. Your mother's an implacable snob. And your dad, too.'

'What class are you, then, Laurie, to be so despised by my parents?'

'Well, I'm not English, and I'm not from Gawpassat.'

'True enough.'

Laurie hailed from out west somewhere, poor thing. She came from a routinely tragic background, for which modern psychology had devised dozens of convenient categories. The old-fashioned way of putting it is that her father was a bastard and her mother was a terrified punching bag. Laurie had left all of that behind, and didn't bore people with her early troubles or use them as an excuse for her own shortcomings, if she had any.

I could see the fellow's feet now. He wore dark leather sandals with loops over his big toes – the light from the verandah revealed that much, plus two inches of white ankle, but I still couldn't see his face under the bill of his hat. I tried to tense my body without appearing to do so, so that I could spring on the maniac when he made his move. I imagined an axe or machete sundering the screen, and saw myself leaping from the chair before it was cleaved in twain. Then I would either run away or be all over the intruder, depending on my mood. It would be entertaining for Laurie, either way.

'Let's not talk about that, I'm sorry,' said Laurie. She sighed again. 'Where are you actually sitting, anyway? I want to visualize you.'

'I'm on the verandah, in my boxer shorts.' As I said this, an idea struck me. With my heart beginning to beat almost visibly in my naked chest, I said, 'I'm on the verandah with the light on. It's really dark outside, but not so dark that I can't see that there's a guy in a baseball cap standing about five feet away, watching me.'

The toes twitched.

'What?'

'You heard me. A Peeping Tom, I guess. He'll go away, now, because he can hear me. Probably some lunatic murderer come to kill me.'

'Matt? What? Come on, don't be such a—'

'It's true, Laurie. These things aren't supposed to happen, in Gawpassat. Don't worry, he'll run away now. Go away,'

I said, to the shadowy place where the man's head ought to have been.

The toes twitched again, as he considered what to do.

'Matt? Don't tease me.'

'I'm perfectly serious.'

'Well, *do* something. Do you want me to call the police?'

'No. Just relax. Sorry to have made you anxious. Just listen. I'll put the phone down while I chase this bastard away. Won't be a moment.'

I rested the phone on the coffee table. I stretched my arms and legs, then stood up. I walked to the screen door and opened it, peering into the darkness. There was an outdoor light switch I intended to turn on, hoping it would frighten the man away. I could still see his feet, and he hadn't moved. I took a quick breath through my nose, then lunged out and flicked the switch, whose location had been ingrained in my tactile memory by decades of use. The light came on overhead.

The man had turned and started to walk towards the corner of the house. I could just make out his shape, and the awkwardness of his gait as he reached the flagstone path, like the amble of a slightly injured person wearing uncomfortable sandals. I could have gone after him, but I decided to return to the telephone so that Laurie wouldn't worry – and what is more, I was barefoot and I have a horror of stubbing my toes. I walked back inside, closed the screen door, and picked up the receiver.

'It's all right. He's gone away now.'

'Who was it?'

'I don't know. Maybe a gardener who fell asleep in the heat this afternoon. It could have been anyone.'

'Aren't you worried?'

'Not in the least. This is Gawpassat, Laurie. We have no crime.'

29

I came into some money at law school that made me rethink my place in the world. A college friend of mine named Jimmy, a ne'er-do-well if ever there was one, had struck it rich in the glorious world of pop music. One drunken night – Jimmy certainly was drunk – I dared him to let me contribute the lyrics to one of his songs, just for old times' sake and because he was so obviously blocked. He had begun to take himself seriously as an artiste, so it took some arm-twisting to get him to agree. I drew up what turned out to be an expertly binding contract using my newly learned legal skills, then dictated to him the lyrics to the immortal hit song, 'Brute Force'. Jimmy awoke the next evening clutching a piece of paper with perfect lyrics written on it in his own drunken handwriting. He loved his new song, and rushed the new single into production.

My beautiful and violent words couldn't quite be heard over the din of my friend's incompetent band, but the song made a fortune for Jimmy and, after I unleashed my contract on him, easily paid for my three years of law school and much else besides. At later jobs I would look back in awe at the four or five minutes of work that had created such a magnificent windfall. I made two more stabs at getting my friend to let me 'write' for him, but he had wised up. He died quite soon, anyway, after teaching me the important distinction between income and worth. I suppose the experience contributed to my antisocial view that if I waited patiently, with an expectant look on my face, money would come my way.

30

I slept alone in the big house with the windows open, not worrying about the shadowy man in the sandals. All towns like Gawpassat, when the weather gets hot, have people hovering around at night. A big open lawn like ours seems to attract them.

Even the people who actually lived on Gray Hill in our neighbourhood weren't entirely to be trusted, not that they ever behaved criminally; we've had some awfully strange neighbours in our day, Gawpassat being a deceptively transient town. The Bracknells, for example, were so impressed by our connection with the Great Man that they finally broke down and begged for an introduction – which was out of the question. They spied on the house as best they could, cutting down a rather splendid maple tree to clear the line of sight to our house from a port-hole window in their attic a few hundred yards away, hoping to get a glimpse of Uncle Ian. We knew about this because my sister Jean had befriended one of the Bracknell girls, who invited her up to the attic one day to take a look. Jean mischievously reported that all she could really make out clearly, using a telescope, was the upstairs bathroom I then shared with Melissa.

The Craysons, who for many years lived just down Lincoln Street from us, were also firm supporters of the Great Man. They expressed their devotion by allowing their children to sell lemonade outside the Town Hall, proceeds guaranteed to go straight to the Institute of the Word. Mrs Crayson, in particular, was a Word enthusiast. When I was a little boy I used to worry that Mrs Crayson was going to kidnap me, because whenever I came across her she ran up to me and hugged me and asked me how my family was. Even when I'd grown up, more often than not I took the long way round to the town centre rather than risk an encounter with Mrs Crayson.

People like the Craysons and the Bracknells could be seen leaving Fourth of July barbecues Word-Signing each other and their hosts, but in my day they made up a small minority of Gawpassatans. In my view, God intended the people of my home town to be Congregationalists, and that is the way they used to be. They made such an attractive sight, so prosperous and scrubbed, as they paraded to church on Sundays past the clutch of delinquents, myself included, sitting on the nearest

66

stone wall drinking beer and smoking cigarettes and being as badly dressed as it was possible to be in a consumer-driven society. Their girls wore white socks and pinafores. Their boys wore blue blazers, grey flannels and brown loafers, and their short wet hair was parted sharply. A number of these children would grow up to be temporary delinquents, like me, sitting on the stone wall, others would end up plumbing the depths of the Word on White Hill, most would do the Bad Thing. But for my money, in those days, they made one of the prettiest sights in Gawpassat.

One of Uncle Ian's most surprising and successful early strategies was to join the upright churchgoers, take a pew among them, and glower. His presence caused such a force-field of religious conflict that even the experienced and open-minded Reverend Casey found it difficult not to stutter, or to inject more ecumenical parables than usual into his far from boring sermons. At least, so it was reported to me: only my mother and Melissa ever attended the Congregational church, leaving me on my delinquents' wall, Jean with her delinquent boyfriends, and my father brooding delinquently on Gray Hill.

For two or three years, Uncle Ian glowered in the pews, sapping the spiritual energy of Reverend Casey. He sang the hymns, he fell to his knees in prayer, he sipped cranberry juice with the elderly stalwarts on the lawn outside the church, he patted the neatly combed heads of Gawpassat's adorable, privileged children, he cast disapproving looks in the direction of me and my delinquent friends. Slowly, slowly, resorting to neither bribe nor verbal persuasion, he lured the faithful to his creed. Week after week, Sunday after Sunday, Reverend Casey addressed a smaller and smaller gathering. One week it might be the widowed grandmother of six who failed to appear; the next, her six grandchildren would be absent; the next, the grandchildren's parents would have seen an alternative light and found reasons to excuse themselves from church.

Reverend Casey was deservedly well-loved. A one-church town ought to have been thankful for such a well-meaning, dedicated man. His saint-like wife devoted herself to Sunday school, scouting, picnics and excursions that allowed Gawpassat's children to wonder, in relative safety, at the big city's cultural treasures. His own children were exemplary in every way, so much so that one worried about their futures in commerce. Reverend Casey was forever plotting ways to improve the lives of his flock, hard as that was to do in a rich man's paradise, and asked nothing in return but the satisfaction of seeing so many fulfilled people lining his pews on Sundays, and the right to live in a roomy manse looking out on the most spectacular view of crashing ocean that our state had to offer.

Who would have thought, then, that Reverend Casey himself would succumb to the simplistic temptations of the Word? No-one knew for sure how Uncle Ian pulled it off. In fact, no-one had ever seen Uncle Ian speak directly to Reverend Casey, even over cranberry juice after church services on the most languid summer days. What was even more surprising – though there were few left in Gawpassat to be surprised any more – was that Reverend Casey stayed on in his roomy, ocean-side manse, continued delivering his sermons, and seemed able to maintain the support of his church's highest authorities both locally and abroad. Nothing changed, in other words, except Reverend Casey's message. His message became the Word. His flock returned as one. Uncle Ian had won a Luther-like battle in three years, without bloodshed, without recrimination, really without anyone's taking much notice.

31

Mornings in Gawpassat are almost invariably gorgeous. In winter the water turns black and hostile and the wet rocks glint in a slanting sun. In spring, the three hills come alive; their perfume drifts out to the lobster boats in the bay. In autumn – in the *fall* – there is no more breathtaking sight than the three hills of Gawpassat raging with colour. I have been here and there, from the roof of the world to the God–damned Brazilian rain forest, from Tierra del Fuego to Tahiti, too many places, in fact. The world can be awfully good-looking, but there is no place I have ever seen, impressionable though I am, to match the glory of the Gawpassat hills aflame with their seasonal death.

Unfortunately, it was summer. I awoke just before noon, choking on the heat, caked in salty layers of dried sweat. I dragged myself from bed and leaned out of the open window, only to be drowned by a visible mist of baking heat looking for a person to cook. I fell back on to my bed, feeling and probably looking like a rosy lobster. I could hear the drone of the lawn mower outside. I remembered that I had dreamt of becoming heir to the Word – I had seen those horsy faces of the Trainer's clientele, neighing their congratulations. I had swept over Gawpassat Bay in my canary-yellow chopper, dipped my rotors over Trainer's, shot up Black Hill at treetop level, and alighted on my flawless lawn to be greeted by the devoted staff that made my every living moment a treat. It was a straightforward dream – as, no doubt, Uncle Ian's dream had been thirty-five years previously.

When I was sixteen years old I had a car, a girlfriend and a bank account; I denied myself no pleasure. This privilege was bestowed on me and my friends by an unconscionably blessed group of Gawpassatans, who themselves had known nothing but ease and luxury and the social intrigues that flourished among grown-ups with too much time and money on their hands. It was probably true that my parents were the least financially well-off of all Gawpassatan mansion-owners – they had lucked into their house, after all – but an English accent went and still goes an awfully long way. Their great social coup was probably the curious fact that they worked at all – how exotic, really, to live atop Gray Hill and still take an *interest*. I can remember my mother's annoyance at cocktail or dinner parties when, after disclosing her secret working identity, her bejewelled interlocutors would announce to the party at large, 'Isn't that *something*? Listen to this, girls. Say it again, Margaret, say about your *work*.'

Naturally, most people in Gawpassat assumed my mother was a member of the British aristocracy – OK, thanks to the rumour-mongering of me and my sisters, of the Royal family itself. I encouraged this perception, in the certain knowledge that no-one I knew in Gawpassat would take the trouble to drop by the tawdry, lower-middle-class backwater of a suburb where my maternal grandparents lived and died. Goodness me, were they down-market. It was one of the pitfalls of my worldliness that I was able to recognize their true station. They visited my family every other year, and vice versa. I reckon I chalked up twenty or thirty solid hours in their company during our coincident lifetimes. Because they were virtual strangers to me, I was able to be pitilessly objective about them. I knew all about NHS glasses, about gutter accents elevated, just, for special occasions, about that Queen's garden party that they spoke of daily from the moment they quit the grounds of Buckingham Palace until the day they died. I'm sure their friends liked them, and I'm almost certain my grandfather did everything he could to save us from the ghastly Germans, but it is the duty and prerogative of the young to be disdainful of their elders.

The one time my English grandparents were formally presented to Gawpassat society was one of those epiphanic moments of youth when the true wretchedness of one's relatives seems suddenly to come into focus. It had to be at the Yacht Club. It had to be on my birthday, which I traditionally shared with Claire, because we were born one year and one day apart. The whole family walked down there together, the grandparents cooing in awe at the smaller houses we passed along the way. Uncle Ian, their other son-in-law, had already disgraced himself by divorcing Aunt Charlotte, so he was not in our company. Claire and I walked together, plotting our escape. I was thirteen, she about to turn twelve, a year before her accident.

Claire was the cutest girl – I'm sure I don't allow posthumous propaganda to influence these memories. She was so eager and adventurous, and I . . . Well, my parents must really have been annoyed when she died. Having first-hand acquaintance with the fact that blameless girls like Claire can be extinguished cast a certain pall over their lives.

Anyway, Claire's fantasy of the day was that she would grow up to be a legendary pilot. She was something of a reader – like Melissa, unlike me and Jean – and her imagination had been captured by a book about Amelia Earhart. She loved the idea of ticker-tape parades, and had practised the publicity-shy pout required of grand female adventurers, the one that says, 'It's lovely to be noticed, but who *are* all of you people?' Men can't do that, as I discovered to my cost when Marcus and I were interviewed in a small way after Everest. When a man says, truthfully, 'It was nothing,' he sounds arrogant. Claire's eyes would have twinkled as she dismissed praise, and she would have been called modest, ingenuous, adorable. My own fantasy is that she could have come along to Everest with me, instead of grumpy Marcus. Claire would have made it.

Down to the Yacht Club, then, with the supposedly aristo-cratic grandparents. We all knew Uncle Ian would be there – these were the days when he still took every opportunity to appear in public – and the grandparents had steeled themselves to behave with regal dignity. My grandfather, Harry, had that terrified look of someone who lives in perpetual fear of his social betters, of people who might accuse him of having bought second-rate double-glazing. He was the sort of man about whom relatives are wont to say, 'He never talks about the war,' implying heroics and gore. I suspect Harry never talked about the war because a) he had nothing to tell; and b) he lacked the imagination and vocabulary to make whatever he had seen into an interesting story. My grandmother talked enough for both of them, about nothing at all.

'Fish and chips,' Jean used to say, trying to explain my grandmother's girth. She looked like a sofa. Jolly and innocent and set in her ways, she seemed to enjoy her grandchildren despite their Americanized accents. She was shocked by the luxury and plenty of Gawpassat, and by the wastefulness of its inhabitants. I think she imagined that the whole of America lived the way we did – and I suppose, compared with Britain in those days, she wasn't far wrong. I remember the way Jean used to cringe with class anxiety when our visiting grandmother failed to rinse dishes properly, or preserved the tiniest scraps of food for future use, or insisted on walking all the way to the town centre and back for a carton of milk.

It was a breezy fall day, and the weekend sailors were out in force when our troupe descended on the Yacht Club. A lot of my friends, and their parents, had shown up hoping to lay eyes on my royal grandparents. As the small crowd parted, and a few photographs were snapped, I began to regret having fomented the rumours of their status. I do believe there were a couple of bowed heads as we processed towards the restaurant. My grandparents, stunned into speechlessness by the opulent yachts in the marina and the colourful clothes and shining faces of the club members, were unaware that they were being observed with reciprocal awe. Of course it made sense that the parents of Mrs Richmond – who lived with her equally humbly employed husband in the third-best house in town – ought at least to be a duke and duchess.

The main restaurant of the Gawpassat Yacht Club is enclosed in glass year round, cooled by harbour water on three sides. Our family took its place of honour at a long table on the main ocean side of the room. Each of us in his or her own way was aware of Uncle Ian's presence near the kitchen door; I thought and hoped that he looked like someone explaining a fabulous birthday surprise to the *maitre d'*. He wasted no time in coming over to greet us – his ex-in-laws, the could-have-been grandparents of his non-existent children, his beloved Claire. It struck me right away, embarrassed as I was that my fellow townsfolk were pressing their faces against the windows of the restaurant, that for his own vicarious benefit Uncle Ian might have helped build up the reputation of my mother's side of the family.

Uncle Ian's charisma never failed him, and he quickly disarmed the potentially hostile old folks. In those days he wore his already white hair seditiously long, sideburns and all, and felt comfortable appearing at the Yacht Club restaurant wearing khaki shorts and a rugby shirt open to reveal both collar bones and a tan, hairy chest. His mouth was his most prominent feature, from the point of view of a child, either drawn back hawk-like under his nose in a friendly, clown-like smile, or open and grinning with long, yellow, frightening teeth. His voice – which he had succeeded in modulating somewhat over the years – was soft and pleasant, and still unmistakably that of an educated Virginian. He kissed his ex-parents-in-law, my grandparents, who must have thought the gaping photographers outside were interested in Uncle Ian. He kissed his ex-sister-in-law, our mother, then shook our father's hand. He tousled all our hair, but reserved a special kiss on the forehead for Claire.

There were fifty guests invited to our birthday party – a party that was really a smoke-screen for introducing my grandparents to the town. How long it took my parents to realize that everyone there expected to be introduced to a duke and duchess, I don't know.

What I remember vividly is my normally abstemious mother's face turning crimson with wine and embarrassment as she began to grasp the reason for her fellow Gawpassatans' sudden solicitude. Claire and I sat on either side of her, licking butter from our fingers as we devoured corn-on-the-cob, watching my mother get drunk in public for the first and last time in our lives. She was English, after all, and there probably welled in her bosom some innate, ingrained shame of her station – the only thing worse than which was its public exposure and discussion. She was surrounded by friends who had completely misunderstood her background, and as a good English girl she could not let it go, nor bask in their American preconceptions. She had to set the record straight; in order to do that she had to speak in front of a large group of people; in order to do that, she had to get drunk.

'Are we supposed to call you *Lady* Richmond?' asked Mr Bracknell, from the other side of the table. We had reached dessert and birthday cake, and he could take the social stress no longer. Voices were lowered elsewhere to catch my mother's reply.

Mrs Bracknell tapped her husband's arm with her coffee spoon. 'No, silly,' she said. She wore absolutely the most ridiculous tangerine-coloured wig. 'It would have to be the *Honourable* Lady Richmond. Until he – well, unless her father or both her parents are dead. No offence, your Lordships.'

There was dissent a few seats down, where a woman whose ex-husband's brother had known someone who claimed to be an English earl, said that *Right* Honourable Mrs Lady Thomas Richmond was the preferred form of address, but that it was nevertheless true that at the Gawpassat Yacht Club we could simply call her Ma'am.

I'm sure my grandparents, overhearing this, must have assumed that in Gawpassat titles had something to do with being related, however indirectly, to Ian Armstrong. They listened closely, perhaps wondering if their elder daughter's divorce had robbed them of a title they never knew they deserved.

'What is everyone *talking* about?' said my mother, in a panicked voice, searching the faces of her friends and relations. Claire and I fidgeted with our lobster tails and gave each other clandestine guilty looks. 'Is everyone *mad*?'

'Mother,' said my father, who called his wife Mother. His one word effortlessly conveyed the sentences, 'Not here, dear, not now. You're confused. Not in front of the children. You'll only embarrass your parents.'

'Don't "Mother" me,' said my mother, as if she hadn't been addressed that way by her husband since the day Melissa was born. 'I see what is happening here, and I simply cannot let it pass.'

Her last syllable, so English to Gawpassatan ears, almost had *me* believing that my mother was an aristocrat. She should have gone with a good thing, in my view, but deeper pressures acted upon her now: during her twenty years or so in America, she had taken a few twists and turns in the accent department and landed on about the poshest one imaginable. She sounded nothing like her parents any more. She was therefore doubly, soon to be trebly embarrassed.

'My parents,' she said, fixing Mrs Bracknell's gaze, 'are *nothing*. Is that clear? *Nothing!*'

No-one present would ever forget that silence in the restaurant of the Gawpassat Yacht Club. I stole a look at my grandparents who, having not been let in on the original misunderstanding, were probably more perplexed than anyone at their daughter's sudden outburst.

'Nothing?' my grandfather's grey eyebrows said.

'Nothing?' said my grandmother's watery eyes.

The silence ended only when Uncle Ian rapped his knuckles on the table and announced, 'Right. I have a surprise for our birthday boy and girl.'

The room exhaled. Claire and I gave each other another look, this time of excitement. Uncle Ian was good at surprises. He nodded at the *maitre d'*, who flung open the kitchen door. Out came not a clown, nor a magician, not a bigger, better birthday cake, but, arm in arm, my current professional baseball hero and Claire's favourite female television star. That would have been enough, I suppose, but we were also hustled on to a sea plane and flown out to Clark's Island to have a private picnic with our idols.

My parents hated it when Uncle Ian did things like that.

32

I felt like a stranger in my own home. I went downstairs to make a cup of instant coffee, and had to call out several times to make sure I was alone. I took my mug of coffee back upstairs and outside on to our phoney widow's walk. From that vantage point one could take in both of Gawpassat's other hills, the ocean, and the death-cloud hanging over the city on the horizon. Far from being refreshing, the soft breeze felt hotter than the local atmosphere itself. I could see all the way down to the centre of town, where long-legged girls posed on the sea wall and, if memory served, remarked on the quality of their male contemporaries' automobiles.

A young girl stood on the lawn below me, wearing a green bikini and a matching sun-hat: one of Ian's angels, if Jean was to be believed, and possibly a relative of mine. I watched her for several minutes, to see if she would move. At last, she brushed an insect from her shoulder, and I thought I heard her mutter a word or two of frustration. She didn't wear a watch, and I wondered how she would know when her shift had ended; no doubt one of her Word-fearing parents would drop by to pick her up.

I found it disturbing that the Word had incorporated children into its idiosyncratic workings. In the old days it had been easy to write off the Word as a refuge for neurotic, credulous rich people with gaps between tennis lessons and marriage-destroying cocktail parties. To find that they had taken the Word seriously enough to farm out their little girls seemed to me a worrying development. I resolved to brush up on the latest Word, just to remind myself what it was we were teaching our young people.

The city, far over the horizon, seemed to be burning. Its carpet of smog, sharply offset against what I imagined to be a mostly natural summer haze, clung to the skyline. Gawpassatans liked to tell war stories about the city, about close calls or cultural epiphany or, more to the point, what a good idea it had been not actually to live there. The city, Gawpassatans agreed, had deteriorated into a shameful symbol of a degraded country.

A degraded country – a phrase, now that I think of it, from *The Third Word*, Uncle Ian's stab at political and social analysis. More than a stab, to be fair; *The Third Word* was a whole catalogue of fairly obvious social ills set against stark solutions. I always thought Uncle Ian had bitten off more than he could chew when he attempted to encapsulate America. It seemed to me a large topic. Uncle Ian's point, apparently, was that if everyone would suddenly love each other and work extremely hard and behave selflessly at all times in their private lives, things would sort themselves out.

76

There was a folksiness to Uncle Ian's *Third Word*, an anec-
dotal tone harking back to his days chopping wood for his
invalid parents outside their one-room cabin. If we would
all just go out and chop wood for our invalid parents, he
seemed to be saying, any number of domestic and foreign
policy problems would be swept aside.

The little girl in the green hat turned around, looked up,
and noticed me. I raised my coffee mug to her and smiled.
She smiled back, then remembered her terms of employment
and looked back out to sea. I worried about her prolonged
exposure to the heat and sun. I thought about Jean's theory
of Uncle Ian's angels, and wondered if he employed little boys
as well. Then it occurred to me that there were already plenty
of boys hanging around town looking surly. The girls I had
seen certainly were more decorative. The one standing in the
centre of our lawn had the makings of swimmer's shoulders,
long, brown legs, thin hips and slender arms.

America, according to Uncle Ian, was an abstraction. Other
countries, he noted, lived up to their historical and cultural
reputations. America, no. He liked to quote the Gettysburg
Address – or one word of it, at any rate – when he described
the manner in which the United States had been 'conceived',
rather than painstakingly honed or eroded by long periods of
internal and external influence. Connoisseurs of the Word liked
to believe that the Great Man considered America's conception
to have been immaculate. In the eyes of the Word, so they
said, the American experiment had far from run its course;
the results were not yet in – not conclusively – but most of
the signs pointed towards self-immolation. This pessimistic
line of thinking led Uncle Ian to complain that, unlike rats
undergoing massive injections of toxic chemicals, the subjects
of the American experiment were free to alter their doses. The
actions they took would determine the outcome of the great
social and political experiment. I think his conclusion was that
people had to be awfully damned careful.

33

Uncle Ian had to be careful, too. It is axiomatic that any American possessing even a grain of celebrity is a marked man. Sooner or later, someone will try to murder him. The most famous Gawpassatan after Uncle Ian, an Olympic skier turned Senator, was shot dead on his Washington, DC doorstep by a man claiming to have found links between his victim and a lost civilization living miles below the earth's surface in the crater of a Hawaiian volcano.

Uncle Ian had shown me his hate-mail and death threats. He kept them in a special cabinet in a room of their own in the Black Hill mansion. I was sixteen at the time, considerably in Uncle Ian's thrall, and fascinated by the violence and perversity contained in his intimate files. Even the most innocuous fan mail can contain hints of threat. 'Your books have changed my life,' many of them began. There usually followed a personal anecdote describing the correspondent's recent domestic travails – his inability to pay bills, his belief that certain unnamed parties held potentially murderous grudges against him, his loathing of women – leading to the conclusion that if someone were to put a bullet in Ian Armstrong's head, the world would be cleansed of its sins. One of the more worrying letters I was allowed to read came from a woman, who wrote, 'I can make you different. I can make you different. I can make you different. I can make you different. I can make you different. I can make you different. I can make you *DEAD*,' in a left-handed, loopy scrawl. She had enclosed a return address, which allowed the authorities swiftly to detain and interrogate a frustrated hairdresser in Boca Raton whose policeman husband turned out to be the dangerous one in the family.

Uncle Ian's hate-mail contained voodoo-related talismans, strips of human flesh, dung, canisters of poison gas, satanic verse, bloody razor blades, teeth, erotic photographs, and the universal refrain: 'You are a dead man.' Women, who statistically made up the large majority of Word consumers, sent Uncle Ian hair (roots and all), rent underclothing, marriage proposals, seventy-five-page single-spaced letters confessing to selfish longings, and, in one case I was allowed to see, a big box of wet barnacles.

Uncle Ian hired security early on. For those of us who longed to be rich and well-known, my uncle's experience was a cautionary tale. He made the best of a bad deal, pretending to relish his enforced seclusion, but those reasonably close to him saw how terrifying was the gaze of the public eye.

Only one man ever got close to murdering Uncle Ian. He had written hundreds of straightforward death-threats, and his identity was well known. His extensive psychiatric care had been deemed a success, and no-one could have predicted that after his release he would surface at a Word seminar in Aspen, Colorado, brandishing what was later found to be a beautifully sharpened section of a military helicopter rotor blade. Disarmed of this cumbersome weapon, he produced the more conventional handgun, and fired twice at the podium where Uncle Ian had already been lain upon by six dedicated, flak-jacketed security guards. A taxidermist from Omaha was grazed, a Russian ballet dancer's thigh was punctured. The assailant was returned to the loving bosom of his hospital.

Uncle Ian's headquarters security was one of the wonders of Gawpassat. The expensive consulting services of two ex-Israeli Defence Force officers had not been paid for in vain. Nothing short of suicide could kill Uncle Ian in his bunker bedroom. We had to keep reminding ourselves that Uncle Ian was only slightly famous, only moderately rich in the big scheme of things. One had to wonder to what lengths truly popular people had to go to protect themselves from the violent adoration of the masses.

34

I heard a car enter our driveway. A door was clicked open, then slammed shut. I watched an impatient-looking mother stride round the corner of the house and towards the centre of our lawn, aerating it with her spiked heels. Her daughter didn't move until touched on the shoulder, as if being awakened from deep hypnosis. Her shoulders heaved with relief. She followed her mother back to their car, but not before looking up over her shoulder and smiling at me in the natural, girlish way she had done when she first saw me, before remembering herself. She and her mother disappeared around the corner, car doors were opened and slammed again, and their car's tyres hummed away down Lincoln Street.

Now that I was alone in my mansion and on my grounds, and the strong black coffee had organized my mind, I began to experience a powerful nostalgia. Jean's surprising revelations about Uncle Ian had centred my thoughts on my relationship with the Great Man. There was no point in denying that I had, at one time, been almost as special to him as my sister Claire. I have no idea how my parents felt about it, but Uncle Ian went well out of his way to coddle and protect us. As the example of our Yacht Club birthday party illustrates, he was shameless in his indulgence of his youngest niece and only nephew. I suppose it is fair to say that he was every parent's nightmare vision of a well-to-do in-law; it was so easy for him to enthral and amaze us, and impossible for my parents to compete. He even took it upon himself to perform a service for me that most would say was not any longer within the remit even of a father, much less an uncle.

Uncle Ian was a highly literate man. His rugged youth had not deprived him of books, and his tastes leaned in the direction of . . . rugged youth. One of the themes of the novels he preferred – rugged novels of American youth – had to do with that supposedly fundamental rite of passage, the young man's loss of virginity. In these books, if memory serves, the rough, alcoholic, distant father softens one sodden evening – after being laid off from work – in order to pay for his son's initiation at the hands and loins of a reputable prostitute. The encounter is brief and humiliating, but lives in the initiate's memory long enough for him to record it with suitably corrosive resentment in his first coming-of-age novel. Perhaps inspired by his reading and, for all I know, himself a beneficiary of similar indoctrination, Uncle Ian took it upon himself to usher me into the ranks of the not altogether inexperienced, on my sixteenth birthday.

As I recall, the pretext Uncle Ian used to deceive my parents was that he wanted to take me to the opera. We listened to an opera on his limousine stereo as we swept into the city in the opposite direction from the traffic jam of homeward-bound commuters. He sang along with the major arias and advised me to remember the gist of them in case my parents were to quiz me later on. He said he had seen the show the previous week, and that I ought to report to my parents, if asked, that the modernist set design consisted of overabundant foliage and plenty of mud.

Our excursion excited me. Concentrated, individual attention from Uncle Ian was in itself a thrill. The quaintness of the project he had in mind was surprisingly moving. We engaged in a memorably man-to-man conversation as the blackness of the city reared up before us. True to his Word, Uncle Ian lectured me on the subjects of responsibility, gallantry, chivalry and prophylactics. He told me I would shortly be making the acquaintance of a Miss Harvest Moon, and that I ought to comply with her every request. She was, he said, startlingly knowledgeable for her tender years, and awesomely beautiful. She was extremely expensive, he added, but worth it at ten times the price. I was not going to forget Miss Harvest Moon, Uncle Ian said, and he was right.

Miss Harvest Moon lived and worked in an anonymous but quite attractive brownstone in one of the city's more desirable streets. Our driver found the way without instruction or map consultation, as if he had driven there before. It was still light when he pulled up to the house, and I remember that Uncle Ian looked both ways before opening the car door and escorting me to the threshold. I wore a white shirt, navy-blue cashmere V-neck sweater, tweed jacket and grey flannels. My hair had been cut for the occasion. We were met at the door by a young man dressed as a butler, who turned out actually to be a butler. I have never seen a butler since. The house was not designed as a brothel. We were ushered into a normal, if overdecorated drawing room, and served very cold champagne. Uncle Ian smiled hugely at me, and my good health was toasted at least three winking times. My glass was refilled. I drank. I felt so happy and expectant, so grown up and appreciated, that I consciously prayed to Jesus Christ – then my spiritual mascot – to prolong the experience indefinitely.

'Miss Harvest Moon,' announced the butler, and in she glided.

Uncle Ian and I stood up to greet her – he with a single kiss on the cheek; I with what I hoped was not too firm a handshake.

She was beautiful. At the time it would never have occurred to me to guess her age – all 'women' being vaguely old – but today I can estimate that Miss Harvest Moon was twenty-three. She was petite. Her long, long brown hair reached the small of her back. She had the friendliest, most self-assured smile. She wore a socialite's black and white polka-dotted cocktail dress, pearls like my mother's and high-heeled black shoes. Uncle Ian and I might have been the first arrivals at a particularly smart dinner party. Harvest had the brilliant blue eyes that I associate with Ireland, and the most delicate freckles.

It struck me, even then, that this was a far cry from the rugged-youth initiation immortalized in Uncle Ian's favourite novels. A down-market, bourbon-slugging whore in a dusty frontier town it certainly wasn't, not by a long chalk.

'Do call me Harvest,' said Miss Moon, seating herself expertly on the sofa next to where I stood. She patted the cushion next to her, and signalled for more champagne. I sat down, and crossed my legs as manfully as I knew how. I had been told that

I looked older than sixteen, and if liquor-store proprietors were anything to go by, this was the truth. I tried to look Harvest in the eye as she embarked upon a systematic exercise in small talk – and I was aroused. What a beautiful, elegant girl she was.

Uncle Ian, beaming, did most of the talking. Miss Moon, it turned out, was an adept of the Word. She remarked upon the sheer ecstasy of having the Great Man visit her salon. Within twenty minutes, Uncle Ian asked pointedly if he might be left alone to play Miss Moon's grand piano. Miss Moon said of course. She took my hand and led me out of the room to the staircase, saying something about the importance of music in the Word. We walked slowly up the stairs, as Uncle Ian picked out the chords of an antique show tune. I remember the warmth of Harvest's hand as we climbed the stairs, and her scent. I know that men are prone to credulousness where the flattery of prostitutes is concerned, but I hope to live out my days believing that Miss Harvest Moon enjoyed her performance as much as I did. The whole thing was so thoroughly choreographed that a clandestine video would convince the disinterested viewer that true love had blossomed between us.

'You're so . . . I shouldn't say this. You're so *handsome*, Matthew,' Harvest said. 'No, really – I'm blushing. I can't believe I'm saying this to you. Can I – *may* I . . . no, I can't ask. I'm blushing.'

She really did blush. I thought to myself at the time that a woman like Harvest could get anything in the world she wanted. She could enter a crowded room, ask the nearest fellow who the richest, most desirable man was on the premises, and, when told, *get him*. Her power was frightening.

'What do you want?' I asked her. 'Just tell me what you want.'

Harvest feigned embarrassment.

'I don't know,' she said. 'I mean, your *Uncle's* downstairs.'

Harvest put a hand under one of the straps of her dress, softly rubbed her collar bone, appeared to be lost in conflicted thought. We were in a bedroom.

'Never mind him,' I said, ruggedly. And then, in an inspired moment I have since reckoned to be my best, I said, 'Just let me kiss you.'

What a wonderful thing to have said; I must have read it somewhere. I thought Harvest must have been extremely impressed by my poise and *savoir faire*. At any rate, it probably saved her a lot of time. We kissed, we fell on to the bed, our clothes were cast aside. I remember thinking, I'll never be able to afford this again, ever, until I'm dead and, by extension, the world has ended.

I like to think that Uncle Ian found it noteworthy that Harvest and I did not descend the stairs for at least two hours. We had showered, and pulled ourselves together. Uncle Ian, who had never in his life been at a loss for words, complimented Harvest on the quality of her piano, noted the time, thanked her for a wonderful evening, bundled me past the severe-looking butler and into the street. Our driver hastily extinguished his cigarette under his heel and rushed to open the limousine door. We hummed out of Harvest's street – out of her life for ever, in my case; I don't know about Uncle Ian.

'Well, my boy,' said Uncle Ian, or hackneyed words to that effect. 'Are you glad we came to the big city?'

'Sure,' I replied, blowing on the fingernails of my left hand.

'Well, come now, Matt,' he said, dissatisfied with my lack of *esprit de corps*. 'Where are your manners, my boy? Aren't you going to thank me?'

'Thanks, Uncle Ian. Thanks a lot.'

'Well, come on, son, *enthuse*! This is a big moment. Not that we'll ever mention it again, you understand. Don't you worry about that. It's only that I thought right now you'd like to – I don't know – *revel* in the occasion. This is a transition, Matt. I might even be persuaded to give you another glass of champagne.' I could see, even in the gloom of the limousine, that Uncle Ian was desperate to be complimented on his liberalism, his consideration, his generosity. 'You're a *man*, all of a sudden,' he said, almost pleadingly.

'That's what makes you a man?' I said, crossing my legs.

'Well, of course it is. In a manner of speaking.'

'In that case,' I said, staring him straight in the eye, 'I've been a man for about two years.'

35

'Boo,' said a deep voice behind me, and I almost leapt over the edge of the widow's walk.

I wheeled around and saw that it was my nephew and namesake.

'Hello, Uncle Matt,' he said.

Holding my chest with my free hand, I breathed a similar greeting. 'You frightened me,' I added.

Little Matt now stood over six feet tall, and looked a great deal like me. He was sixteen years old, suddenly, and if I remembered correctly the last time I had seen him he had been a weedy, awkward child. It occurred to me in a flash that he was the age I had been when *my* uncle took me to the big city; from the cocky looks of him, he needed the initiation about as much as I had.

'Is Mel – you know, Miss – Melissa,' I stuttered. 'Is your *mother* downstairs?'

'Naw,' said my huge nephew, who wore cut-off jeans and an untucked white tennis shirt. 'She just sent me over to say hello. I walked.'

I felt at a disadvantage – not simply because my nephew dwarfed me, but also because I was dressed only in boxer shorts.

'So, how are you, Matt?' I said.

'Sure, great.'

'School?'

'Yeah.'

'Your mom and dad?'

'Yeah.'

'Summer job?'

'Yacht Club, you know. Yeah. I've been playing some golf.'

'Good for you.'

'Yeah.'

Our conversation over, we went back downstairs. I told my nephew I would meet him in the kitchen, then hurried into my bedroom to get dressed. When I caught up with him, my nephew was seated at the kitchen table washing down a whole pineapple with a jug of milk.

'I have to go to a wedding today,' he said, between bites, looking at his watch.

'Oh? Anyone I know?'

'Yeah. Little Dave Periman.'

Little Dave Periman was a contemporary of mine.

'I didn't know Little Dave was getting married.'

'Yeah. To Beth Rhodes.'

Beth Rhodes, roughly speaking, was a contemporary of my nephew's.

'Did Beth invite you?'

'Yeah. I taught her to sail, last summer. Aren't you invited?'

'No. I suppose I've lost touch with Little Dave. I haven't even seen you in – I don't know, four years?'

'I don't remember. I've seen pictures of you, though. With that black guy on the mountain.'

'Marcus.'

'Right.'

'Everest.'

'Right.'

He had finished his pineapple and milk. He stood up, show-ing no intention of clearing up his plate, knife, fork and glass.

'Where's the wedding?'

'White,' he said, meaning White Hill, on the lawn of the Institute of the Word. There had been a day when Uncle Ian performed wedding services himself, including Melissa's. In recent years, those duties had fallen to his minions, though Uncle Ian still sometimes appeared electronically to bestow a special blessing.

'What are you going to wear?'

My nephew squinted at me. 'Wear?'

86

'What do people wear to Word weddings these days? It used to be that we wore pretty informal clothes, in the summer.'

'Mom got me a uniform. The boys wear uniforms, now. They're good.'

'Oh,' I said.

'I'm sure they wouldn't mind . . . '

'I don't have a uniform, Matt. Have a good time. Don't pass out in the heat. It really is so hot.'

'Don't worry about me. Anyway, I guess I have to go.'

'Right you are.'

My nephew walked towards the kitchen door to let himself out, then turned around as he remembered something.

'Mom wanted me to tell you that Grand Uncle wants to see you.' My nephews and nieces called him Grand Uncle. Anyone even remotely related to the Great Man made the best of it.

'Oh? I hadn't told him I was in town. I don't even know how to reach him.'

'I don't know about that. Mom told me to tell you. She said to tell you that Grand Uncle expects to see you this afternoon. Around five? That's during the wedding. That's all she said. I assume that means up on Black, but don't quote me.'

'Well, thanks, Matt. Thanks for delivering the message.'

'Sure. You're welcome.'

My nephew had huge feet and hairy legs, and yellowing sweat stains under his arms. He had healthy Richmond skin, and his father's crooked nose. I failed to detect any trace of humour in his eyes.

'Do you have to go?' I said. 'Do you want a cup of coffee?'

'I don't drink coffee.'

'It's only a manner of speaking. I mean do you want to sit down and have a chat? It's been a long time.'

'I really have to get going. I have to put on my uniform.'

'I'll walk you out to the street, then.'

'If you want.'

We walked outside into the blast furnace. I was barefoot, and the flagstones leading to the driveway were wet and cool from a sprinkler someone had turned on earlier in the day.

'I saw your mom last night. She seemed fine to me.' My nephew didn't reply. 'She seemed fine to *me*,' I stressed.

'Yeah, she's OK.'

'Do you know there are brothers or sisters of yours, or both, I haven't even met?'

'Me neither, at this rate.'

'That's very funny,' I said.

Matt looked at me seriously.

'Well,' I said. 'She does love children.'

'I guess she does. She's having another one.'

'What? Mel? Another one?'

'Yeah. She told us about it a week ago.'

'She didn't say anything to me.'

'She probably forgot.'

We had reached the driveway, away from the sprinkler. I had to walk on the grassy verge, it was so hot underfoot.

'You know it's funny, Matt,' I said, fraternally rather than avuncularly, looking up at my nephew. 'Jean – your Aunt Jean – says the Word has really taken off in Gawpassat. It's like the whole town, everyone, has been swept up by the damned Word. Do you find that to be the case?'

'It isn't right to talk that way,' he said.

'I beg your pardon?'

'*The Last Word* is coming, Uncle Matthew. The Date, too.'

'Well, so?'

My nephew stopped abruptly and looked at me. '*The Last Word* is coming. And the Date.'

'That was inevitable, Matt, but let's not—'

'Shut up,' said my nephew. 'Just shut up.'

'Matt?'

'Yeah?'

'Don't *ever* tell your uncle to shut up.'

'I won't if you won't . . . won't be . . . blasphemous.'

'What did you say?' It was strange, really, to feel physically threatened by my nephew. I was not, by any stretch of the imagination, a small man. I was a conqueror of Everest. But my nephew, I now realized, was a giant.

We continued walking down the drive, until we reached the top of Lincoln Street.

'You said – I can't say what you said. *The Last Word* is coming, the Date is coming, and you can't say those things or you'll be killed.'

'Killed?'

'Accidentally.'

'Accidentally?'

'Like Aunt Claire,' said my nephew, referring to my dead sister – who had never, technically, been Matt's aunt.

'Uhm, right.'

'I'm sorry I said shut up,' said my nephew.

'That's quite all right, Matt. Thanks for apologizing.'

'Mom would never allow it, is all.'

'Well, she's very pure.'

I found myself hopping back and forth from foot to foot on the hot asphalt at the gate between the rhododendrons. It was then that my nephew gave me the most elaborate and sincere Word Sign I had yet encountered, adding an unnecessary and humiliating bow. My nephew loped away down Lincoln Street, past a little girl in a sun dress stationed at the first bend.

36

I would have been the last person to dismiss the Word as yet another light-weight self-help programme for dim-witted malcontents. It is too easy to laugh at the expense of true believers, of any persuasion; one has to see faith from their point of view. The power of the Word lay in its all-encompassing simplicity. It often occurred to me that a religion as ornate and profound as, for example, Catholicism, would naturally be lost on those with short attention spans. The Word, on the other hand, was clearly spelled out in half-a-dozen breezily written books – or on audio and video tape, the increasingly popular methods of assimilation. There was practically no hocus-pocus involved. God had spoken to Uncle Ian, dictated his Word in up-to-date lingo, issued a few instructions, and let humanity take it from there.

Hell, as classically conceived, did not exist. According to Dr Sohlman's latest projections, Hell was the equivalent of lousy television reception: no way to tune in on the world, no way to be tuned in upon. At its worst, Hell sounded to me less like eternal damnation than mild but rather prolonged frustration. Heaven – perfect reception – turned out to be a relaxed, almost lazy affair. An inhabitant of Heaven could take or leave his paranormal options, taking aeons out for sleep, if he chose.

The important matter of how to conduct oneself when alive was covered by the Twenty Laws, each of which Uncle Ian had expounded upon at some length based on how he had gauged God's tone of voice when He dictated them. God turned out to lean very much in favour of egalitarianism and fair play. He had no time for personal violence (war was another matter), and He seemed particularly to detest torture. Marriage, He took with a pillar of salt: adultery was no sin, though polygamy was frowned upon where prohibited by law. God thought America was almost certainly the most interesting, beautiful and advanced civilization in the history of creation, and promised to do what He could to protect her from even the most cunning of enemies. Americans, it was implied, were to consider themselves the Chosen.

As is so often the case with religions, the Word itself was far from objectionable: what people *did* with it was the problem. There were politicians and role-model professional athletes and car salesmen who seemed to be able to talk of nothing else. People tended to put their own spin on the original Word. Early on, there were highly profitable offshoots in other parts of the country, and several times Uncle Ian had been forced to sue. Independent interpretations abounded, even close to home: one Gawpassatan zealot, Martin Elland, took it upon himself to 'decipher' *The Fifth Word* (Uncle Ian's advice on sexual relations), and came up with an apocalyptic treatise that appeared to blame the imminent self-immolation of the world on lesbians, of all blameless people.

Misinterpretation is one of the guaranteed pitfalls of the religion business; by founding the Institute of the Word and its assembly-line publications, Uncle Ian managed to stifle most dissent and keep his creed ticking over. Another disadvantage of being a prophet is that one's followers tend to focus their adoration on the individual, rather than on his message: if they weren't writing death threats, they were climbing the hills of Gawpassat in down-market vehicles, rubber-necking passers-by, photographing the gates on Black and White and Gray, generally making a nuisance of themselves.

A concession and souvenir stand had to be built next to the church, outside of which were parked vulgar cars with out-of-state licence plates. Gawpassat had become a tourist attraction – something generations had tried to avoid by keeping the profile down and the property prices up. My sisters and I – and later my in-laws, my nieces and nephews – were accosted in the streets by Word worshippers who had done their research and knew who we were. At a minimum we were asked to pose for photographs. Sometimes we were offered money to divulge any conversation we might have had, ever, with the Great Man. Jean, at seventeen, had been paid two hundred dollars to tell a man and his pregnant wife that Uncle Ian had recently decreed that children born within the next six months would inevitably be healthy, wealthy and wise. She was severely disciplined when I ratted on her.

I was the only one of my extended family ever to be kidnapped in earnest. It happened in early summer. I was fifteen. A girlfriend and I had perfected the technique of crawling along the timbers under Trainer's pier, and clambering up through the mossy scaffolding to Trainer's bar. Once there, and lost in the crowd, liberal-minded patrons ferried drinks to us and kept us hidden from the paranoid and authoritarian staff. On that particular night, perhaps the fifth or sixth time we had attempted to penetrate Trainer's, my girlfriend and I were snatched from the sea wall as we snuck down to the pier, thrown into the back seat of a station wagon, blindfolded and driven away. A few minutes later my girlfriend was abandoned when our husband-and-wife abductors realized she was of no interest to them. I was taken for a long drive, put through the usual kidnapping routine. I was released by the sea the next day, and I walked home along the beach. My parents told me the kidnappers had asked for nothing more than a brief chat with Uncle Ian, just to pose him three questions. Uncle Ian was indisposed – in Ceylon, or Sri Lanka, I don't remember which – so it was arranged for my father to be put on the line to pretend to be Uncle Ian. The kidnappers were satisfied, not to say bowled over, by my father's first succinct, almost threatening reply.

'We want children,' the male kidnapper had asked. 'Is that wise, or will the world come to an end before they have any fun?'

'Do not have children,' said my father, adopting as best he could Uncle Ian's gentle southern accent. 'And "fun" is not the point.'

'The world won't end?'

'I didn't say that.'

'You didn't?'

'No.'

'Oh, well, then, how about—'

'Your three questions are up,' said my precise, cartographer father – I have the police tape-recording, one of my consolations for having been through the supposed trauma of kidnap. A brief argument followed, during which my father uttered the words, 'Your loyalty to the Word is unquestionable. I absolve you of guilt if you release the boy unharmed – release him, or suffer like a worm in salt.'

I was dumped on the beach twenty minutes later; the kidnappers were caught almost at once. My father, like an emotionally scarred war veteran, refused ever again to discuss his masterful intervention.

37

I trotted back into the house, wondering what to do. It was so hot. There was no-one in town I wanted to see except Jean and, of course, my supposedly dying Uncle Ian. I went into the kitchen and poured myself a glass of orange juice. I picked up a telephone and dialled England. Laurie answered right away. I told her I wasn't interested in listening to her stories about torture, I wanted to talk. I wanted her to know how perfect she was in every way. She thanked me, but told me lots about torture anyway.

Laurie had taught me much more than I wanted to know about torture. One of her conclusions was that if asked to devise her own torture she could concentrate, for weeks if necessary, on the most grotesque imaginable outrages against body and mind, fuelled by her own deepest fears, and emerge with a method that an expert would only scoff at for its watered-down ineptness. The great torturers were as skilled as master craftsmen, they honoured their horrible traditions, and they raised their trade to a grisly art form. From the noble rack to the humble thumbscrew, from the thousand cuts to the glorious strappado, torturers had built up a canon of technique and technology in its own way as impressive as that of printing or optics or instrument-making.

Laurie was frequently asked what, in her opinion, was the very worst torture ever devised by man. Ah, but there were so many. At the simplest level, there was the pure, fundamental inflicting of physical pain. In this area, surely the fracturing of all the bones in the body – carefully, slowly, the victim must not lose consciousness – followed by the drilling of all the teeth, followed by fastidious burning of every inch of flesh, yes, surely this had to be the flagship of the torturer's fleet. But there was so much more that could be done, so many ways to amplify the horror. Laurie usually said that in the end torture wasn't a proper topic for informal conversation, arguing that even as she spoke there were men, women and children undergoing mock executions, flayings alive, electric shocks and every conceivable cruelty ever born of man's brutal mind.

Yes, people said, but what's the *worst* torture you've ever heard of? When pressed, Laurie usually told about the practice of torturing the prisoner's *mother* while the prisoner is forced to look on. This wretched business is only an hors d'œuvre, of course. Once the mother has been tortured to death – let's say this takes three or four days – her naked corpse is then tightly bound to the prisoner's body, and he is left to experience its slow decay at close range. After Laurie had described this particular brand of inhumanity, people usually agreed that it was improper to talk of such things, that one felt sickened and helpless and would rather not know.

How often I thought that it was a peculiar world indeed that simultaneously produced, on the one hand, torturers who killed women and strapped them to their sons' bodies; and on the other hand, Laurie. She was as unlike pitiless torture as she could possibly be. I met her on a bus in Brussels – where I had been sent to retrieve a consignment of precious gems from a crooked Norwegian tax exile, and where Laurie was to be briefed by an expert on some of the most appalling examples of torture ever known (recent, German). I got on the bus, saw her, sat next to her, and we felt romantically linked from then on. I could see right away that she had been rattled by something. It turned out that she had just that day met her first real-life torturer. She had studied them in the abstract for quite a long time – but to shake hands with one and look into his lively eyes, to hear about his love for his grandchildren, this brought some of her nastier discoveries straight home. The meeting had upset her. It embarrassed Laurie, as a scholar, that she had been so choked with revulsion that she had been unable to ask more than half of her prepared questions. The unoriginal realization that all people had a latent capacity for unimaginable cruelty – this had made Laurie un-comfortable. I told her I thought she ought to take a break.

We went walking together in the Alps, once our duties had been fulfilled. I remember standing next to her in a saddle between two insignificant peaks, looking out over the mountain range on the purest of days.

'You must be bored by this,' she said, 'after Everest.'

I replied that she had to be kidding.

38

I phoned Uncle Ian's private line, only to find that it had been changed. I phoned the Institute, only to be told that I was not the first person to pretend to be related to the Great Man. I phoned Jean's house, where there was no answer. I phoned the Institute, and demanded to be put through to Dr Max Sohlman. I reached a male secretary in the Department of Death, who told me that Dr Sohlman was in California, lecturing on the Afterlife, but I could speak to his second-in-command.

'Alice Schultz,' said a woman's deep voice.

I introduced myself. Mrs Schultz said she remembered me, not only as the Great Man's nephew, but as one of her best pupils in the old days, when she had been a teacher. She used to work on the publishing side of the Word, but Dr Sohlman had taken a shine to her and brought her over to Death. She was known to be efficient and organized – two qualities especially prized by Dr Sohlman – and not a great deal of fun.

'I need my Uncle's new number,' I said, coming to the point. I knew it would be unwise to give the reason for my sudden interest. Who knew if Jean's information was correct or, come to that, if the Institute staff had been told of his deteriorating condition?

'Well now,' said Mrs Schultz, whose husband was an alcoholic. 'That, of course, is impossible.'

'Are you saying that it is impossible that I need my Uncle's new number?'

'Don't be smart with me, Matthew Richmond,' she said.

'Well, then,' I said, 'can you confirm or deny for me that my Uncle is in Gawpassat? That he is at home?'

'I cannot.'

'May I leave a message for him? So that, for example, if he felt like giving me a call, or having someone else call me, I might in that way be put into communication with him?'

'Don't be smart with me,' Mrs Schultz said again. She used to teach me geography at the Middle School – not a discipline known for its flexible thinking: you either knew where you were, or you didn't. Not at all like the Department of Death, I wouldn't have thought.

'I'm sorry to have troubled you, Mrs Schultz. You must get an awful lot of crank calls.'

'You have no idea,' she said.

'Particularly now,' I said, fishing.

'What do you mean by that?'

'I mean now, what with the, with his, with the whole . . . ?'

Nothing. Mrs Schultz said she had work to do, she wished me luck, and rang off.

I remembered Mrs Schultz's daughter, Tanya. She embarrassed me badly one night as we walked home from a party. She asked me why I didn't have a car. I replied that there were plenty of cars awaiting my sixteenth birthday, then only days away. I said that she would be one of the first people I drove around, if she wanted me to. She said I didn't understand, that she merely wanted shelter, so as to have her way with me. I said I hadn't thought of that. It was drizzling. Tanya asked me what I was going to do about it. I thought for a moment, then suggested that we ought to break into the Mannings' house – they were in Florida. We did so (finding the keys in the flower pot outside the back door, like every house in Gawpassat). We spent the next few hours in Mr and Mrs Manning's bed. Tanya got pregnant but, as boys used to say about such things in their horrid, cavalier way, she was a good sport about it.

39

Jean roared into the driveway in a pickup truck bearing the logo of her dog farm. She was barefoot and wore the blue-and-white shorts-and-shirt uniform of the Gawpassat High School girls' field-hockey team. Jean had a great body, even by our town's high standards. The sleeves of her tee shirt were cut off at the shoulders, her shorts rode high on her hips, her legs were long and brown. My sister hadn't changed a great deal in the past fifteen years.

'OK,' she said, removing her dark glasses as she burst into the kitchen. 'Ian's fading fast.' She seemed to relish this news. 'I need you at his deathbed. This is heavy.'

'I tried you at home,' I said. 'No answer.'

'I'm not surprised. I wasn't answering,' Jean said, in a more pronounced English accent than the rest of us affected.

'Why not?'

'Why not? I'll tell you why not. May I have a beer please?'

'Do we have beer?'

'Of course we have beer.'

'I'll get you a beer, then.'

I fetched a can from the refrigerator, from behind a rotten cantaloupe, poured it into a glass and handed it to my sister. Jean took a swig and sat down on a stool at the kitchen counter.

'I made a mistake last night,' she said, wrapping her calves around the legs of the stool and smiling wickedly.

'What mistake was that?'

'You saw that boy I was with.'

'Yes, but I don't know who he is.'

'A youngster, no?'

'Certainly.'

'He's twenty-one years old, as of a week ago.'

'A youngster.'

'As I said. Whew.'

'What's the problem, Jean?'

'I'm only telling you because you're my little brother.'

'Of course.'

'You saw how disgracefully we behaved.'

'It *was* disgraceful.'

'And I did go home with him.'

'You *did* go home with him.'

'Yah.'

'And?'

'Well, and, the usual, in a kind of very *young* way. The point is, *who* he is.'

'Who is he?'

'He's the Sherman boy.'

'*The* Sherman boy?'

'All right, *a* Sherman boy.'

'I remember him. He played a mean third base, in Little League. Sure, I remember him. Billy Sherman. Billy Sherman's nine years old, Jean.'

'Last time you saw him.'

'Time has frozen for me, Gawpassat-wise.'

'So, he's not nine any more, he's twenty-one.'

'Twenty-one.'

'And I was ruthless in my seduction. No-one does this any more, you know. I'm a throwback, a dinosaur.'

'I hope you had fun.'

'I did,' said Jean, pulling her shirt down over the elastic waistband of her shorts.

'Good.'

'No, not good.'

'Why?'

'Because, I'll tell you why. Because you remember who the Sherman boy's father is?'

'Willie Sherman Junior, is the father. Your boy Sherman must be Willie the third.'

'Correct.'

'And Junior, his old man – let me guess. Junior is an Elder.'

'Correct again.'

'You slept with Elder Willie Junior's boy?'

'Again correct.'

'Oh.'

It was never a good idea to sleep with Elders' boys. It was even worse, for some reason, to sleep with Elders' girls. The Elders, elected every other year by a secret 'committee' at the Institute, were Gawpassat's guardians of the Word and its works. They wielded considerable power, especially when it came to selection for membership of the Yacht Club.

All Elders were men: Uncle Ian's religion was of the I-only-bar-women-because-I-worship-them variety. I have heard this argument used in contexts other than club-segregation or back-to-family-values political platforms. Often it can be useful to point to the supposedly divine qualities of Woman when one makes an argument against their suitability for mundane activities such as golf or dinner-party conversation, or work.

Women were allowed to work at the Institute, though none except Uncle Ian's sister was a departmental director. They were allowed to use all of their charms as fund-raisers. They basked in Uncle Ian's admiration in every edition of his Word. *The Second Word* had contained an elegiac tribute to Uncle Ian's mother that moved even me, and echoed some of the nicer things Christianity had to say about the mother of Jesus.

Elders had to be married – it went with the territory. Although it was nowhere specifically expressed that I know of, in my experience they were also required to have or to purchase full heads of hair. One of their most important functions was to ratify the Laws of the Word as soon as they tumbled down the slopes of White Hill, thus lending a semblance of democracy to the process. They were paid modest stipends, to give them credibility, but their perks were invaluable.

'No-one will find out,' I said to Jean, realizing full well the social ostracism – not to mention media exposure – that could result from a wanton relation of the Great Man's consorting with an Elder's son.

'Oh, yes they will.'

'How?'

'I didn't leave until this morning.'

'Someone saw you?'

'No, it was Willie himself. He had a bit of a crisis of conscience. He said he had been taught not to behave that way, and that it must therefore have been my fault.'

'He's – let me get this straight. He's accusing you of rape?'

'Sort of.'

'Preposterous. Anyway, he won't tell. No man would complain of being raped by a girl, not even little Willie Sherman.'

'He said he's going to confess.'

'Come on.'

'That's what he said. He said he *has* to confess to his father.'

'This is silly, Jean. You're just tired. He's scared. He's so young. You probably frightened him. There's no confession, in the Word.'

'There is, when the Date looms. And I believed him. He put on a suit before I'd even got out of bed. A black suit. He said he was going down to the church.'

'They don't confess there, do they?'

'No, they pray. They confess afterwards.'

'And confessions aren't confidential?'

'Are you kidding? Where have you been? This is the *Word*. They practically print them in the *Gazette*.'

The *Gawpassat Gazette*, our alliteratively titled local newspaper, given over completely to dissemination of the Word. The *Gazette* was one of Ian Armstrong's first purchases after he arrived in Gawpassat.

'So,' I said, as I got Jean another beer. 'We need damage control. First, you don't want your boyfriend to know.'

'Right. Poor guy.'

'Second, you don't want to be ostracized.'

'Right. Poor me.'

'Third, you don't want every other guy in Gawpassat to steer clear of you when they see what kind of trouble you are.'

'Please.'

'Well?'

'OK, I suppose so.'

'There's something very important you're forgetting, Jean.'

'Is there?'

'Yes. Just think for a moment. Do you think Willie Junior – Elder or no Elder – is going to want to publicize his son's disgrace in the arms of Ian Armstrong's *niece*?'

'I've already thought of that. I think it makes my position even more dangerous. You don't know what the climate's been like, Top. An Elder like Willie Junior would be *more* likely to use his son's disgrace with me as an example. It would prove to the people how strong his convictions were, if he took a stand on something so serious.'

'I don't believe it.'

'Well, listen to me. *The Last Word* is on the way. The Heir will reveal himself on the Date, et cetera. Old Sherman will think this is a test of his faith, that Ian sent me along as part of that test. He's probably already convened a crisis hand-holding family meeting, and they will have decided to go for broke, call Ian's bluff, make the best of a bad thing.'

I could see how agitated Jean was, but I had an awful feeling she might be right.

'You're the lawyer, Top. Tell me what I ought to do.'

40

Only technically was I a lawyer. After law school – admittance gained thanks to a strongly worded recommendation from the Great Man, funded by my four-minute lyric-writing escapade – I saw clearly that one of the main ways people with law degrees earned their living was to become employed as lawyers. In this enterprise I was joined by what looked like a majority of my liberal-arts contemporaries. There seemed no point in doing anything else.

With my education and connections, I was hired before I had sweated out the pertinent Bar exam, which turned out to be a mere formality. Uncle Ian organized, but did not attend, a celebratory dinner in the city for me and my family, as if by falling into line with everyone else I had attained mankind's highest calling. For a Gawpassatan, becoming a lawyer was the rough equivalent of a Welshman going down the mines, or a Bordelais trying his hand at viticulture. I took my kudos where I could get it, but inside I already suspected that I had taken a wrong turning. It wasn't the law I objected to – it was the lawyering. My one brief summer stint as a paralegal had shown me what to expect: a Sisyphean mountain of work, which was infinite in the sense that when one reached the top one plummeted down the other side to one's death. Of course, these were the thoughts of a young man, and in retrospect a somewhat arrogant one, but they saved me from the inevitable blow of realizing too late that I wasn't cut out for the law. I may not have liked the law, but the law didn't like me, either.

What with everyone and his sister joining law firms up and down the country, I had to be very careful to appear élite – that's just the way we Gawpassatans are. I had pulled only one or two of the thousands of strings available to me, and was signed on with great big grins and country-club handshakes and embarrassing 'You'll go far, my boy' pats on the back. My direct supervisor, a newish partner only five years my senior, asked if they could mount my Everest summit photograph on the wall in reception, enlarged to life size. This would do me a lot of good, they said, and might give the firm that Roof-of-the-World feeling so conducive to competitiveness.

So it was that on my first day at work, itching in my only real business suit, I was greeted by a giant photograph of myself standing on the summit of Everest, holding up a gloved thumb and smiling through my fetching, frosty beard. The jealousy of my fellow associates was palpable. They knew about my Uncle Ian, and must have assumed he had bought the firm. Work came my way relentlessly, like barges down the Mississippi – great stacks of reading material so fabulously boring I found it hard to believe that the wheels of advanced society turned on the details couched within their pages.

Before lunch on my first day I looked over the edge of one such document and inspected my colleagues in our modern, open-plan offices. The young ones looked fresh and pressed; some smiled to themselves as they dabbed their incisive comments in the margins. The slightly older ones, the almost-partner ones, looked haggard and put-upon, like some climbers I have known who one could tell were going to go down with altitude sickness with the next step. The senior types, when I got a glimpse of them, looked hale enough, and cheerful, but I had to assume something hormonal happened to old lawyers that made them look back on their years of drudgery with proud satisfaction.

I fell into my routine. I made a few mortifying mistakes at the beginning, but the gang covered for me. At the end of the second week I went out with half-a-dozen colleagues, and much *bonhomie* was in evidence. These were good, diligent, serious, earnest people – the sharpest tacks of their generation, some would say. They seemed to look up to me, if only because I was a few years older and had taken some time out, however briefly. One would think I had been to war, the way they asked, respectfully, if I might share with them a few tales from the mountaineering front.

We were paid fortunes, all of us, but the consensus was that we deserved what we got. Many of my youngest colleagues were married or engaged to other lawyers; a few had tiny proto-lawyers crawling around at home with the hired help. They spoke of their *pro-bono-publico* work with self-indulgent reverence. I found them all to be conscientious, sincere, and honest to a fault. I suppose corruption didn't wiggle its way into a lawyer until the partner stage.

I cracked in my fifth week. It was a fairly dramatic scene by my phlegmatic standards. I had been thumbing along through my huge work load, working at home until late at night, numbing myself against the thought that I would be performing these same tasks *ad infinitum* by telling myself that I could be doing something equally scary and stultifying for a fraction of the money. It occurred to me only every hour and a half or so that I ought to down tools, grab my jacket and storm out of the place. I thought I could probably get a reasonably cushy job at the Institute, and just *live* with the accusations of nepotism. 'Nepotism,' I reminded myself. 'From the Latin for *nephew*. That's me.'

An announcement came over the loudspeaker overhead one morning. 'To whom it may concern,' said a voice we all recognized as Pete Dayer's. A senior partner, Dayer was allowed to be jovial because he was indisputably a crack lawyer. 'I have the pleasure of announcing to you that today is Alex Booth's sixth wedding anniversary.' A smattering of applause, a cat-call or two. 'I'm sorry to say that we don't have a gift for Mr Booth, *per se*,' Pete continued, 'but if Alex would step into Boardroom A for just a moment, we might be able to make it up to him.'

This remark had everyone on their feet, applauding and whistling. I found their behaviour undignified, but I joined in just to be a good sport. I got a look at Alex's face as he walked down the centre aisle of our office, pulling on his jacket, being shaken by the hand, patted on the back. Everyone beamed. Alex's face turned red over its usual exhausted grey, and I was certain he would soon burst into tears. What was the meaning of this? Why, a promotion, of course. Alex was to be a success.

I began to plot my resignation. Something in my upbringing prevented me from simply stating the reasons for my decision, packing up my meagre desk accessories and departing. I had to stage an elaborate alibi. Chronic illness, perhaps? An allergy to air conditioning? Another death in the family? A mysterious, inexplicable offer from out west to direct a major motion picture? A fabricated conflict of interest? It even crossed my mind that I ought to fake my own murder.

In the end, I strode into my boss's office and explained to him that I had fallen in love with a Hong Kong real-estate heiress, and that I was torn between a long career at our élite law firm and the life of the billionaire. He urged me to leave – he frog-marched me to the elevator, in fact – and he promised strong recommendations if I ever decided to work again.

41

Jean was on her third beer and her fourth cigarette. Unlike our sister Melissa, she perspired. It worried me that she might have become an alcoholic. Who wouldn't, in Word-mad Gawpassat? It was shameful, inexcusable that someone with Jean's background had failed to find a niche in life – but that is one of the problems with having so many advantages: there are few challenges that don't involve years of disagreeable hard work to surmount, which defeats the purpose of privilege. In my case it was the law that had seemed simultaneously over my head and beneath me. Perhaps one shouldn't mock the prince who complains that he is unable to walk the streets with the common man, unnoticed and independent. Jean had done everything required of her and her social group: college, a year in Italy, a conscience-salving eighteen months in Latin America, a master's degree in international relations, then home to Gawpassat for a summer break that never really ended. Her dream, ever since I could remember, had been to become a 'casting director'. She must have got the idea from the credits of a film or television show. Everyone thought she was kidding, that for year after year she harped on the subject of her illustrious career in casting only to annoy us. As time went on, she complained more and more bitterly that her business had gone nowhere, that work had 'dried up', that she could count her clients on no fingers. She seemed really to believe her own fantasy. Her expertise grew and grew as she followed the trade news, gauged who was in and who was out, who was affordable and who had grown too big for his britches. She read novels only to cast them. She watched films only to criticize the choices her imaginary colleagues had made. What she simply could not understand was why no business ever seemed to come her way. When anyone suggested that she might want to hang out a shingle, or at least move a few thousand miles west to where the actors lived, she took offence. She claimed she had gone nowhere so far because no-one believed in her, that she would show us all in the end.

Years after her graduation, I went with Jean to her university careers office to see what she might do with the rest of her life. A pleasant woman in a tweed jacket sat across from us, with some sort of employment bible open before her. I said I thought Jean ought to be a congressional aide. The woman liked this idea, and suggested that Jean, given her background, should latch on to a senator with a special interest in Latin America.

'Right,' said Jean, who was in a peculiar mood that morning. 'And I really know a lot about arms sales.'

'Development, Jean, development,' I said.

'Sure,' said Jean, making a nuclear-weapon noise.

'I see,' said the woman, undeterred. 'Then perhaps government isn't exactly right for you. Have you considered non-governmental aid agencies? Charities? Health? There are some terrible diseases—'

'I'm sick of diseases.'

'I see,' said the woman.

I felt sorry for her. Maybe she didn't adore *her* job, either, but she tried to make the best of it. Spoiled rich kids dropping by to be ungrateful must have made her shout at her children in the evening.

'And those things don't pay,' Jean added, ruthlessly.

'Er, no.'

'Come on, Jean,' I said. 'Everyone's only trying to help.'

'You want to be highly paid?' asked the woman.

'Who wouldn't?'

'I see. Well, have you considered law school? Business school? You wouldn't have any problems—'

'Just stop,' said Jean. 'My brother here is the lawyer in the family.'

'Congratulations,' the woman said to me, somehow still smiling.

'Thank you. Jean, maybe you should just collect a few . . . *dossiers*, whatever they are. Some literature about Latin America.

Nothing is permanent. Just apply for a couple of jobs that sound interesting and see what happens.'

'See what happens? *See what happens?*'

There were a couple of young men waiting nearby for their turn with the careers counsellor, and Jean's outburst had them worried. They looked at each other and winced.

'Jean, come on.'

'Come on? *Come on?*'

'Stop repeating everything I say. You're getting exercised,' I said, sounding exactly like our mother.

'You sound exactly like our mother, Top. Don't get exercised, *Jesus.*'

'Look,' said the unflappable careers lady. 'Why don't you take a nice long break, and think hard about what it is that interests you. You're a very lucky and accomplished young woman. I know it can all sometimes seem futile and daunting. Your brother is right when he says nothing is permanent – except children. Relax, have a good time, try to regain your enthusiasm. Life,' said the careers lady, as tears welled in my eyes, 'is about experiences, about love, but also about responsibility. Someone with your talents will find great satisfaction no matter where you are. Also disappointment, frustration, a sense of loss, of time passing too quickly, of—'

'Oh, God, stop, please,' said Jean, bursting into tears. The two young men had panicked looks on their faces. I wiped my eyes with my jacket sleeve.

'Here's a tissue, dear,' the careers lady said to Jean. The woman suddenly looked divinely beautiful. 'Just don't you worry.'

'May I have a tissue too?' I asked.

'Here you are, dear.'

'Oh, God,' said Jean.

The careers lady continued to smile. Perhaps this was her entertainment, her revenge.

'Now,' she said, as Jean sniffled, then blew her nose. 'Why don't I just let you have a couple of brochures?'

42

'Everything will be all right, Jean,' I said, in the kitchen of our parents' house. 'You have to stand up to these people. You must assert your own morality. Worse things have happened, I'm sure.'

'You mean deny everything? Stonewall?'

'Exactly. And go to the source, if necessary. A word in Ian's ear might not hurt, if it ever comes to that. You say he's on his deathbed? So soon?'

'No-one can truly be believed, but this is what my contacts tell me. Be a good little brother and fetch me another beer? It's so hot.'

If we were not overly concerned about Uncle Ian's health, it was because his was a deathbed in name only. There was a special room high in his mansion that he had furnished and decorated for the purpose of his demise. It contained mementoes of his life, fresh flowers, excellent music and, of course, the sacred deathbed itself. The deathbed had belonged to his parents, both of whom had died in it within weeks of each other. It was a rickety, badly sprung old bed, but Uncle Ian insisted on changing nothing, not even the sheets. Jean's news, if true, would send tremors though the Word faithful around the world. In Gawpassat, it would be the most exciting thing that had ever happened. If the Great Man had taken to his deathbed it did not necessarily mean he would soon die, only that he was in a dying frame of mind. The antennae of potential heirs would be twitching.

I told Jean of my visit from our nephew, and his message that Uncle Ian wished to see me. I asked her if this was credible.

'Could be,' she said, clearly excited and jealous. 'You would be the first to see him in ages, unless someone isn't talk-ing.'

'I suppose I ought to go, then?'

'Absolutely.'

'What do people wear, to see the Great Man? Our nephew said something about uniforms, at weddings.'

'Oh, Christ, that reminds me,' said Jean, looking at the kitchen clock. 'I have to go to Little Dave Periman's wedding this afternoon. Do you want to come along?'

'I wasn't invited. And I don't have a uniform.'

'Little Dave would be thrilled. Are you kidding?'

'I don't think I want to go. You have a good time.'

Jean snatched her keys and dark glasses from the counter and said she would see me later at Trainer's. As a rule, Gawpassatans were tolerated in their drinking and driving. We Richmonds were virtually immune from prosecution. Jean turned her truck around, backing into a hedge in the process, and flew out of the drive into Lincoln Street with a casual wave out the window.

Alone again, I made myself a sandwich and a pitcher of iced tea. I moved slowly, and concentrated on not sweating. I could hear the buzz of a lawnmower outside. I ate my lunch on the verandah, missing Laurie in the worst way.

43

Laurie and I – uncharacteristically in both cases – had taken our time getting physically acquainted. We met on that bus in Brussels, we ate lunch and dinner together, we met the next day for coffee – but it wasn't until after our trip to the Alps that proper love-making could be said to have taken place. I had heard about people who behaved this way; I had even heard about quite long-term platonic relationships between men and women. It was a first for me, though, and I found it powerfully erotic.

She told me about her ex-husband, I told her about my ten or twelve most recent girlfriends. She struck me from the outset as awfully strong, to have made so difficult and final a decision so young. In a way, I understood my parents' view of divorce: it was an admission not just of defeat, but of having made a terrible mistake in the first place. 'Bad judgement,'

I could hear my father saying, through his moustache, as if Laurie had lost an inheritance at the tables of Monte Carlo. I thought Laurie was brave and inspiring; only later did I exhibit irrational jealousy of her ex-husband, the bass player, but this she managed to quell in her typically sane and sweet way.

It is not in my constitution to peer back in time searching for explanations, nor do I court remorse. I prefer to keep hung in my mind a portrait gallery of relatively happy memories, chief among them those early days with Laurie. There was nothing special about us; we were just another couple wheeling into love. As an individual, there is very little else I have. I find it interesting that such tender memories survive, whereas the specifics of the countless hours 'entwined in brute passion', as my father once alarmingly described the act, appear as retrospective hallucinations. Never mind the brute passion: I remember lying chastely next to Laurie in an Alpine cabin, inches away, and if it is possible to recall a scent it would be hers – the faintest healthful glow of our day's exertion in the mountains. I edged closer, my face nearly touching her shoulder. I lay so long propped on one arm that I was stiff for three days afterwards. It is heartbreaking to fall in love, but of course one has scant choice in the matter. She slept in a clean white cotton blouse with thin straps at the shoulders, which she would hike in the following morning. Brute passion would not be long in coming.

I made it my plan to kiss Laurie's collar bone without waking her. Her breathing was slow and shallow, even at altitude. My lips were dry from the day's sun. Her soft brown hair, short in those days, brushed against mine as I drew closer. I closed my eyes and softly inhaled her delicate, delicious scent. I exhaled slowly, slowly through my nose on to her skin. I gently pressed my lips to her collar bone, stayed there for a minute or more, then felt Laurie's hand on the back of my neck. I settled next to her and we faded in and out of sleep and love for the short hours until dawn. I think of that night as a good experience.

44

Despite the heat, I decided to put on a jacket and tie for my visit to Uncle Ian's house on Black Hill. I gave myself forty minutes to walk there. I took the short-cut off Lincoln Street, a path that led down through the woods to a shallow valley. Needless to say, my friends and I had employed this path for all of the private needs of youth, memories of which came back to me as I picked my way down the hill through the trees. In the valley I crossed the mighty Gawpassat river, its flow so reduced I ignored the footbridge upstream and merely hopped from bank to dry bank.

Not wishing to arrive at the gates of Uncle Ian's house in a sweat, I climbed Black Hill extremely slowly, stopping every few steps to let the faint breeze dry my face. Inevitably, I was reminded of Everest and those painful steps up the wall, sometimes one minute apart for long stretches, with only the rapid whistling of my own breath for company. I truly hated that part. In fact, Marcus and I agreed that there was almost nothing enjoyable about the physical act of climbing that silly mountain. The views could be beautiful, but repetitive: who looks out of the window of an aeroplane any more? Whatever joy there was, for lucky amateurs like me and Marcus, came in retrospect, and vainly so.

I joined Jefferson Street halfway up Black Hill, and walked up past the most desirable houses of our highly desirable town. Their lawns and gardens, their driveways and automobiles – as well as the houses' façades themselves – were groomed to a perfection that suggested their occupants lived in perpetual fear of unannounced inspection. Their perfect children played basketball, swatted tennis balls, ran through sprinklers, leapt into swimming pools. I had been told that, of late, Gawpassatans' lives had become somewhat frayed at the financial edges, but it didn't show. They still frolicked in peace and safety: fathers unloaded golf clubs from second or third cars; mothers scolded baby-sitters and lectured nannies; teenagers roared about in sports cars or on high-performance motorcycles; children returned home by gleaming yellow bus from Saturday hot-house school. Superficially, nothing had changed. If they were worried about anything, they weren't letting on.

Near the top of Black Hill there was a long stretch of road that cut through what could only be called a forest. There were no houses within a half-mile radius of Uncle Ian's mansion. I paused before the massive gates at the end of Jefferson Street and mopped my face with a paper towel I had brought along for exactly that purpose. I was already being watched by closed-circuit cameras, and in the distance I heard the whine of the golf cart that would arrive to ferry me to one wing or other of Uncle Ian's spread. The golf cart ferrying was only one of the innumerable vulgarities I actually liked about Uncle Ian's setup. The gates hummed open a few inches, and I squeezed into the grounds. A boy wearing some sort of white tunic pulled up in the golf cart. I introduced myself, but his mind was elsewhere. I climbed in, and we lurched off in the direction of Uncle Ian's splendid pool under ancient maple and oak trees.

The boy stopped the golf cart at a stone path that led through a white wooden gate and down to the pool house. Without a word, without looking at me, in fact, he made it clear that I ought to disembark. Adjusting my tie, I walked down to the pool house and entered through the back door. This was a long, low building with screens and French windows running the length of the pool. A banquet table had been laid with glass bowls of fruit, ice chests of beer and wine and soft drinks, simmering dishes of lasagna and chicken, wooden bowls of salad. This feast did not necessarily indicate a likelihood that guests would soon arrive; food was part of the furniture on Black Hill.

I walked back outside, on to the green plastic surface that surrounded the pool. Uncle Ian, wearing goggles, crawled lazily along in the centre lane. There was no-one else about, only the dead eyes of video cameras posted on the roof of the pool house. I sat down in a deck chair and watched my uncle swim. He was a tall man, and his long strokes looked strong and efficient. His big white feet fluttered under the surface of the water. Except for the goggles, Uncle Ian swam in the nude. On a chair near where I sat lay Uncle Ian's discarded clothes: a white tennis shirt, khaki shorts, a baseball cap and a pair of large leather sandals – the kind of leather sandals with loops for the big toes.

45

Uncle Ian still hadn't noticed me, so I had a few minutes to ask myself why he would have wanted to spy on me the previous night. I tried to remember if I had said anything incriminating on the phone to Laurie, something that might have insulted my uncle. I thought not. I supposed it was just one of those built-in eccentricities of the rich, a rarefied form of amusement. If I had been as wealthy as Uncle Ian, I probably would have snuck around more than I normally did.

From an early age, I had been fascinated by very wealthy people. It was a bonus to be related to one, especially of the self-made variety. I dated the middle Periman girl for a spring and a summer, but that liaison did not prove to be instructive: I think her parents were waiting for her eighteenth birthday before breaking the news that if all went well she would some day inherit a dozen million strictly legitimate dollars. Little Dave Periman, whose wedding I had chosen not to attend, had seemed more on the ball than his younger sister. He spoke to his trust fund manager on a daily basis, even at prep school, and had the temerity to write to his father with investment advice. There was something shallow, though, about Gawpassatan wealth. It seemed to me that our very richest fellow townspeople failed to take sufficient advantage of their money, as if it were something to be ashamed of. The lives of the most élite Gawpassatans – except for Uncle Ian's – were really not that different from the run-of-the-millionaire families scattered farther down our three hillsides. I thought at the very least that they should make grand gestures designed to cause envy in their neighbours, or, among the younger generation, engage in perilous degeneracy.

Rumour had it that Uncle Ian had accumulated between sixty and seventy-five million liquid dollars over a career spanning thirty-five years. There is something about that kind of money that tended to make accusations of charlatanism or cupidity ring hollow. This was what Little Dave used to call, when tipsy, 'So-*what* money.' Evidently, once a certain threshold of wealth had been achieved, the point became one of subtly lording one's impregnability over less fortunate people. In Gawpassat, this meant pretending not to care what other people thought, and, more importantly, pretending that money made no difference to their perfectly balanced and fruitful lives. Some quirk of popular culture tended to back up this stance, since very wealthy people were invariably portrayed as flawed, corrupt, unhappy, perverted and doomed. The best thing that could happen to them was to lose all their money, or give it all away, so that they could rediscover the essential elements of life that no amount of money could buy: love, spiritual wholeness, the gratification of honest toil, profound and equable relationships with their children.

Well, *horse puckey*, as my Uncle Ian might have put it. He argued persuasively in *The Fifth Word* that there was absolutely no point in living in a society that professed a devotion to social and economic advancement, unless one were prepared to gloat over the proceeds and bar the door. Any fool could see that properly managed money meant freedom, and it was up to the beneficiaries to decide how to use it. A glance at history shows how great wealth and power invariably bred wonderful follies of self-indulgence, exclusivity, cruelty, passion and, significantly, sex. How it came to pass that our few extremely rich

Gawpassatans decided that real money had to be accompanied by responsibility, social graces, charity and liberalism, even Uncle Ian could not explain.

46

I watched Uncle Ian pull himself through the water, and loosened my tie. His body was tan and smooth, and his flesh sagged only slightly at the hips. His physique was a good advertisement for the Word. After a few more laps he stopped in the shallow end and stood up.

'Hello, Uncle Ian.'

He turned around, not in the least surprised. He must have known I was there all along.

'Hello, son,' he replied. A towel lay on the deck, which he used to dry his fairly long white hair while still standing in the pool. With the agility of a much younger man, he hoisted himself out of the water, stood up, and wrapped the towel around his waist.

'I hate swimming laps,' he said, as he walked over to join me. 'I don't do it very often.'

'You look good,' I said, rising to shake his hand. Uncle Ian slapped his free hand wetly on the back of my neck as he made his usual solid eye contact. I didn't know if that meant I was supposed to half-hug him or not, so I held back.

'Great to see you, son.'

'And you.'

He sat down with a grunt and asked me what I wanted to eat and drink. I said I would have what he had. He made a hand signal in the direction of one of the cameras, and seconds later a young man wearing what looked like a purser's uniform bounded out from the pool house. Uncle Ian ordered two bacon, lettuce and tomato sandwiches on white toast with pepper and extra mayonnaise, two cold draught beers – no, make that four – and four aspirin.

'In case you have a headache, too,' he said, when the servant had jogged away.

'It's so beautiful here,' I said. 'It's been a long time.'

It really was beautiful, too. The far side of the pool was lined with boxwood hedges and, behind them, a tall row of pines. If you stood on the diving board and looked down the length of the pool and over the edge, there was the ocean and the rocky loop of Gawpassat Bay. There were even two tall palm trees growing on the lawn nearby, that some expensive miracle of botanical science allowed to survive our vicious winters. There were such sweet smells on the air, and such dead quiet.

'The first thing you do, my boy, before the food comes, is get those hot clothes off you and take a dip. I'll fetch us both a robe while you do that. Come on, now, hop to it.'

I kicked off my shoes and undressed, walked down to the diving board, took a look into the hazy distance, then dived deep into the cool water. I swam two lengths on my back, looking up into the grey-blue sky. I climbed out and put on the yellow terry-cloth robe my uncle had left for me on the diving board. I rejoined him at a table in the shade of a Japanese maple just as our snack arrived, borne by two women wearing tunics similar to the golf-cart driver's. Uncle Ian smoothed back his thick white hair, then tucked into his sandwich and beer. I did likewise, reinvigorated by my swim. The faintest breath of breeze whisked through the trees and cooled my neck. Uncle Ian leaned back and spread his legs wide under the table.

'You've got to feel that cool air on your balls,' he said, sipping his mug of beer. Rich people are allowed to be as earthy as they want, when it suits them.

I nodded, and adjusted myself to take advantage of his suggestion.

'My goodness,' said my uncle, finishing his sandwich and appraising me. 'I don't believe you've changed one bit, Top. I can remember you with those cute things you used to bring by, those cute things in their cute little, you know, bathing costumes. It just isn't *fair*, Top.'

'No, sir,' I said. 'It isn't.'

'Don't think I wasn't looking.'

'Of course you were.'

'You dog.'

The Word said, in so many words, that it was OK to be lustful in one's heart.

'Hell,' said Uncle Ian, remembering something. 'Have you got the time?'

'No, sorry. I left my watch at my parents' house.'

Uncle Ian leaned down and squinted into the pool house, where there was a clock mounted over the banquet table.

'Oh, hell, look at that. Benjamin!' he shouted. 'Benjamin, bring the transmitter! Step on it!' He lowered his voice. 'Sorry about this, Top.'

'That's all right.' I had no idea what was going on.

Benjamin, the man in the purser's uniform, scrambled over to us carrying a heavy aluminium case. He knelt down on the deck and opened it.

'Hurry, for goodness sake. Come on, it's twenty past,' said Uncle Ian.

Benjamin unpacked cables, a microphone and stand, and what looked like a fairly old-fashioned two-way radio. He set up the microphone so that Uncle Ian could speak into it without changing his position. He plugged in a lead here, a lead there, with some dexterity and without breaking into a sweat, as I had already done.

'Plenty of echo,' said Uncle Ian, as Benjamin patched in a more modern effects device. 'Come on, now, hurry. Sound check?'

Benjamin turned on the radio, adjusted levels, donned headphones, then nodded.

'Right, Benjamin, here I am,' said Uncle Ian into the microphone. 'Mairzy dotes 'n dozy dotes 'n liddle lamzy divy. OK?'

Benjamin gave him the thumbs up.

117

'Patch us through,' ordered Uncle Ian.

Benjamin threw a switch, and over the radio came the voice of Little Dave Periman, reciting his ghost-written marriage vows: ' . . . companion, lover, best friend . . . take you into my heart . . . declare this day eternal . . . '

Uncle Ian took a swig of beer, turned away from the microphone to clear his throat. It was Beth Rhodes's turn to repeat the same home-spun vows: ' . . . surrender my soul . . . trust, openness and caring . . . uniting of fate and fortune . . . '

A few solemn words of introduction were then spoken by Reverend Casey, the ex-Congregationalist sell-out to the Word, then Uncle Ian leaned closer to the microphone: 'So shall it be,' he said, in a strangely weak voice, as if pretending to speak from his deathbed. It must have had quite an effect, down on the lawn of the Institute. 'May you be granted all happiness and prosperity. May all your striving be rewarded, may your love endure and increase . . . '

Uncle Ian's eyes were closed, as if he were concentrating on remembering his lines. His voice diminished to a whisper until, at last, he breathed the words, 'God bless you.'

He looked at Benjamin and signalled the end of his transmission by drawing a finger beneath his jaw; Benjamin switched off the radio and began immediately to pack up the equipment.

'Sorry about that,' Uncle Ian said to me. 'The Perimans have been awful loyal over the years.'

'Of course they have.'

Benjamin lugged the suitcase away, and we were alone once more.

47

The man across from me – in a yellow robe, his wet white hair plastered back from his suntanned forehead, his genitals airing in the whispering breeze – was the true idol of tens of thousands of people. Some of them would have given the life of a loved one in exchange for an audience similar to mine. He had a pointy nose, a prominent chin, a long neck, a grey-haired chest, slender, bony arms, unmuscled calves and large feet tipped with yellowing toenails. His teeth were long and yellow and frightening. When his mouth was closed his brown lips sagged at the corners and pursed in the middle, which in concert with his twinkling brown eyes gave him the almost permanent expression of someone who had scored a devastating point in an intellectual debate.

He had aged imperceptibly over the years, the way older relatives will, and if it hadn't been for all the photographs of him in my bedroom I would have said he hadn't changed since the days when I was allowed to bring my girlfriends over for a swim. His hair was his best feature, his trademark. It would have been impressive even on a man whose business was not helped by a white mane's carrying divine overtones. His hair had been white as long as I could remember, though yellowed by nicotine in the days when he smoked. He had announced his wrenching departure from cigarettes when I was a young boy, incorporating his defeat of painful withdrawal symptoms into the Power of Will section of *The Second Word*. Thousands of people quit with him, or tried to, and only those of us who knew him well were aware that he continued to smoke for sixteen years after the official announcement that he had beaten his addiction. He finally stopped, all of a sudden, when he was injured in a spear-gun accident and a doctor showed him a section of his charred left lung.

That spear-gun accident was probably the moment when I realized that my uncle really was famous. Every newspaper carried the story, every television news broadcast at least mentioned the Great Man's brush with death. The accident occurred in the Red Sea, which was technically part of the Holy Land, and therefore good for business. I am quite sure the facts were muddied or glamorized for the consumption of his followers, but the way I understand it a girlfriend happened to fire off a spear from aboard ship just as Uncle Ian surfaced from a shallow scuba dive. He was struck in the back, his lung was pierced, and a French doctor in Tel Aviv was the one to hold up the piece of spongy black fuzz that put a halt to my uncle's smoking for ever. No-one ever asked if the girlfriend might have shot him on purpose.

48

'Tell me about yourself, Top,' said my uncle. He gathered me in with his intelligent eyes, grinned at me with his self-assured, worldly mouth. 'It's been a long time.'

'Last time I spoke to you must have been on the telephone, from Cyprus. What, two or three years ago?'

'Cyprus. Of course, that's right.'

'I'm sorry about that.'

Uncle Ian snorted. 'You were a drunken boy, were you not?'

'I was indeed. I was a drunken boy.'

'You just talked and talked. Of course I remember.'

'I must have called everyone in my address book. Your people wouldn't give me your new number today, by the way. I was lonely, I guess.'

'Lonely and drunk.'

'Yes, and I'd found an open hotel room with a telephone just sitting there, waiting to be abused.'

'Ah, so *that's* it.'

'Sure. It just felt like minting money, talking on that phone hour after hour.'

'Good for you.'

'As I recall, I had discovered a few key secrets of existence that I thought might be useful to you. How embarrassing. I'm truly sorry.'

'Sorry? Never you mind. I can play you the tape, if you want, or show you the transcript. It's all in the archive. And what a lot of good suggestions you had, too. If I remember right you were concerned about collecting deuterium from the world's oceans. Big, mobile, ocean-going deuterium collectors.'

'You have an amazing memory, Uncle Ian.'

'Your name used to come up at dinner parties, as part of a game I liked to play.'

'Oh?'

'Everyone would write down the name of a place, I'd get out the world map and a piece of string, and the person who guessed closest to where you were won a holiday there. Very amusing. We called the game "Where's Top?".'

'But how did you know where I was?'

My uncle smiled and ran a handful of fingers through his drying hair. 'That was easy,' he said. 'And sometimes, if I was too lazy to find out exactly, I'd just make it up. I was the umpire, you see. I had invented the rules, I could invent the answers. No-one complained if I said, "Congratulations, Dick, you're on your way to Java. Bring the wife if you want."'

'No, I don't suppose they would.'

'Usually I did know where you were.'

'How unnerving.'

It is well known that self-made rich people tend to become fanatical about control. Uncle Ian's behaviour bore out this rule, and then some. His house was a nest of advanced intelligence-gathering equipment. Like any sensible person in the public eye, he knew he was being watched; his reply was to watch back. I had personally seen only a small selection of his toys, but it was enough to convince me that my uncle would not have been at a technological disadvantage *vis-à-vis* your average country. He had most to fear from the Internal Revenue Service, like everyone, but even that organization's tentacles would have been stretched.

I have noticed an instinct among rich men for sparing no effort in simplifying their routine activities, and damn the cost. Telephones must dial themselves and always be within reach, preferably with hands-off speakers and receivers; yachts must be navigated by satellite, even if their longest journey never takes them out of sight of land; limousines must be equipped like Wall Street trading rooms, and endowed with the amenities of a penthouse hotel suite. The point is one that even moderately well-off people seem to take for granted in an age of inexpensive gadgetry: greater streamlining equals better life.

Uncle Ian took this assumption to amazing extremes. I had just witnessed a minor example of this in his benediction of Little Dave Periman's wedding. It must have taken a great deal of organization at home and at the marriage site to provide the link for Uncle Ian, just for the sake of the supposed convenience of not having to move a muscle when the time came to deliver his brief address.

I always used to imagine that it wouldn't be long before Uncle Ian succumbed to classical symptoms of the tycoon's paranoid obsession with germs, and locked himself away in a sterile glass chamber. While this never came to pass, he did insist upon indulging in such wasteful practices as always having a full buffet on hand when he went for a swim. Every contingency had to be planned for in advance: what if, what *if* he suddenly felt a strong desire to eat a slice of watermelon? Watermelon there would be. To go water skiing? The boat would be fuelled, ski and wet suit arranged on the dock. To play golf in failing light? His jet would race the sun back over the horizon and deposit him on the first tee in a better climate, a more appropriate time zone, caddy on hand polishing his titanium driver, course cleared of *hoi polloi*. The running costs of a life based on catering to one's every whim must be shattering even to the very-rich-indeed.

I have noticed in my own small way that appetites sated or thirsts quenched are soon replaced by other, slightly more powerful cravings. This is a corrupting influence on mankind, and one of the reasons wealthy and powerful people are supposed not to be trusted on any account – likewise wealthy and powerful nations. I was not surprised, therefore, to learn from the Great Man's mouth that he had been tracking my movements over the past few years, nor that his sandals suggested he had been spying on me the previous evening. It was unfair, that's all, and a bit scary.

49

'How's, er, Agnes?' I asked, to change the subject. I supposed I was allowed to call his second wife Agnes. She was no relation of mine – but that hadn't stopped Jean and me from referring to her over the years as Auntie Intellectual. Agnes was a socialite who lacked the successful hostess's quick mind, now in her early forties. This is not to say that she was useless. Her *modus operandi* was to be frenetic and strident at all times, a whirlwind of high-volume social point-scoring and, needless to say, blind consumerism. Something must have gone terribly wrong inside Uncle Ian's brain for him to have married her. Jean and I suspected a sexual allure visible only to older men.

'Agnes is in Paris,' said Uncle Ian. 'Doing you'll never guess what.'

'Shopping?'

'You could say that. Do you want to watch?'

'I beg your pardon?'

'Oh, you're going to love this, Top. This is new. Come on, now.'

He put on his baseball cap, stripped off his robe, put on his shorts, shirt and sandals. I dressed as quickly as I could and followed him through the pool house to the main lawn.

There was Uncle Ian's mansion, similar to my parents', but twice as big. It was a grand old place, covered in believable ivy.

'It's staff day,' said Uncle Ian, when I noticed that the tennis court was occupied. 'What time is it in Paris, do you think?'

'Elevenish?'

'Perfect,' said my uncle. 'She dines late.'

We entered the house through a side door, straight into one of Uncle Ian's situation rooms, which had been completely modernized since I had last visited. Consoles, television screens, recording equipment, banks of telephones, speakers, microphones, headphones and a wet bar.

'Grab us a beer,' he said. 'I'll set up. The engineers are all on court.' He was excited, and showing off. He capered about the room, as the sun broke through one of the sound-proofed windows. He turned up the air conditioning, the main console, a monitor or two, then seated himself in a leather throne. 'Come in, Paris,' he said, theatrically. I opened a beer and handed it to him. 'Sit here,' he said, patting the arm of his chair. 'This won't take long, if all goes smoothly.'

'If you're about to be able to do what I think you're about to be able to do . . . '

'Beautiful, isn't it?' he said, as one of the monitors flickered to life and introduced us to a wide-angle view of a hotel suite.

'I'm not quite sure about that.'

Uncle Ian adjusted a volume knob, and we heard a low, steady humming sound.

'Isn't it working properly?'

'Of course it is. That's a hair dryer, my boy. You have to be patient, in this game.'

'I'm sure.' So it really was true: egomaniacs with unlimited funds will set themselves up like spy-novel villains.

'That's Agnes, there,' he said, pointing at a corner of the screen. Sure enough, there was a trace of silk dressing gown visible through what must have been the bathroom door.

It has to be said that society considered Agnes to be a beautiful woman. I disagreed. It went without saying that women like Agnes were put in an impossible situation by the natural ageing process, but her futile retaliation seemed to me to make matters worse. She dressed too colourfully, after starving herself, in *haute couture* even the catwalk seventeen-year-olds who flogged it to her must have thought vulgar. It is tiresome even to have to report the basics of her daily toilette, her two-hour coiffure that ended up looking like cotton candy, her rumoured (and perfectly obvious) dabbling in plastic surgery. When I was old enough to understand the tragedy of Agnes's appearance, it was not beyond me to draw parallels between her cult of beauty and Uncle Ian's religion business: each was a tax on stupidity.

Agnes turned off the hair dryer and flounced into the bedroom, spritzing her face with what I hope was an atomizer containing water. She went over to a full-length mirror on the wall near the bed and spent more time looking into it and adjusting her appearance than I probably had in the previous five years, and I am on the vain side.

'I can't believe you're watching this,' I said, hoping it wasn't completely out of line for me to say so. 'Anyway, how is it possible?'

'Where have you been? I just bounce it right in here on satellite, transmitted off the roof of her hotel. You just pay for satellite time, which is a steal, considering what you get. The signal is encrypted, of course. Not for general consumption. Look, she's putting her dress on.'

'But surely just about anyone with any knowledge—'

'Let 'em watch,' growled Uncle Ian.

I had to admire how up-to-date my uncle was with his spying gadgets. I thought satellites were young man's work.

'I take it she has no idea you're watching. This isn't some sort of two-way link because you . . . because you *miss* her so much.'

My uncle and I shared a laugh.

'This, my boy,' he said, after a soothing sip of beer, 'is evidence. I don't want to break your heart, but I'm afraid the arrangements for our legal separation have been in the pipeline for about three years. The time has come for me to part company with Auntie Intellectual.'

'You knew we called her that?'

'Naturally.'

'Anyway, Uncle Ian. That's too bad. I had no idea. And what do you mean, evidence?'

'If you want to sit right here for a little while, you will see your evidence.'

'Oh?'

'Yes.'

'I see.'

50

'Trust in your love,' Uncle Ian had written importantly some-where, and here he sat at the controls of a round-the-world spying machine, watching his wife preparing to dine romanti-cally in her hotel room with a paunchy, grey-haired Frenchman named Michel.

'This is too much, too sordid,' I said. 'I can't possibly watch.'

I couldn't tear myself away. It was fascinating beyond all pornography. Uncle Ian stretched, clasped his hands behind his back, settled into his great leather throne.

Michel, it turned out, was hilarious. In fluent English he teased my Auntie Intellectual, told her how naughty she was, how tantalizing and irresistible.

'Michel sells toothpaste,' Uncle Ian remarked over his shoulder.

'How can she . . . ? How can he . . . ?'

'I know, I know. What a silly woman. Can you imagine? How long was I going to live, anyway?'

'Don't say that, Uncle Ian.'

This was special, to say the least, to be so close to the Great Man, to see his real life. He had indirectly mentioned his own demise, an event for which perhaps one million people waited in solemn anticipation.

Uncle Ian had predicted his own death in *The First Word* – an act I would have thought was ill-advised, even for prophets. It did lend some eerie credibility to his supposed conversations with God, to have been told the *exact* date of his removal from existence. People took it for granted that God knew the future, which I found not necessarily rational. I searched my mind for the Date, that fateful Date, supposedly etched into my memory when I learned the Junior Word in elementary school. All followers of the Word knew the Date, repeated it like a mantra in their prayers and meditations and weight-lifting repetitions.

The Date came back to me with the ease of the Lord's Prayer, or the year Columbus sailed the ocean blue, and with a quick flexing of my brain I calculated that my uncle, if he were to live up to his version of God's will, had roughly two days to live.

'Look here, look here,' said my uncle, leaning forward to touch a corner of the screen. 'Do you see that? Do you see that?'

'I can't watch.'

I had to watch. Auntie Intellectual and her Frenchman were having a fabulous time with a plate of *charcuterie* and a carafe of red wine that had been brought to their room.

'The best part,' said Uncle Ian, 'is when he asks about me. I'm not huge in France,' he added sadly, 'but Michel here, he's interested.'

I have to say Uncle Ian looked childlike in his electronic playroom. He seemed almost to have forgotten about me, and spoke mainly to the satellite monitor or to the ceiling.

'If we're lucky they'll talk about my death.' Uncle Ian turned up the volume, so that we heard some rather unpleasant smacking of chops and licking of lips and gulping of wine. 'They've talked about my death quite a lot over the past few evenings. Quite often. They are hopeful, they are looking forward to it, but they don't – they can't bring themselves – to *believe*.'

'He's in toothpaste?'

'Toothpaste. Look, there.' He touched the screen again. 'I'm *paying* for this, you know.'

They had moved on to the duck.

It amused me to hear Uncle Ian complain about the trivial expense of dinner for two in a five-star Parisian hotel. He had managed in his life to forge two contradictory popular images of himself: he was seen at once to be a public benefactor and a private skinflint. He ran his business with fanatical attention to detail. He wrote in *The Fourth Word* that an American ought to make every dollar *count*, because 'counting means adding up'. On the other hand there had always been evidence of grand generosity, not least where his nieces and nephew were concerned. The famous island-hopping birthday party for Claire and me was a typical example. Another was the permanently unresolved question of my parents' obligations regarding rental arrears. Whose house was it, anyway, up there on Gray Hill? He lavished luxury on himself, yet there were those who complained that even his highest-ranking employees could not afford to live in Gawpassat. They drove in from dreary row houses in towns nearer our ghastly city.

'Why do you watch this?' I asked my uncle, as Michel and Auntie Intellectual held hands across their hotel room dining table, gazed into each others' eyes and laughed at the beauty of their secret liaison.

'That's easy,' he replied, turning to look at me for the first time in half an hour. 'Because I *can*.'

51

There had always been an argument in my family about the sincerity of Uncle Ian's Word. The hated, atheist press took it for granted that Ian Armstrong's programme was nothing more than an unsophisticated scam at best, at worst a cynical exploitation of credulous people. On the other side were the true believers, growing in number every year, who took it on faith that the Great Man was committed to his teachings, which by their nature had to derive from his spirit rather than from the needs of his wallet.

I thought both views were simplistic. I could readily see how he might have started out with a cold, commercial view of the Word, but like a politician whose hypocritical slogans caused historical movements of large numbers of people, he probably began to believe in the Word as an extension of himself. Some corner of Ian Armstrong's mind must have conceded long ago the meaninglessness and redundancy of the Word, if not its unmitigated crassness, but who would not come to trust in his own magic when the masses clamoured at the gates for more?

Only once, that I know of, had anyone dared ask Uncle Ian if he believed in his own religion. I could have done so on numerous occasions, I suppose, but the question had always seemed inherently rude. The moment in question was a television interview, of black-and-white vintage, in which my uncle was asked point blank whom he thought he was kidding with his talk of a pipeline to God. The interviewer, sucking on a cigarette, asked if Uncle Ian didn't think most people would agree that if God wanted to reveal all to a human being he would speak some language other than a kind of rustic, southern, aphoristic lingo full of colourful, even licentious metaphor. Uncle Ian's response was to issue a full thirty seconds of hostile, withering glare, followed by the words, 'Don't you mind yourself about that, then, little man.'

52

Uncle Ian had been married to Agnes for more than ten years. None of Aunt Charlotte's relatives was allowed to go to the wedding, by Agnes's decree. Practically no-one attended, in fact, as it was thought in those days that too much attention paid to a second marriage might put a dent in Uncle Ian's business. This fear proved to be unfounded, for when the news broke, much was made of the bride's supposed beauty and refinement; the conclusion was drawn that the prophet of the Word must be a virile fellow indeed. Women, already converts for reasons of their own, bought the collected works for their husbands.

My parents, still reeling from Uncle Ian's divorce from Aunt Charlotte, despised Agnes Rush. They could probably *just* have tolerated her had she been from Gawpassat, slightly older and less showy. If they could have seen what had just appeared on the monitor at Uncle Ian's house, they would have felt vindicated in their prejudices.

'I can't, can't, can't watch this,' I said, watching, watching, watching. 'Uncle Ian, you're a masochist.'

'Not at all, son. Better him than me, if you want to know the truth.'

'I've got to leave. I've got to go outside. I need air.'

'Go on, then. Suit yourself. Ask someone for . . . for whatever you want. I won't be long. I want to talk to you.'

Like Jean, he seemed to want to talk to me without making the effort actually of forming words and uttering them. Without replying, then, I made my exit just as Agnes and Michel seemed to have decided that their *digestifs* were best enjoyed abed.

53

Sitting at a table in the shade of a tree on Uncle Ian's lawn, I decided to pretend I owned the place. Benjamin scurried over to me when I waved at him, and stood silently before me as I made up my mind about what it was, exactly, that I wanted.

'A pitcher of iced tea,' I said at last. 'With plenty of ice. Leave the sugar and squeezed lemon on the side.'

'Yes, sir.' It occurred to me that Benjamin looked familiar.

'And I would also like a plate of baby shrimp, with mayonnaise.'

'Yes, sir.' Now I remembered: Benjamin had been a classmate of mine, a rather good pole-vaulter and the captain of the debating team.

'And an avocado, cut in half, filled with cottage cheese and sprinkled with paprika.'

'Yes, sir.'

'Thanks, Benjie, that's all.'

Off he went, leaving me alone, master of all I surveyed. Well, not quite alone. There was a skinny girl in a white tutu not far away, burning her shoulder blades in the sun. I hadn't remembered Gawpassatan pre-adolescent girls being so thin, in my day. It was conceivable that Uncle Ian's creed of leanness had affected even the very young. This girl's mosquito legs stuck out from her tutu in two straight brown lines. I thought perhaps that was where Jean had made the connection between Uncle Ian's sentries and our sister Claire: her legs had looked like tennis racket handles. She probably would have grown up tall and clumsy, perhaps scholarly. If so, she would have had an uphill battle. Gawpassat wanted its girls to look enticing and, later on, to learn how to drive automatic-transmission minibuses to chauffeur their children to and from sporting contests. Professional women in Gawpassat were outnumbered twenty to one by women who lived lives balanced between gruelling child-care and fantastic pampering. This indicated to me that people who didn't have to work tended not to.

'Ah, Benjie, thank you so much,' I said, in my master's voice, when my second snack of the afternoon arrived. 'Perhaps we should offer a glass of iced tea to the little girl over there? She must be thirsty, in this heat.'

Benjamin's eyes bulged. 'Oh, no, sir. No, not possibly, not at all.'

'I'm sorry I mentioned it. Relax.'

'Thank you sir.'

Away he went. I mixed sugar and lemon juice into my tea, ate a shrimp or two, and soon Uncle Ian emerged from the house to join me. A lot of people would have thought I was the luckiest man in the world, to be in a position to wave casually at the Great Man and urge him to join me in the shade for a bite of shrimp or avocado, the black, placid ocean at our feet. My uncle had a smile on his face, and shook his head wryly as he sat down with an older man's attention to knees and back.

I felt comfortable enough to speak at least part of my mind.

'That's one of the strangest things I've ever seen in my life,' I said. 'Spying on your wife that way.'

'Ex-wife, as of almost immediately. You can't imagine what a struggle this has been. Don't go into marriage lightly, if you can possibly avoid it. Anyway, don't look so shocked. It isn't really spying when you find exactly what you expected,' said my uncle, displaying the same slippery logic that was the foundation of much of his philosophical oeuvre. It astonished me to think that somewhere, as I sat chatting quietly with Gawpassat's richest man, a cast of ferreting lawyers were banging out settlements, compromises, threats, counter-threats, all to preserve as intact as possible the fortune he had amassed during my lifetime. 'She knows it's coming,' he said, with what simply had to be a note of honest sadness. 'She just doesn't know how soon. She'll sign right away, after this. There are a couple of terms yet to iron out, but basically the war's over.'

'I'm really very sorry to hear the news. I honestly had no idea. No-one had any idea, that I know of.'

'I'm glad to hear it. Security is paramount.'

'Of course.'

'I don't hate her, you understand.'

'No?'

'Certainly not. This is simply one of my last business acts.'

'I was going to ask, yes. About the Date, and all.' I felt bold, and privileged. Even for unbelievers, the advertised date of Uncle Ian's death carried profound subliminal meaning. 'To tell you the truth, and I'm sorry to say so, I hadn't remembered that it was so imminent. I must have blocked it out. It's not lost on the town, from what I've seen. The place is humming.'

Uncle Ian gave me a long look, his old face so famous and familiar. He looked in perfect health, when I had expected to find him on his deathbed, fizzing with cancer. He said nothing, so I felt I ought to continue.

'You're going to survive, of course. I mean, aren't you?'

Uncle Ian gazed out over the lawn. 'Look at little Lizzie, there,' he said, extending an arm to point at the skinny girl in the tutu. 'Is that sweet? Is that adorable?'

'Sure. I only worry about sunburn.'

Uncle Ian frowned. 'It's character building.'

'Is that why you've put them there, around town? I'm confused about that.'

'I do it,' Uncle Ian replied, looking back at me, twining his fingers and cracking his knuckles, 'because I *can*.'

'Ah.'

A tinge of anger in Uncle Ian's eyes made me think I ought to have let him take his time saying what he wished to say, that I had gone too far in asking directly about the Date. I hoped I hadn't offended him too much, then realized I had when he put both of his palms on the table and looked crossly at me, like a judge at a lawyer speaking out of turn.

'I *can*,' he said, 'so I *do*. Understood? Understood? So I spend some time checking up on the wife. So I teach these spoilt brats a thing or two about self-control, about working for a living, about the contemplation of the passage of time.'

Jean hadn't mentioned those salutary effects of hiring little girls to stand around doing nothing.

'There isn't a lot of time, as I've now reminded you,' said Uncle Ian. 'It isn't a laughing matter, either. The Date, I mean.'

'I'm not laughing.'

'Any power I have I intend to use,' he continued, growing somewhat agitated, in a frightening way. 'This town, this Gawpassat – do you have any idea what it has meant to me? I first came here before you were born. I took a boat out into the bay, there, and I looked back ashore at the hills and I thought, There's the place for me. My place.'

'You were inspired.'

'You could say that. I bought this house that very same day. I walked right up Black Hill, the way you came today,' – Uncle Ian knew everything, apparently – 'and introduced myself to the old Mayflower-descendant son-of-a-bitch of an owner, and explained to him that his house was about to belong to me.'

I had heard differing versions of this story. Conspiracy theorists claimed that Uncle Ian had simply hypnotized the owner on the spot and walked away, deed in hand. Others said he had made so outrageously high an offer that the proud scion of one of Gawpassat's oldest families had swallowed his pride, taken the cheque, and moved with his loved ones back to England. My parents' recollection of events was that Uncle Ian had charmed the old guy, converted him to the Word, and promised him everlasting life in exchange for the Black Hill house.

'But did I gain respectability?' asked Uncle Ian, as if reading from a prepared text. 'Not on your life. I made it my business to crack this town.'

Sure enough, the other two houses fell swiftly into his hands; my parents, grateful but dubious, were able to move up the hill from my father's more modest house near the water. It was possible, it seemed, to ascend in half a generation from socially unacceptable southern snake-oil salesman to revered spiritual leader and acknowledged wealthiest man.

'People are small-minded, Top,' said my Uncle, as the sky darkened overhead. He waved a hand in the air, and Benjamin appeared at his shoulder. 'I'll have a glass of sherry,' he said, without looking at his servant. 'And tell Lizzie to come over here.'

Benjamin, who looked worried, went out into the middle of the main lawn and tapped the girl on the shoulder. He pointed in our direction and spoke to her. She nodded, danced over to us in her tutu, gave Uncle Ian a kiss on the cheek, then sat down. I didn't know a lot of children, but this one looked like an example of the way they ought ideally to be. She put her elbows on the table and clasped her fingers together at the end of her spindly arms. 'Good evening,' she said to me brightly, with a trained child-actress's cock of the head. 'I'm your niece, Lizzie.'

'Well, hello there.' How many nieces did I have? Was this the same one who had worked the night shift at Trainer's? 'Last time we met you must have been . . . ?'

'I was too young to remember you. I've seen your picture, though. On the mountain?'

'But *I* remember, now. Last time I visited you were too busy to see me. You had ballet, piano, French, aerobics, birthday parties with your friends, tennis, golf, sailing. You must have been about seven years old.'

Uncle Ian looked on, enchanted, as my niece and I got to know each other. It had never been lost on me how much he regretted not having children of his own, while being for some reason philosophically set against adoption. His sherry arrived, along with a glass of orange juice for Lizzie.

'Lizzie is our star,' said Uncle Ian. 'She helps organize the scheduling and plan the sites for the other girls. Don't you, Lizzie?'

'Yes, I do,' she said, with a precocious child's overly precise articulation. 'Only until next spring, when it will be Sally's turn.'

I gathered that Sally was the next of my nieces in line for the honour of being head foot soldier of the Word.

When Lizzie had finished her orange juice, Uncle Ian told her it was time for her to run along home. I thought for a moment he was going to make her walk all the way to Melissa's house, but a golf cart whirred across the lawn to give her a lift. She gave us both a formal, skinny-armed Word Sign, and departed.

54

My prying question about the Date, and Uncle Ian's sour-grapes lecture on his struggle to tame Gawpassat, still hung between us. I decided I would not be the first to speak. He drained his sherry glass and stared meaningfully out to sea. His dark-brown eyes squinted beneath suitably god-like, wispy grey eyebrows. From what I remembered about his conversational style, he was likely to say almost anything, from a simple question about one of the countries I had recently visited, to an offer of a low-altitude helicopter ride over the rolling inland countryside, to a curt statement of his wish to be left alone. He enjoyed his image of unpredictability. One of his publicity stunts, ever since the first years of the Word, was to drop by unannounced at a subscriber's house on his own birthday, bearing gifts and food and signed editions of his books. The people he barged in on were vetted for heart disease, because he didn't want any Word-related coronaries on his lawyers' hands. These visitations were featured glossily in the Word's monthly magazine (circulation: 250,000), with photographs of the at first bewildered, then ecstatic victims – though no pictures of Uncle Ian himself. There were those who believed Uncle Ian sent along a double for this unpleasant annual chore.

'I'm going to need your help, son,' he said, which was encouragingly direct. 'The next couple of days are going to be a tad hectic. Are you free?'

'Are you kidding?'

'Good.'

In just a few moments I had gone from an intrigued, nostalgic nephew to feeling somewhat dizzy with nerves. Uncle Ian employed dozens and dozens of people who could help him make whatever arrangements were necessary to skirt over the embarrassment of not being ripped into immortality by his old pal God in a couple of days' time. If he needed me to do something, logic suggested that it would probably be clandestine. Before Uncle Ian began to explain, I had time to shudder at the thought that there might have been something to Jean's wild speculation after all. Had I just sat through my first formal interview for the job of heir to the Word?

'You know, don't you Top, that your parents are about the closest people in the world to me? I mean, despite everything, your Aunt Charlotte, all the mistakes – still we have known each other for a lifetime, *your* lifetime. Except for my sister I think of them as my only family.'

I nodded. Then, because there was nothing I could really say in reply, I asked after his sister, Barbara.

'She is not all that well. She stopped working – or I had to stop her working – a couple of years ago. She's never been a happy woman, you know. She doesn't like being seventy-five one bit.'

As a child I had always been terrified of Barbara Armstrong. She was a tall, heavy-set woman, grey early on like her younger brother, and had a reputation for severity and impatience with children. She was the only adult woman ever to strike me in my life. I can't recall precisely what my crime was, except that it had something to do with not being a good sport where a lesser classmate of mine was concerned. Barbara took my punishment into her own hands. Where my mother might have let a mildly disapproving rebuke suffice, Barbara thought she ought to stride over to me, pinch my biceps so hard my knees buckled, and slap my cheek once I had fallen to the floor. I vowed that day that I would grow big and strong so that I could knock Barbara to the ground when she least suspected it, but when that day came I decided there was not a lot to gain, not even justice and revenge, in beating up an old lady.

It was believed that Barbara's were the financial brains behind the early Word, and she was often credited with the relatively clean image of Uncle Ian's affairs. While various hints of scandal had attached themselves to his dealings, his record was still the envy even of people in conventional businesses. This was all the more unusual because so much of Uncle Ian's corporate income over the years had taken the form of grubby used banknotes, mailed to the Institute in envelopes addressed directly to Mister Armstrong. Some of these funds were accompanied by letters thanking the Great Man for showing them the way to what was called, for no reason I could divine, 'a community of thought' – and, incidentally, for recent weight-loss. It would have been the simplest of swindles to see these filthy, untraceable ones and fives and tens and twenties safely into an amenable foreign bank, but I can imagine that Barbara Armstrong would have ruled her department with unfailing probity. She had grown up alongside her brother in that legendary log cabin, after all, chopping wood for the invalid parents, and knew the value of honest dollars – especially if those honest dollars flooded in at such a rate that only someone greedy to the point of mania would risk deceiving the authorities.

'Is she ill?' I asked.

'Not in the slightest. I just couldn't let her go on at the Institute. She was getting excited about all kinds of new-fangled financial products that don't have any business in the same room as the Word. She had lost sight of what made us tick over in the first place.'

Uncle Ian's first tenet of making a million was, 'Be your own product.' This struck a chord with Gawpassatan aficionados of the American Dream, who believed that reinvention of the self was a not just a fundamental characteristic of their compatriots, but *a good idea*. I don't think my uncle had any such sociological ideas in mind when he said 'Be your own product.' I think he meant it cut down on overhead.

'Is she still living on White?'

'No, no. I had to get her away from the Institute. She's on a well-deserved world tour.'

'Organized by you?'

'Well, *paid* for by me, I can tell you. I handed over a year's budget at five grand a day to someone who knows how to make people comfortable in dirty, unpleasant countries where there are sights to see.'

It was one of Uncle Ian's un-Gawpassatan characteristics that he dropped sums of money the way social climbers dropped names.

'I'll get most of that back, though,' he added. 'Old Barbara wouldn't stand for spending a tenth of that much, even of someone else's money.'

'She devoted her whole life to the Word.'

'That she did.'

'The two of you are so close.' I was trying to steer the conversation back to that tantalizing exchange of a few minutes ago.

'Not the way you might think. She tried to mother me, and I hated that. You don't have to pretend she wasn't a fearsome woman, Top.'

'Nor could I.'

'Right, well. I just wanted her gone during this difficult time. She ought to be in Salzburg as we speak.'

'You could check up on her by satellite.'

'Don't be cute.' Uncle Ian silently gestured over his shoulder for another sherry. 'Join me?'

'No thanks.'

He crossed his legs. 'It's like this, Top. I need you around for a lot of reasons, but one of them is I want you to – how shall I put it? – *cushion the blow* for your parents. I wanted them to stay away, but they'll be back tomorrow.'

'So I'd heard. Cushion what blow?'

Uncle Ian looked at me with impatience. 'What have we been talking about here? For God's sake, boy, listen up.'

'I'm listening.'

'It isn't that I'm saying that your folks haven't been disappointed in me, and who can blame them. But I just bet you there's more of a soft-spot there than they let on.'

'I'm sure that's so.'

'Which is why I don't want them getting all upset when I check out.'

'Check out?'

'You're not all there, are you, Top. Can't you concentrate?'

'I'm concentrating, but you have to be more specific. I'm unprepared for this. I've been out of the swim, that's why. Can't you tell my parents yourself – whatever it is you have to tell them?'

'Let me just put it bluntly, then, if you're going to be so thick. Do you honestly think your parents will like it when people start accusing their only boy of murder?'

55

Murder? That was not a term often heard around Gawpassat. Our senatorial assassination had taken place in the nation's murder capital. There had been talk years ago that Mr Ingell's wife hadn't really 'disappeared to South America', as he claimed, but only gossip – no criminal charges – ever stuck to the husband. No-one ever claimed that anyone had deliberately tampered with my girlfriend's Peter Pan flying machine. One stevedore from a neighbouring town had nearly been killed by his cousin in a drunken, broken-bottle fight outside Trainer's Restaurant (to which they had been refused admittance on account of the stench of fish). Even the wider brotherhood of the Word seemed statistically clean of murder, if the Institute's numbers were to be believed. Only one case drew any unwanted attention, when a teenaged boy confessed on Uncle Ian's radio call-in show that after listening to one of the Great Man's tapes on the subject of self-assertiveness, he had poisoned one dog, two kittens, three guinea pigs and a step-father.

For years after my sister's death, I believed that Claire had been a victim of murder. She was an excellent sailor, and the conditions were not unusually severe on the day she failed to return to the Yacht Club. Her routine was to sail alone out around Clark's Island and back, timing herself with a stopwatch from the last channel buoy outside Gawpassat Harbour. Claire was a self-contained girl, and made her own entertainment. She had made the average five-hour round trip on dozens of occasions, sometimes twice a day for a week during the summer. She never read a book on board, she never listened to the radio, and she never brought along a friend. She sailed as hard as she could, against the clock. Everyone in my family remembers her excitement when she came home from the Yacht Club on a blustery day, watch in hand, and showed us that she had completed the round-trip journey in just under three hours. After Claire died I used to stay awake at night wondering what she thought about all that time alone at sea.

I was convinced that someone had boarded Claire's little Bering sailboat – christened the *Diffident* – committed unspeakable crimes against her person, throttled her with the main sheet, tied it around her neck, and fixed the tiller so that she sailed straight out into the shipping lanes. In my imagination I saw her killer swimming a mile to Clark's Island, picking up a motorboat and buzzing back to his mud-stained, uninsured pickup truck on the mainland. I simply couldn't conceive of her creating some sort of knot in the main sheet underfoot, perhaps lifting it overhead to inspect it in the sunlight, accidentally dropping it over her head, then choosing that exact moment – in a swell, perhaps? – to stand up and fall overboard.

There was an investigation. The breeze had been just strong enough, the seas just rough enough, to send a little girl overboard; no-one saw why the wind might not have been blowing in the right direction to set the *Diffident* on a free course towards Europe. My friends and I kept our ears to the ground, hoping to pick up any scuttlebutt on a potential murder conspiracy. A bungled kidnap of the Great Man's favourite niece was a popular theory. Claire would have put up a fight, we decided, when the powered rubber dinghy pulled up alongside the *Diffident* and she was confronted by cruel-faced men wearing dark glasses and berets, knives drawn and clenched between their teeth as they stormed aboard. Having killed her in the ensuing struggle, surprised by such a little girl's grit, they would have done their clumsy best to make her death look like an accident.

I even suspected Uncle Ian – as did Jean, I'm sure. Carried away by his love for Claire, and driven insane by the frustration of having no children of his own, Uncle Ian would have resolved to steal Claire from us. He would have plucked her from the *Diffident*, and replaced her with a previously strangled blond girl collected elsewhere. Oh, it all made sense to me when I was sixteen. My sisters and I were never told the condition of Claire's corpse, but we could guess. Dead and washed in the ocean for twenty-four hours – well, one could imagine. Of course, forensic tests were unnecessary. The identification of her body, performed by my father, would have been made through tears and squints, if at all. Uncle Ian would long since have imprisoned Claire on Black Hill, never again to be seen by the outside world. He would have treated her like a princess. 'See?' he would say. 'I've named my fabulous yacht after you. Your *parents* never do things like that, now, do they? Wouldn't you rather have a daddy like me?' It seemed to me just the sort of thing a rich, lonely man was likely to do. We thought about and discussed every conceivable scenario, except one: no-one ever, *ever* mentioned the possibility that my introverted, quietly spoken little sister might have killed herself.

56

'Murder?'

The lights had come on outside Uncle Ian's house. I remembered that I had always been puzzled that there seemed to be no insects on the Black Hill property. At my parents' house, clouds of moths and mosquitoes and daddy-longlegs swarmed in the lights, flapped against the screens, smacked against the windows. I suppose Benjamin, or his equivalent over the years, was charged with their extermination.

'Murder? What do you mean, murder?'

Here was Benjamin now, bearing another sherry and a kerosene lamp to set between us on the table.

'You really ought to keep your voice down,' said my uncle, when Benjamin had retreated into the shadows. 'I'm going to try to explain to you. In my own time.'

'Fine. You can see why I might be curious.'

This had turned into a most interesting evening, when I had arrived expecting no more than a handshake from my bedridden uncle and a cursory question or two about my errant progress through life.

'I know I can trust you, Matthew,' he said, reverting to the use of my most formal first name. 'I know I can.'

That wasn't a question, so I remained silent. My uncle's face flickered in the wavering kerosene flame. The furrows around his mouth, the half-moon shadows under his eyes and the creases in his forehead were thrown into more pronounced relief by the light beneath his chin. I folded my arms on the table and leaned closer to him, relishing despite myself my proximity to a morsel of history. This audacious man had probably changed a million lives.

'Assassination,' he said, 'would have been perfect.' He sipped his drink, swallowed a baby shrimp, drew his tongue along his front teeth. 'And it still might be. It still might be.' He coughed quietly into his fist. 'On the other hand, no. No, no. You can imagine that I've given this some thought over the last thirty-five years or so. Can't you?'

'Yes, of course I can.'

Did he believe it? Did he believe his own Word? I don't think it had ever occurred to me for a second, not until that moment after sunset, over the shrimp and the lamp, that Uncle Ian believed in his own prophecy, his own preordained death. I almost wanted to laugh out loud, to call his bluff. I needed more information. It reminded me of my brief spell as a lawyer, when the big picture never seemed to reveal itself beyond the bumph, until one of my more experienced colleagues pointed it out in all its obviousness.

'I made a statement that seemed reasonable at the time. I really did base *The First Word* on that bit of news, and it was the most thrilling revelation. The date of my death had been delivered to me. Think about it. After that, everything was easy. It seemed a long way in the future, back then, I can assure you. I was younger than you are now, for God's sake. And here we are, right?'

'Right, here we are.'

'It is time for the reckoning.'

'How worrying for you, Uncle Ian. Do you just lie down and let it happen?' I couldn't resist asking questions, and I couldn't help that they sounded sarcastic. 'Or do you take precautions?'

'Precautions? Preparations, more like. It is going to happen, you know.'

'Is it?'

'Of *course* it is. It *has* to, you little . . . ' Uncle Ian exhaled loudly through his nose. His temper made me believe him.

'I don't mean to be insolent,' I said. 'I'm only trying to understand.'

'What you don't seem to understand, right from the get-go, is how urgent it is that no mistakes are made. You're here for a reason. I get the feeling your sister didn't exactly fill you in.'

'Jean? She hinted darkly, I suppose you could say. To tell you the truth, and no offence, I expected to find you on your deathbed, for real.'

'Is that so? Is that so?'

'I have to be honest. That is the impression she gave me. She seemed to think the whole town was under that impression.'

'Well of course they are, Top. Of course they are. Of course they are. The Date is just ahead of us. The Date, son, the Date.'

143

It could have been the light, but Uncle Ian's eyes looked wild. He hadn't completed a coherent thought since the topic of his death had been raised. I had to conclude that Uncle Ian's shot-gun attempts at communication were the scattered, panicked ramblings of a man who actually believed his death was only days away.

'Jean's a good girl,' he said. 'She's a good girl. This is need-to-know, and she understands that. Jean understands.'

All I understood was that Uncle Ian seemed to have come unhinged.

'How well do you remember *The First Word*, son?'

'I remember the Date. I remember about half of the Twenty Rules, but I could guess the rest. I remember the "Will to live, live to will" part pretty well, I suppose. Look, Uncle Ian, I'm sorry. I'm not what you'd call up to speed on the Word.' This honesty seemed to upset Uncle Ian, so I added, 'Of course, just *knowing* you is enough, maybe better than the book-learning. Don't you think so?'

'I'm disappointed in you. This is bad. This is very bad.' He stroked his chin and looked up at the sky. 'Or maybe it isn't so bad. Maybe it's not so bad at all.'

'OK. If you say so.'

Now Uncle Ian began to rant in earnest. He spoke of assassination, of murder, of suicide. He bemoaned a certain lack of communication from God's quarter, which would have made his options clearer. I assumed he referred to the manner of his death, and I could see how a word in his ear from the ether might have helped him keep a steady hand as the Date neared. Unless he was acting – which was not beyond him – he sounded like a death-row convict waiting for a reprieve from the Supreme Court.

No-one had ever accused Uncle Ian of being mentally unbalanced; on the contrary, even his most vehement critics tended to applaud his cunning and acuity. Now I began to have my doubts. For one thing, he seemed to give me a lot of credit for inside knowledge I simply did not possess. Perhaps, in his inevitable prison of egotism, he assumed I had done all

I could over the years to understand the ins and outs of the Word and the Institute, and that like every other male who had ever come close to meeting him, I coveted the position of Heir.

57

I was a failure, and I supposed Uncle Ian knew this. There had come a point when I had to admit that my glamorous allergy to honest work – a trait that a generation ago might have turned me into a popular icon – had left me defeated and rudderless. For a while I revelled in my individualism – for a few months, even – until the days seemed to grow rather too long even for the few ingredients necessary to survival I felt I had to inject into them. I knew other failures, but they weren't friend material, somehow. I was alone.

Failure is relative. If the seventh child of a handicapped sharecropper decides to lounge around the shack for a few months, who is to say he has failed? By the same token, should the sharecropper's son manage to reach college, he need never again be branded anything but a wild success. In my case, nothing so spectacular had ever been expected of me: only to hang on for thirty or forty years to a perfectly interesting and highly paid job that was mine for the asking. By the time I broke the tape of retirement, I would have been judged an achiever.

My sister Jean was a failure, too, but she relied on her fantasy of an entertainment-industry cabal conspiring to keep her casting-direction business on ice. I made no such excuses for my own failure: I went about my business hoping no-one noticed. I had the foresight to know that for people like me, money had a way of turning up. Everywhere I went I simply made myself available to be paid. I think it was my lack of personality that made the difference. Rich men in bars or nightclubs were for some reason compelled to ask me where I fitted in; when this produced no satisfactory reply, they quite often asked me if I wanted to work for them, on an informal basis. In the few cases when this did not entail illegalities, I took them up on their offers. I made deliveries, I carried suitcases, I taught children to ski, I loomed threateningly and pretended I was armed. Anyone who has taken this path in life knows that sooner or later one ends up working for the Central Intelligence Agency, whether one knows it or not. This is the impression I liked to give my parents and siblings, at any rate.

Seeing the world has its charms, especially when one travels with the special passkey of a famous uncle. It amazed me that the majority of the people I met had at least a passing knowledge of the phenomenon of the Word, and an even more detailed acquaintance with the Great Man and his ever-increasing fame. Wherever I went I was asked if I worked for Uncle Ian, if I could supply literature, if I *believed*.

58

'I want to know that I can count on you to do everything I say,' said my uncle, sounding a lot like many of my employers over the last several years. 'I may say some things that are disturbing to you. Are you comfortable? Are you comfortable?'

'I'm fine, Uncle Ian.'

'Are you sure you don't want a drink? It's still so hot. This climate, I tell you. The sun goes down, it just seems to get hotter. Won't you have a drink?'

'No, no thanks.'

'What's with you, son? You're not on the wagon, or something?'

'Not really, no.'

'That Laurie – she hasn't been a bad influence on you, has she? Turned you off the stuff. I know how Laurie can be.'

'Do you? I don't remember . . . I haven't introduced her to

you, actually. You must be thinking of someone else. She'd love to meet you, of course.'

'I know Laurie. You just trust me. The lovely divorcée.'

'I don't understand. You've met her?'

'Let's say I've *seen* her, and leave it at that.'

'As you wish,' I said, wondering if Uncle Ian had spied on us via satellite.

'Where is that God-damned Benjamin?' Benjamin materialized at Uncle Ian's side. 'Just bring me the God-damned bottle,' he said, and less than thirty seconds later the bottle stood on the table next to the Great Man's glass.

'I want to get drunk,' he said, once Benjamin had evaporated. 'I think I have to.'

'Fine.'

'I've been thinking about this conversation for a long, long time. For years, in fact. I don't want to shock you. I don't want you to be afraid.'

'I'm not afraid.' Maybe not afraid, but distinctly uncomfortable. I thought I knew what was coming. If Uncle Ian had rehearsed the telling in his mind, I had rehearsed the hearing.

'You're old enough to know how complicated life can be.'

Technically, I was old enough to be a grandfather.

'You know about compromise. You know about loyalty. You know about love and betrayal and the dark places in your heart.'

When coherent, Uncle Ian sounded as if he were reading from a prepared text, like a sermon.

'Have you ever thought about this – that you can live your life without fundamental information, crucial information, information that would make a *huge* difference? An analogy would be the atheist, who wanders about lacking any of the basic information he needs to operate morally. It can work that way on a more practical level.'

I nodded dumbly.

'What I have to tell you is only a *version* of the truth, but you must know it. Your mother and I,' he said stiffly, like a bad joke-teller reaching a punch line, 'were more than friends, years ago.'

I arched my eyebrows.

'I can't put it any plainer than this. Your mother and I were lovers, Top.'

I lowered my eyebrows.

'I firmly believe that your sister Claire was my daughter.'

I tilted my head to one side.

'And I believe that you are my son.'

I fixed my eyes on my uncle, or my father, and succeeded in not twitching. I had been prepared, after all, by years of fantasizing.

'There you go, I've said it. I've said it now, haven't I?'

I adjusted my mouth.

'Now come on, son, speak to me. Don't you have any-thing to say for yourself? Come on now, I'm twisting in the wind, here. Say something, boy.'

'Could you please pass that bottle over here?'

59

It was the consensus around my home that the most glamorous thing about my mother was her wartime childhood in London. There was nothing quite like the raining-down of bombs to add spice to a girl's life. With my grandfather off deafening himself with his own artillery, my grandmother and her two non-evacuated little girls were left back in London to fend for themselves.

My sisters and I used to pester my mother to distraction by begging to be told the Story of the Blitz, when she had already told us the relatively humdrum truth dozens of times. We insisted that the story ought to improve with each retelling, so that by the time I was a teenager my mother had commandeered the Spitfire of a wounded pilot and single-handedly shot down eight German bombers and a handful of Messerschmitts – at the age of twelve. But what about *romance*, we wanted to know. The passionate cauldron of war? Living for the moment? The look in the pilot's eyes that says he won't be coming back this time? My mother was sixteen when the war ended, but we wanted her to admit to torrid, back-alley, up-against-a-bomb-damaged-wall love-making, and secret trips to the country to give birth to the babes of dead Canadian airmen. And the V2 rockets, Mum? Tell us again how your neighbourhood was razed by a V2 rocket as you cowered in the local shelter, cradling your terrified sister Charlotte in your arms. No such luck, I'm afraid, but she tried her best to make rationing and blackouts sound interesting.

My sisters and I wished we'd had a good war. Melissa wanted to be a nurse in an RAF burn unit. Jean wanted to be a daredevil front-line correspondent and film-maker. I wanted to be a spy, armed only with my wits and a cyanide capsule. Claire never grew old enough to put her finger on what she wanted to be, but showed an early preference for the Pacific theatre. The only real war we had was distant, useless and depressing, and not a single Gawpassatan ever got close to it.

My mother and Aunt Charlotte were attractive young women. They were both on the bookish side, or perhaps they only seemed so compared with my generation. I imagine that they were close, what with having such a grand war and all of that cowering in shelters in common. They looked alike, my mother being by a narrow margin the prettier of the two. I gather they had a reputation for being 'spirited', which was borne out when they both married unknown quantities – my father and Uncle Ian. During the short time before Melissa was born, the quartet travelled together, drank together, schemed together and became best friends. My guess is that Uncle Ian's *First Word*, whether he believed in it or not, was a source of amusement to the others, and carried with it the *frisson* always generated by a large windfall of cash.

Whenever I contemplated an affair between Uncle Ian and my mother, I decided it would have been *hot*. Assuming for the sake of argument that it was possible for one's parents to have carnal urges, I imagine that their attraction, evolving across barriers of marriage and sisterhood and friendship, must have been extremely erotic. My mother would have been a great challenge to Uncle Ian, who was by then already accustomed to the forelock-tugging housewives who worshipped him and believed in his Word. Employed for her intellect, and not in the least interested in what she called Ian Armstrong's 'publishing concern', she would have stood out among Gawpassatan women even if she hadn't been his sister-in-law. The necessary amount of sneaking around would have been arduous, and, if my experience is anything to judge by, would have contributed to the intensity of their assignations.

Over the years, the idea that Claire and I were Uncle Ian's children had required me to step up to another rung of thought. Why not Melissa and Jean as well, while we were at it? A glance at our colouring might have suggested that Jean and I were the likeliest candidates to be products of the illicit union between my mother and Uncle Ian, while Melissa and Claire were legit – or vice versa. Only a certain look in Claire's eye, which I would always remember and identify with, hinted that she and I might have been the odd ones out.

60

'I don't know what to say.'

'Well, I didn't know any other way of putting it to you. You'll probably want some time to let it all sink in.'

It dawned on me that the wild look in Uncle Ian's eyes wasn't egomania, it wasn't worry, it was as close as he could come to love. Uncle Ian loved me like the son he thought I was. I had practised not coming apart at the seams when confronted with this dubious information, and at that moment I felt that I had handled it well: a shrug, a sigh, a meditative look that said life was awfully interesting after all.

'Who knows this?' I asked seriously, as if I had managed to absorb his cataclysmic news and launched immediately into sorting out its ramifications. 'My mother, of course. Did Aunt Charlotte ever know?'

'No, no. It's so hard to say. You know how your mother is. She may not have been able to admit it to herself. Certainly not Charlotte, no. And not your mother's husband.'

'My mother's husband. Goodness gracious me.'

'Now, don't get angry. I know you're surprised. You're in a kind of shock.'

I was nothing of the kind. I was somewhere between excited and appalled. My view was that only a man of Uncle Ian's towering self-regard would think his supposed 'news' would make a real difference to me. He probably thought I had always longed to hear this version of my derivation, which was only true to the extent that anyone will fantasize about the last-minute discovery of their princely origins. To believe this, he also had to have a low opinion of my feelings for the man I had grown up to think of as my father. There was time that evening on the Black Hill lawn for it to occur to me that Uncle Ian's revelation was in bad taste, and about twenty years too late.

'I'm not angry. I'm intrigued.'

This seemed to please my uncle. I was only glad he didn't think that this might be the time for us to stand up, fall into each other's arms, and weep shudderingly for several hours at all the lost opportunities, the unspoken emotions, the man-to-man fishing trips that might have been but now could never be.

'I was never going to say anything, you know,' he said. 'I thought it wasn't right. Just not *right*. But now, with the Date so close – I just don't think I have any choice.' He took a deep breath. 'You are my son. You are my heir. And now I expect you to behave like my son and heir. Understood?'

'Wow.'

A whole new life had opened up before me, a life right there on Black Hill, wealthy beyond calculation, revered by my people, envied by my critics, surrounded by my adoring staff and a high electric fence. It sounded perfectly ghastly, but like anyone I liked the idea of all that money.

61

Uncle Ian tried to explain to me about the atmosphere that he wished to surround his death. He said he wanted to keep the Christian parallels to a minimum, though elements of betrayal and resurrection were to be encouraged. I listened to him with my neck craned forwards and my eyebrows almost touching in concentration. In my flexible line of work I had to be a good judge of people, but I honestly couldn't tell if Uncle Ian had worked out a brilliant plan to ensure the continuation of the Word, or had completely lost his mind. Everything he said made at least some sense, except that at the root of his speech lay his own extinction; it wasn't supposed to be in the make-up of man to be able sanguinely to contemplate imminent death. I had to assume that decades of living off the Word had convinced my uncle of his god-like stature. Certainly Dr Max Sohlman's dim view of heaven did not warrant a premature exit – unless one were going there to run the show.

I hope that I maintained my expression of intensity, even as I told myself that Uncle Ian had finally gone round the bend. The convoluted intrigue he described, and an insistence on 'need-to-know' that made it nearly impossible for me to understand my own role, did nothing to bolster my confidence in Uncle Ian's desire – or even his ability – to follow through with his fateful prediction. I listened, I nodded, I spoke only to urge him on. I tried not to flinch when he spoke directly of what had begun to sound like a combined disappearance and suicide, with overtones of murder. I committed myself to nothing – did not, in fact, necessarily indicate that I believed him.

In an hour, he had finished. Vague stars had appeared in the humid Gawpassatan sky. He announced that he was exhausted. He instructed me to think over what he had said. He apologized for, as he put it, 'unloading' on me.

'I'd have you choppered home,' he added, 'but I hate to wake the neighbours' kids.'

He stood up and extended his hand to me for our first father-and-son shake. He looked proud, and almost misty in the lamplight. He patted me firmly on the shoulder as I went on my way, with a final plea to think hard about what he had said. 'Think it all the way through, son,' he said, employing one of his standard forms of address, but one that now carried an entirely new and more literal meaning.

62

Puzzled and a little afraid, I skipped down Black Hill. I needed advice, but there was no-one to turn to. I couldn't very well ask my mother if, by the by, she had neglected over the years to tell me that my real dad was actually the multi-millionaire megalomaniac on the other hill. I couldn't ask Jean, because I couldn't bear having to tell her that there was even a possibility that we were only half as closely related as previously thought, and that my new half owned most of Gawpassat and the souls of thousands of human beings. That would make her furious. I couldn't ask Laurie, either, if I knew her at all well: for some unfathomable reason she believed in unequivocal above-board behaviour; she would tell me to go to the police, go to my parents, go to the Institute, go to Agnes and Michel, go to the media.

The colourful, uneven light of televisions flashed and glimmered in the living rooms of Jefferson Street. The odours of popcorn and lawnmower exhaust mingled on the air. The faint strains of a whiny electronic orchestra reached me from the slopes of White Hill, where Little Dave Periman's wedding had evolved into the dancing stage. Running lights winked in the harbour and on the bay. A sprinkler on a steep lawn sent a stream of green dye trickling into a roadside drain.

I walked past the house of a high school friend of mine, Roger, who used to mope about with me, talking about girls.

I no longer remembered his surname, but I vividly recalled something he said to me when we were about fifteen years old: 'There aren't any problems I have right now,' Roger said sagely, 'that a whole lot of money wouldn't solve.' In due course Roger inherited a position in his father's law firm, but I doubt that he had much reason to change his sentiments over the years.

At the bottom of Black Hill, near the water, stood the house of my father's birth – my Richmond father, that is. It was a lovely old place, yellow with dark-blue trim, a small garden in front and a brackish pond out back. After we moved to the top of Gray Hill, the house was turned into a 'living museum' of colonial life. Women wearing hilarious bonnets ground meal in the kitchen, planted corn next to the pond, tried to burn damp faggots in the stove. Later on, it became Gawpassat's central dissemination point for the literature of the Word, which drew considerably more tourists than the 'living museum'. In the lighted window I could make out the main display of Uncle Ian's fundamental texts. A small bust of Uncle Ian as a young man had been erected on a white marble plinth and pedestal in the front garden. Unlike our statue of the Minuteman, Uncle Ian's likeness was never, ever vandalized.

I reached the sea wall and stopped to breathe the cooler air. To my right was the base of White Hill; I could no longer hear the music of the Periman wedding over the hissing surf below the wall. To my left was the centre of town, where Trainer's Restaurant jutted out on the main pier near the Yacht Club. The moon had come and gone, but I could still make out power boats and dinghies on the water, ferrying people to the dock that led to Trainer's. The cars that swished past me on the waterfront road were uniformly luxurious and clean, their occupants smiling and well-heeled. Girls in loose T-shirts leaned out the windows and waved at me. Boys made hostile, condescending, anti-pedestrian faces at me from the driver's seats of convertibles.

'If you only knew,' I said aloud, heading off towards the pier.

63

I arrived at Trainer's to an even more effusive greeting than the night before: Word Signs abounded, the crowd parted, drinks were proffered, Jean was swept towards me like a bride at a tribal wedding. My sister was surrounded by thugs, as usual – including Noel, the odious monster. Several women wore formal dresses, and were accompanied by men in what I gathered was the Word wedding uniform: a tight-fitting black suit, *sans* tie, silver cummerbund at the waist. These were some of Little Dave Periman's guests, who had slipped away from his wedding because they couldn't bear to miss another routine session amid the Trainer's tacky scrimshaw decor. Jean, who had changed out of her wedding gear and into her casual evening attire, had me outside in a private corner of the deck before I had a chance to turn and flee.

'Tell me everything. Right now.'

'There's nothing to tell.'

Jean punched me in the shoulder. '*Tell* me.'

'Really, there's nothing.'

'What did you talk about, all this time?'

'We reminisced, that's all.'

Jean scowled, then smiled knowingly. 'I know what it is,' she said, leaning close to me. 'The walls have ears, right?' She winked. 'Gotcha. We could go down to the rocks for privacy.'

'Seriously, Jean. I'd tell you if there were anything going on. Really I would.'

'You're a terrible liar, Top.'

Actually, I was a very good liar.

'Is Elder Willie Junior's boy here?' I asked. 'I didn't see him in the crowd.'

'He wouldn't dare. And don't change the subject. You just spent hours with Ian. I have witnesses.'

'Lizzie?'

'Exactly. Our most perfect niece. So don't you give me this nothing-to-tell stuff. What about the Date, for God's sake?'

'Well, *I* wasn't going to mention it.'

Jean squinted at me in frustration. 'If you're keeping something from me, I swear,' she said. 'I mean, I'm your *sister*.'

Sort of, I thought.

'There may be one or two things of interest,' I said, to mollify her. 'I ought to digest them, though. He can be awfully opaque.'

'*Opaque*? So you *did* talk about the Date.'

'Well. Let's just say the Date resonated on the table between us.'

Jean cursed. It embarrassed me, for no good reason, that my sister was dressed as provocatively as the younger, less well-bred girls at Trainer's. She was deeply tanned, and when she raised her arm to brush back her hair, I saw the natural white of her breast through the baggy sleeve of her light-blue cotton shirt.

'This is *so* unfair. I've hardly left town for a day in ten years, and you just sweep back in here and straight up Black Hill like you own the place.' She paused. 'You don't . . . *own* the place, do you?'

'Not yet.'

'What?'

'Only kidding.'

'You'd better be.'

I apologized to Jean, used the excuse of jet-lag, and left Trainer's through a gauntlet of handshakes. I walked up Gray Hill as fast as I could, thinking as shallowly as possible. Two cars slowed to offer me a lift, but I waved them on. I reached my parents' darkened house after midnight. It was not quite late enough to give Laurie a call, but I couldn't resist. I used the phone in the kitchen.

64

'Don't wake up, it's me.'

'Matt?'

'Sorry, don't wake up. I had to hear your voice before I went to bed.'

'It's OK. It's almost light, here.'

'Go back to sleep.'

'No, no. I want to talk. I found the awful man and the awful book, yesterday.'

'Good.'

'It's worse than I expected, if anything.'

'Oh?'

'I don't hold out a lot of hope for mankind, in case you were wondering, if people can behave that way. I mean, if *men* can behave that way.'

'You sound awake.'

'If I were writing about female torturers, I'd be done by now.'

'I'm sure that's right.'

'How did I get into this racket?'

'All doctoral candidates ask themselves that question, sooner or later. You'll find your answers in time.'

'I've got to tell you about this awful man, Matt, this torturer.'

'Please don't.'

'He used no equipment at all. He was a purist.'

'Please.'

'He could flay your tongue into fifty neat strips with his teeth and fingernails.'

'Please, Laurie.'

'He used hypnosis, to accentuate the pain and the horror. He could make a victim think the pulling out of a single hair on his chest was like pulling a finger out by the roots.'

'Laurie, please.'

'And then he *would* pull a finger out by the roots. And the toes. And the penis, if there was one.'

'Laurie?'

'Yes?'

'Maybe you need to take a break. You're getting bogged down in specifics. You're losing sight of your theme.'

'Could be. Still, I spend most of my time shuddering. No-one can stand talking to me. I'm losing my friends.'

'Oh, Laurie. You'll be fine.'

'I hope so. Anyway, tell me about you. Have your parents come home yet?'

'They'll be back tomorrow. I've had a busy day, though. I was summoned to meet my uncle, at his house.'

'Wow. You didn't actually see him, did you?'

'Yes, I saw him. We had a long chat, for the first time in years and years.'

'Well come on, Matt. What about the Date?'

'How do you know about the Date? I never told you about the Date, did I?'

'Don't you ever read the newspaper? Your Uncle is either mad, or his days are numbered. Do you think he's going to do himself in?'

'Laurie, he's my uncle. This is a very stressful situation for him.'

'Well, he did ask for it.'

'That's one way of looking at it.'

'What did you talk about, then?'

'Nothing much. We reminisced. He's a fascinating man, you know. Nothing like his reputation. We had a swim, a bite to eat. It was all very normal.'

65

When I put the phone down, I felt restless and awake. I didn't like being alone in the big, dark house. I filled a glass with ice cubes from the dispenser in the refrigerator door, then couldn't decide what I wanted to drink. I put the glass down, feeling hot, uncomfortable and bored. I went through the door to the verandah. I reached out to turn on the overhead light, and as I did so I heard a creak of wicker. The light flashed on. I jumped back and bumped my shoulder against the door frame.

'Boo,' said Uncle Ian, sitting cross-legged in the big chair.

I regained my balance and stared at him, bug-eyed.

'I couldn't help overhearing,' he said calmly. 'You've been a good boy.'

I lowered my hand from my chest, where it had been gripping my shirt over my pounding heart.

'You didn't say much to Jean, either, I was glad to hear.'

'How can you . . . I mean, Uncle Ian, how can you *possibly* know that, already?'

'Well son, this is the sort of thing you're just going to have to learn, if you want to be good at the game. Take a look in your left inside jacket pocket, if you will.'

Uncle Ian must have bugged my jacket when I took a swim at his house.

'That's . . . dirty pool,' I said, because that was the expression that sprang to my agitated mind. 'How can you do that to your own . . . you know, to *me*.'

'Where's your sense of humour?' he said, standing up. 'Goodness, look at the time. I must be off. Benjamin?'

The Cyclops headlight of a golf cart blinked on outside.

66

I felt I knew what I had to do. I climbed the main staircase and walked down the hallway to the library. There, alphabetized under non-fiction, were Uncle Ian's collected works; and first in line was our most prized volume, a valuable, intimately inscribed copy from the tiny print-run of the original edition of *The First Word* (Mountain Press). One of my parents had carefully wrapped the book's jacket in cellophane, and I doubt if anyone had opened it in twenty-five years. I took it down from the shelf and sat behind the mahogany desk by the window. I turned on the reading light and opened the book as if trying not to leave fingerprints.

'To my dear, dear friends,' read the inscription, 'Margaret and Elliot – on a beautiful afternoon aboard the *Cerise* on Gawpassat Bay – I think I like it here – You are marvelous – I inscribe this humble number – Looking forward to continued happiness in the paradise we all call home – With lots of love from me and Charlotte – Ian.'

I flipped gingerly through the yellowed pages, scanning the short paragraphs to find the famous passages pertinent to the Date. I had never properly read *The First Word*, only skimmed it, but as I turned the pages some of Uncle Ian's most cherished epigrams and aphorisms came back to me from years of having heard them quoted elsewhere. He had written his first book at a time when people's preoccupations were directed outwards: they feared a foreign power to the point of lunatic paranoia; they were motivated by a desire to improve their material lot in life, rather than by conceited striving for physical and spiritual perfection; they wanted the best for their children, rather than wanting their children to be best for them. *The First Word*'s message reflected such outdated concerns, and it is a tribute to my uncle's flexible virtuosity that he was able, over the course of his next five books, to direct his lessons towards vain and spurious self-improvement.

Forgetting for a moment that *The First Word* purported to be the word of an impatient and disillusioned God, its commonplace parables and stilted aphorisms held a certain amount of charm. Its text was well organized, as one might expect from the pen of a lawyer. The deity's case was more often argued than stated. God had a sardonic streak that one suspects was the product of what my atheist father once called 'a misspent death': if you don't like what I say, He implied, I'll simply wash my hands of you and on to the next.

God called Uncle Ian 'Friend'. God frequently said 'Look', or 'Listen' at the beginning of His sentences.

Listen, Friend. A man is no better and no worse than the character and resolution he brings to his challenges. Look, are you the kind to ask his fellows where lies the uphill path? Friend, you will feel the incline underfoot.

Compared with the deluge of literature that would eventually pour down White Hill from the Institute, *The First Word* was a spare and easily digestible work. It was said by its close readers to be devoid of allusion and cliché, which must have made it unique. It reeked of 'honesty', they said, and 'sincerity'. Uncle Ian, who had reputedly gone into some sort of trance to produce the manuscript at his Rocky Mountain retreat, was said to possess the unquestionable credentials of a 'vessel' – an evaluation based, it was whispered, on the poor expository writing skills he had displayed in college. Early on, he had been accused of relying overmuch on the 'typing skills' of a female amanuensis (scholars could evidently discern gender from short samples of prose). The woman was later named, by a daring critic, as Louise Parks, a law-school classmate of Uncle Ian's whose main accomplishment in life was to be a tragically early victim of cancer. The allegation was swiftly debunked by Uncle Ian's damage-control specialists, and those of us close to the Great Man never doubted that he was the true and only author of *The First Word*. He simply had to be: the book *was* Uncle Ian, to anyone who knew him remotely well.

That being the case, I often wondered about the practical, physical process of writing *The First Word*. His Rocky Mountain cabin, long since destroyed by relic hunters, used to stand on public land at eight-and-a-half-thousand feet on the slopes of an undistinguished peak. He reached it not on foot but, appropriately, on the back of a donkey. The earliest, cheapest biography of Uncle Ian included black-and-white photographs of the sacred spot, including a close-up of the rough wooden table near the window where the prophet had taken his heavenly dictation. Outside was a small system of beaver dams, and one large pool where the animals' work had cleared plenty of casting space on the pebbly banks. I wondered what it had been like during the months when young Ian Armstrong had lived there, all alone, hauling up supplies once every two weeks or so, wondering what he was doing with his life, maybe even believing he was talking to God every day.

He caught a lot of trout, that's for sure. Fish and fishing figured prominently in the metaphors of *The First Word*. He wrote about the early mornings casting rhythmically into the pond or upstream, his mind wandering, when the loudest sound to be heard was the dripping of water from his reel and the squelch of his boots in the mud. He compared the strike of the rainbow trout to the first spiritual tugs from above. I seem to recall that when I was eleven years old I unwittingly embarrassed a table full of my parents' dinner guests by gravely pointing out that the trout stream that led to Uncle Ian's beaver dams had been stocked by human beings.

Uncle Ian could not have had any idea that his book – whether he believed in its authenticity or not – would act like a match in a dry haystack. It took two or three years, but when the fodder was ignited it burned uncontrolled, fed only by an injection every five years or so of a corollary *Word*. His swift social climb up the Gawpassat hills was complete by the time *The Third Word* was published. These were the kind of books no-one outside the religion would ever admit to buying, but they turned up with inexplicable regularity on the minor, paperback shelves of people's summer houses, yellowed and well-thumbed.

Friend, I will tell you this: My Word is my gospel and I entrust it to you. I offer you the time and place of your death, so that preparations might be made to secure the future of our simple teachings.

People assumed that Uncle Ian must have trembled as he committed the Date to paper, but those were the believers: why would he have worried at the time, when for all he knew not another soul would read about it? I liked to think that he cackled to himself in his mountain retreat, totting up the years on his fingers, generously allotting himself a rough three-score and twenty, and adding,

The water, the womb of mankind, will envelop you and take you home.

God went on to inform my uncle, in a roundabout and murky way, that it was the greatest of advantages to be given such an ultimatum, and that he ought to go out into the world and make the best of his privileged information. No-one would deny that my uncle had lived his life accordingly. Even in the early days – or so I hear – he had been one of those big, impressive men who dominated a room on entry, drawing people to him, earning their admiration, standing out in any crowd. He impressed everyone with his good-humoured charisma, his adventurousness, his refusal to quit. When he joined forces with my tall, soft-spoken Aunt Charlotte – who, like my mother, managed to upgrade her English accent within days of her arrival in the New World – they made an unbeatable social force.

True to His reputation for mystery, God did not spell out the transition of power from Uncle Ian to his heir; mention was made of his coming from afar, his being a 'son' of the Word, his having conquered great heights before being 'summoned to the helm'. If *The First Word* hadn't been dictated by God, then Uncle Ian certainly had done a brilliant job of keeping the terms of the transition suitably vague and enigmatic.

Friend, your faithful shall stand guard for the Day, and watch over you.

Were those the foot soldiers of the Word?

Listen: Be calm, but be vigilant.

Was that why Uncle Ian kept spying on me at night?

Look: Your strength will be in acquiescence.

I still don't know quite what that means, but such was God's infuriatingly obscure advice, as presented in *The First Word*. I came away from my first real perusal of the founding text convinced that my uncle would perish at sea, like my sister; that he had somehow hypnotized or programmed me into

163

climbing Everest so that I would fit his ideal heir's profile; and that it was useful all round that I had been given a solidly biblical name.

I took what information I could from that section of *The First Word*, and, after having patrolled the grounds and checked every room and closet in the house for spies, went wearily to bed.

67

A certain amount of fanfare accompanied my parents' return. For two people, they travelled in a lot of vehicles: one taxi for them, another taxi for their excess luggage and two vans for their purchases. I greeted them stiffly at the back door, an operation that would have been even more uncomfortable had we not been surrounded by men lugging suitcases, wrapped paintings and statuary.

My parents were surprised to see me, and overtly pleased. My mother asked me a dozen questions, not waiting for the answers, interrupting me each time she had to issue instructions to the squad of movers who carted her acquisitions into the house. My father grinned at me as I had rarely seen him do before; he rocked back and forth on the balls of his feet, rubbed his hands together, urged the men to work faster. He had discarded his cane.

With everything unloaded and the sweating porters paid off, my parents were able to pay some attention to me. They both sported dry, pink, desert suntans, noticeably different from the darker but oilier Gawpassat version. After not having laid eyes on my parents in at least two years, I was glad to settle down on the verandah for a drink and a heart-to-heart; doubtless there were lots of things they wanted to find out about me, during which time I could inspect my father's features for signs of even the remotest genetic connection to myself.

Our heart-to-heart lasted fifteen or twenty seconds, until my sister Melissa careered into the drive in her twelve-seater van and disgorged her children like clowns in a circus act. Her husband, Reed, wearing his Sunday-with-the-kids costume, tried his best not to look out of place or redundant. After a quick shake of my hand, he returned to the van to begin transporting his offspring's equipment, which included an ungainly badminton net, several hampers of food and clothing and at least two miniature automobiles.

Children were everywhere. I stood with my back to the most isolated wall in the kitchen as the destruction began. Milk and juice and toast and marmalade were flung at me as if on purpose, glasses went crashing to the floor, heads knocked together, all of this amid a din of hysterical shrieks and bangs and a general background noise of devastation. I recognized Lizzie among the throng. As the town's leading foot-soldier of the Word, she sat primly at the kitchen table with her hands in her lap, her impish expression unchanged even when she was splashed with cranberry juice or knocked sideways by a flying child. The grown-ups shouted at each other over this racket, sounding like officers worried about supply lines under artillery fire.

'Did you remember to get the socket wrench for the undercarriage of the − stop it Freddy − stop it Sally − stop it Tommy − stop it Andy − the undercarriage of the − I said stop it, Freddy, Sally, Tommy, Andy − the socket wrench for the undercarriage of the − stop it!'

My nephew Matt stood on the far side of the room in a pose similar to my own, except that both of his meaty hands clutched large pieces of raw food. Suddenly the two ovens were on, and all the gas burners, cooking eggs, hamburgers, corn-on-the-cob, peas, beans: food of high quality, in huge abundance, which is what we were used to in Gawpassat. My mother, wearing an apron over her travelling dress, toiled over her equipment like an assembly-line worker, while Melissa ministered to her howling brood. It was already a hot day; when this was combined with the heat of the kitchen appliances and the stress of standing in the vicinity of my sister's platoon of self-centred little-ones, I could bear no more. In a voice no-one could hear, I announced to my family that I was going for a swim.

68

Our pool, nowhere near so lavish as Uncle Ian's, was set in a peaceful corner of the grounds, protected by a beautiful stand of lilacs. I dived in and floated on my back, looking up at the sky. This had been a popular spot when I was a boy, so tranquil and fragrant, and the Armstrongs were frequent visitors. I was quite grown up before I realized what had been going on around me: the use of illegal drugs, a libertinism countenanced by the literati of the day, dangerous and subversive political conversations. I decided that mine was the first generation in history to behave with more conventional propriety than its predecessor.

There were plenty of stories of marital infidelity in Gawpassat, as everywhere else, but my parents' was the heyday of such behaviour. Husbands and wives were unfaithful not only because it was enjoyable, nor because they were too weak to rein in uncontrollable desires: modern manners simply dictated that they ought to cheat on one another in order that they might be free. Many a fatigued commuter must have dragged his briefcase home on black, freezing winter evenings, dreading the encounter with illicit love that trend-conscious society demanded of him. They were so overt about it – again, the Zeitgeist of my parents' day insisted on unseemly openness – that in elementary school we used to gossip about our friends' parents' behaviour.

Our most spectacular extramarital affairs were the work of Adam W. Dutton, the orphaned son of a very great American indeed. I remember when he used to come to our house for parties, and the women would group together for shelter around the least available or most clearly impotent men – not because they thought Mr Dutton might physically attack them, but because based on his reputation they feared his attractions might prove irresistible. He was so successful, and so convinced

166

that his behaviour would soon become a wider society's norm, that Gawpassat real-estate values actually fell over a period of years as marriages were destroyed and families moved away. Jean and I used to wonder if our mother or Aunt Charlotte – or Melissa, come to that – had ever succumbed to the charms of Adam Dutton. It seemed unlikely, but we argued that if our parents could hardly conceive of what we got up to when they weren't looking, why wouldn't it be equally shocking for us to find out the reverse?

Mr Dutton was of relatively youthful appearance, he was wantonly generous with his hilarious money, and he was set in his avant-garde ways. He never quit behaving – or trying to behave – in the way he used to at the time when the word 'scandal' had lost all meaning. Sadly for Mr Dutton this meant that he found himself, not all that many years later, looking preposterous in his outmoded clothes, weathered by his fondness for the stimulants of his day, and shamed by a reputation that had no place in modern, happily married, Word-reared Gawpassat. He packed up and moved permanently to his *pied-à-terre* in the big city, a place where fluctuations of morality were unknown.

One of my earliest memories was of Adam W. Dutton, wearing a phony skipper's cap and tight white shorts, showing off his tanned legs and mixing powerful martinis for the women around my parents' pool. I suppose I must have been waddling around with even fewer clothes on than Mr Dutton, taking in what I saw for future analysis. My mother and her friends, keen to emulate the European customs they believed to be more sophisticated than our own, shocked Gawpassat's rumour-mongers by sunbathing topless. By the standards of my town, this amounted to unshackled debauchery on a par with bestiality or an avowed approval of trade unions. My father, always a portly man, wore a shirt even when swimming; he and his male friends wore dark glasses at all times when the women exposed themselves. In a typical reversal of generational fortunes, topless sunbathing was forbidden among my sisters and my friends once we grew old enough to make it worthwhile.

I suppose I remembered those early summer days because Uncle Ian's proposition had suggested to me that my mother's dabbling in forward-looking social relations might have extended to a full-blown affair – oh, say, around nine months before my birth. It was ridiculous, of course. I gathered in a mouthful of water and spat it skyward. It was ridiculous to think that my mother – with her children, her responsibilities, her obvious devotion not only to my father but to the social minefield surrounding Ian Armstrong – would dare to be so irresponsible. Still, swimming on my back in the scent of lilac, it was fun to think about.

69

The lawn began to fill with Melissa's children. With the shortest of attention spans in operation, they switched from badminton to croquet to baseball to various forms of physical combat and back again. Several feigned injury, but were shamed back into action by their siblings. My father spent ten minutes trying to keep up with his grandchildren, then noticed me in the swimming pool. Allowing a suitable interval so that he wouldn't appear too eager to talk to me, he found a towel, wiped his face, and walked over to sit down in a deck chair.

'Top,' he said, which was a reasonable greeting. I would have replied in kind, but my father accompanied my nickname with an offhand Word Sign. I reciprocated by pressing my fingertips together, and submerged myself. When I regained the surface, my father was in mid-sentence. ' . . . time, just a great time. You'll be glad to know. I was allowed to limp around exactly nine holes of golf.'

'Hello, Dad.'

'What a lot of fuss these grandchildren are, don't you think?' he asked, not meaning it at all. He looked full of pride.

'I'm not used to it. I don't even know their names.'

'Oh, come on.'

'I'm serious.'

'Anyway. Tell me everything, Top.'

I assumed he meant that I ought to fill him in on the last few years of my life. 'Where to begin? You wouldn't believe the amount of travelling I've had to do. Sooner or later, though, one of these jobs is going to turn into something more—'

'No, not that,' said my father. 'I meant about your meeting with your uncle. We're all dying to hear – if that's the expression I'm looking for.'

So *everyone* knew. My father's inquisitiveness amazed me. He, of all people, with his deep antipathy towards superstition, ought to have ignored the Date on principle. Everything the Word stood for – the exploitation of credulousness; the cynical abuse of a monumentally unjust tax-dodge – ought to have been anathema to my dad.

'Come on, Top, tell me. You can tell *me*.'

I found his unseemly curiosity incredible. I recognized that, based on my various failures since leaving the law, my father might not have held out much hope for a fruitful enquiry along the lines of my own activities; but to jump unceremoniously to my recent conversation with Uncle Ian seemed to fall below the usual standards of our family's etiquette. I stretched out my arms along the edge of the pool and raised my face to the brightest patch of a white-hot sky. I felt like falling asleep.

'He must have said something,' my father pleaded.

'No. No, he really didn't. Ever since I spoke to him I've been interrogated this way. He didn't say anything. Or much.'

'Hah! There you are.'

'He didn't say anything important, Dad. Don't worry about it. Tell me about your trip.'

My father obliged. I lowered my gaze to watch him speak. He was overdressed for the weather, as usual, in a seersucker suit and knitted tie, and despite his tan he looked ill. I couldn't stare at him for too long as he spoke excitedly about his adventures, because one of the most depressing things for young people to witness is the optimism and enthusiasm of the beloved elderly.

When my father had finished telling me about the hospitality he and my mother had met, about the fascinating sights they had seen, about how beautiful the desert could be in the early morning, about the treasures they had brought back to share with our community, he leaned forward in his chair and said, 'Now. You can tell me. What's going to happen?'

I didn't want to be rude to my father, but to tell him anything near the truth would have been even worse. There had sprung up a general trend in the direction of more openness between men, with which I disagreed. It seemed to me that if I were to ask him straight out what the chances were that he wasn't really my father, and that his wife had carried on with Uncle Ian, I risked embarrassing him no matter what his reply.

'You know how Uncle Ian is,' I said. 'I didn't dare ask him anything directly, and whatever he volunteered was clear as mud. I don't know what he's up to.'

'Your mother and I,' said my father, in a low, conspiratorial voice, 'were under the impression that he was trying to get rid of us, or at least to keep us out of town. He certainly did his best to set us up with welcoming hosts, out west. They begged us to stay. Everywhere we went they put on entertainment, bar-becues, all very lavish. We know this was Ian's doing, but the Date was very much on our minds. We cut our itinerary short.'

'I believe he knows you're back,' I said.

My father chortled. 'He probably knew before we did.'

My father was one of Gawpassat's last old-fashioned men. The few of his childhood friends who remained in Gawpassat had transformed themselves into the eternally youthful sort of track-suit-wearing retirees who bragged about their pulse rates until the day they dropped dead from cardiac arrest brought on by overexertion. According to my father, these people had everything backwards: they sought an expenditure of youthful energy they no longer possessed, when they had supposedly earned the right to lounge about, read great books, and reflect on the ebbing away of their existence.

I tried to imagine what our conversation would have been like had I not been a failure. I suppose my father would have asked me how it was going down at Hornpipe, Thorn, Cain and Hewitt, and I would have replied, 'Swimmingly.' He would have asked me how Laura, or Lorna, or Lana was, and I would have said that Laurie was fitting right into Gawpassat life, that her serve was by no means the worst part of her tennis game, that she did not regret at all having abandoned her doctorate in order to give birth to and rear our three sons, that as an academic she was not as depressed as one might have assumed by the degraded cultural landscape of our young, thrusting country – in fact, she had stopped reading altogether.

I wondered if my father felt that he had ever put a foot wrong in his life: born in the beautiful old house near the water; educated exactly like me, only more so; thrown into a friend's family's publishing business, there to discover an eccentric love for cartography that lasted a quiet career; married to a supposedly high-class gal who was, in fact, merely tall, foreign and challenging. Gawpassat was full of men who seemed to do everything right – to own everything, to provide selflessly, to know how to repair lawnmower engines, to read books on how to explain menstruation to their young daughters, should their wives have been found unfit for custody. We were so rich, we were so perfect, we were really pushing back the boundaries of human comfort and happiness.

When people are rich and happy, I have observed, they tend to go that one step too far and demand an explanation. It is for that reason that those who say that religion is invented by the powerful to subjugate the meek are probably wrong: the powerful invent religion to satisfy themselves, and the meek pick up the crumbs that fall from the table. I was lucky enough to hear the Great Man himself declare that, to him, the strangest, most inexplicable thing he had ever seen, heard of, or read about in the history of all human history was the enduring success of Christianity in the Americas. Just when a clean break was called for, he had said, popping a black olive into his mouth, the clumsy authorities reverted to Jesus, of all people. Granted, as a colleague of Christ's, if not a contemporary, Uncle Ian had only the highest regard for what

Jesus had managed to accomplish, and no doubt he envied a religion that showed no signs of quitting two thousand years after its foundation in a distant, long-discredited land.

70

'Top?'

'Sorry, I nearly fell asleep. It must be jet lag, Dad. I'm really awfully sorry. You were saying?'

Some of Melissa's boys raced about on the lawn wearing realistic combat gear, firing hundreds of rounds of imaginary ammunition at each other. The girls seemed to be practising their swoons.

'I was just saying how seriously everyone takes the Date. I'd hate to think you were being disrespectful or . . . or cavalier in not reporting something. You've been away, you know, and . . . and you may not realize that there's almost a nation-wide watch on here, to see what happens. You're the only one he's spoken to—'

'Don't ask me why.'

'Well, yes, no, of course. But you're the only one, so what you may know may be valuable.'

'It's good to see you, Dad.'

'What?'

'I said it's good to see you. Really.'

'Oh? Oh.'

'Are you well? You look tired.'

'No, I'm fine. And of course I'm tired. I'm sorry if I sounded . . . if I sounded *preoccupied* with Ian's – with your Uncle's . . . *project*. We all are. Everyone is. What I mean is, how *are* you, Top?'

'Ah. Extremely well, thanks for asking.'

'You've been . . . on the move?'

'As usual. I've just flown in from Tel Aviv,' I admitted, dropping the Dublin story. 'Have you ever been to Tel Aviv? I can't remember.'

'Only to say hello to,' said my father.

Melissa came down the lawn to join us. I could see now that she was indeed pregnant again. She walked slightly duck-footed, and wore a martyr's expression on her flushed face.

'Some of the children want to know if it would be all right if they went for a swim,' she said, looking at me.

'If it would be all right?'

'Yes.'

'With . . . with me? All right with me?'

'Yes. I mean, if you're done, and if you don't mind.'

'If I'm done . . . with the *pool*?' I gestured at the water with my palms, from my crucifixion-pose at the edge of the deep end.

'Yes.'

'Mel?'

'Yes?'

'Please tell the kids they have my blessing.'

Did my sister actually *bow* as she thanked me?

71

It made sense to me that one of the reasons Uncle Ian might have given my parents his beautiful Gray Hill house was that he wanted to keep his mistress and illegitimate children close at hand; what a lucky break for my nuclear family that he reasoned the way he did. Rich people have a good deal wherever they may live, but to grow up in the Gray Hill house, in Gawpassat, in an age when strict education was neither necessary nor enforced, during a time of convenience and abundant electricity – that was surely the most *lenient* childhood a human being ever had. I inspected my nieces and nephews as they splashed noisily about me in the swimming pool. This was paradise, and they had no way of knowing it. They would grow up to be surly and selfish, just like their Uncle Top and Aunt Jean.

My father stroked his moustache as he assessed his grand-children in the swimming pool. It was impossible for me not to reappraise him in light of what Uncle Ian had told me, much as I tended to dismiss the Great Man as deranged. My father was the most familiar man in the world to me, but a few words in my ear from Ian Armstrong had made me look at him sideways, from underneath my wet hair.

It had to be said that, by Gawpassatan standards, my father was an inconsequential man. I grew up with friends whose fathers were bankers, judges, chairmen of multinational corporations, disgraced former White House advisers; or that most prestigious category of all, the mysterious life-long coupon-clipper blue-bloods who lived in Gawpassat only two months a year and wandered around wearing the vacant expressions of people who simply had no idea what to do with their lives because they had never been presented with any challenges. These men were my father's arm's-length friends and tennis partners, but I'm sure they must have wondered why old Elliot insisted on *working*, of all things to do with one's life.

My father had retired at fifty-five, and spent the next twelve years being suspiciously cheerful – with the exception of a four-month period of recuperation from his stroke. I remember having to look up the word 'stroke' in the encyclopedia – at the age of twenty-five – before sending my written condolences. I sensed that Gawpassatans didn't or weren't supposed to have *strokes*, that there was something *déclassé* about *strokes*. This paranoid view was confirmed for me when I began to receive mail from my mother and sisters insisting that what he'd really suffered was an *embolism*, which sounded far more grand.

My father's best friend, whom he probably saw once a month, was a retired movie star whose name was unknown to my generation. He had made a great deal of money for himself just before the war, narrowing his eyes and speaking lines like, 'So, we meet again, El Bastardo!' He hadn't worked in nearly forty years and he was, as they say, without a family. He was older than my father, and they made a touching sight on the tennis court, one limping with age, the other limping with partial paralysis.

'Top?'

'Oh, sorry. Sorry again, Dad. My mind is all over the place.'

My father looked unwell. There were too many grandchildren about. I imagined that for a man to sit in the same chair as he had when young and childless, then suddenly to see a parade-ground full of grandchildren running and yelping, that this might have a telescoping effect on one's retrospective lifetime.

'You've been travelling, I take it?' my father asked me.

'A great deal.'

'I don't have the energy for it. I just go there and stay for a while and come back.'

'Go where?'

'Well. To my destination. I simply mean that I won't put in a lot of to-ing and fro-ing once I've arrived wherever it is I've planned to go.'

'I see.'

'Your mother is the same way.'

'Is she?'

'Certainly.'

'So you agree with each other on what it is you ought to do once you get to where you wanted to go?'

'Exactly.'

'That's very good.'

'Yes, it is.'

My father was a cautious, and therefore not very dynamic man. If I have his personality gauged at all accurately, he lived mainly for the avoidance of controversy and embarrassment. The sight of so many grandchildren swimming about – so many potential sources of scandal, tragedy, disgrace – must have been awfully disturbing for him. I can remember only one time in my life when my father lost control, and he had the usual excuse of having drunk immoderately. God knows what kind of indiscretions he may have committed without getting caught, but in this particular case he could do nothing but throw himself on the mercy of his family and his town.

72

Valery Young, she was called, and rare was the Gawpassatan man who would not cringe upon hearing the name. Her only crime was to have been beautiful and rapacious. Men like my father – the old guard of America – were her favourite targets. Valery herself was a descendant of those early, creepy Americans who decided they preferred danger, starvation and the unknown to some mild ribbing from their religious antagonists. The decadent Gawpassat of my childhood had begged for someone like Valery Young to wash up on her shores; when Valery finally arrived, in the flesh, she was welcomed by the men like rainfall on a drought-stricken plain, by the women like bubonic plague.

One by one, Valery Young seduced the helpless men of my town. It is hard to imagine that during her heyday she was seven or eight years younger than I am now. To the children of her victims, she was just another grown-up with a martini glass in her hand and freckles on her legs and a throaty laugh. She refused to be distracted by us, and seemed not to understand that ten-year-olds could speak fluent English. In my day I have met women almost in Valery's league, and I know that there is nothing any mortal man can do to resist such a person's advances, short of having himself killed. Uncle Ian, targeted first, succumbed first; my father, targeted last, held out longest of all. Ah, but when he fell, my old man made sure we all heard the thud.

It was winter, and that meant snow. In Gawpassat it always snowed hard at night. My father and mother went to a party over on Black Hill, near Uncle Ian's house, where Valery Young began to work her magic on my father within moments of his arrival. He combated her attentions with alcohol. My mother became unhappy with his sloppy condition, and announced that she would go home alone. He shouted at her to be *bloody* careful driving the *God-damned* car in the *fucking* snow.

His next *faux pas* – and even I have only gossip to go on, for the event was never mentioned again in my father's earshot – was to announce to several other guests that he and Valery were 'in love'; perhaps this was the only way he could justify touching the small of her back. His claim was perfectly believable from my father's point of view, but it was presumptuous of him to speak for Valery. When she heard what he had been saying to people, Valery wisely and characteristically decided to call his bluff. She forced him to dance in the ghastly, ritualistic style of my father's generation, which I'm afraid he would never live down. Some reports suggested that peer pressure led my father to smoke a particularly forward-looking guest's marijuana, which I find only *just* credible. At some point around midnight, after Valery had found a less *tense* person to entertain, my father decided to walk home. Head down, hands deep in overcoat pockets, he would have set out down Black Hill through the picturesque but very cold snow, with a warm feeling in his belly and in his limbs.

This would have been in my father's pre-embolism days, when he was fit and robust. He would have walked the route a thousand times. His briefly heightened sensitivity would have opened up to nostalgia as he reached the bottom of the hill and the house of his birth. That might explain why he opened the gate, walked up to the front door and, as the police were later obliged to report, 'attempted to gain ingress.' In those days the house was not yet in the hands of the Word; it was still a 'living museum' of colonial life. My father was greeted at the door, whose lock his scratching key did not fit, by a young lady so keenly professional that she wore an authentic Pilgrim nightgown to bed.

Turned away from the home that would still have been his had Uncle Ian not crept into town, my father angrily turned on his heel and disappeared into the snow. No other sightings were made of him – not at Trainer's, not near the playing fields, not on Lincoln Street. In fact, it was I who made the next visual contact. I awoke with the dawn, excited by the prospect of sledding on our lawn, and threw open my bedroom window to measure the quantity and quality of the previous night's snowfall. One of my windows gave on to the drive, which had automatically been ploughed by Mr Genovese at midnight.

Mr Genovese seemed to have missed a spot. I leaned out the window and squinted. It had stopped snowing, and it was a clear, cold day. Yes, Mr Genovese had missed a spot – a man-in-an-overcoat-sized spot. I put on a bathrobe and a pair of shoes and went outside to investigate. There was my dad, lying face up in the drive, his house keys in one hand, the collar of his coat pinched around his neck in the other. His trousers had ridden up on his legs, which I saw were purple once I had brushed off the half inch of snow that had fallen since midnight. I started dragging him towards the door, thinking he must be dead and that I would somehow be blamed, but he mumbled something about his lapsed Yacht Club membership so I knew he was OK. I could not have known then, as a mere adolescent, how often our roles would be reversed over the next several years.

73

Jean turned up at the swimming pool, wearing dark glasses and avoiding the children where possible. She hadn't changed her clothing from the previous night. The scene at my parents' house had now broken into the realm of the idyllic. Melissa and my mother turned the kitchen upside down to provide fuel for the young, and served it wherever the kids wanted: poolside, on the verandah, on the lawn, down on the rocks where my oldest nephew had gone to fish.

'Oh, my God,' said my father, which made me look up. 'It's . . . your uncle.'

Uncle Ian came down the lawn wearing white shorts, panama hat and blue blazer. The children flocked to him, grinning and Word-Signing. He gave each a benedictory pat on the skull. He had brought Benjamin with him, two other servants, two bodyguards and a golf cart trailing a wagon full of ice and cocktail ingredients. This was going to be one of those fabulous, drunken afternoons I remembered from twenty years ago, when the children would exhaust themselves and go inside, leaving the tipsy adults to crack open lobsters and talk softly in the cooling air of their regrets and their resolutions.

It was uncomfortable, at first, as Uncle Ian's servants drew a table and chairs around the barbecue at one end of the swimming pool, and the Date hovered over the Great Man's greetings with my parents. I gathered from their conversation that they hadn't spoken to each other in several weeks. The children went quiet; those who had been swimming wrapped towels around their shoulders and sat silently on the sloping lawn like an audience at an open-air play. It was good of my uncle to have brought along his own bartender, who set to work uncapping bottles and slicing lemons and spreading out the ingredients of whatever exotic drinks might spring into one of our minds. He looked familiar to me, and soon I was able to place him as a near contemporary of mine who used to be good with automobile engines.

I climbed out of the swimming pool and was handed a towel by the ever-alert Benjamin. I dried myself, then went over to shake hands with Uncle Ian. He was one of those men who had looked steadily more ruggedly handsome every day of his life. I didn't think he looked much like me. I have a slightly bigger build, broader shoulders, fairer skin. As he spoke to my parents, I stood close by taking a good look at him, wondering if all my life everyone I knew had spoken amongst themselves about the eerie resemblance between me and my uncle. Perhaps one couldn't tell these things operating from the inside, the same way tape recordings of one's own voice sound unfamiliar. If so, my friends and relatives had been awfully good at hiding their suspicions – so good that I simply had to rule out Uncle Ian's assertions as fantasy.

Fantasist or not, Uncle Ian seemed to have lost none of his mental sprightliness. He joked in a relaxed way with my parents, without mentioning Agnes, the Date or his true intentions *vis-à-vis* dying. He asked Benjamin for a scotch and soda with plenty of ice – the staple cocktail of old–school Gawpassatans.

He stood erect, with one hand in the pocket of his baggy white shorts. His brown legs sagged just a bit around the knees, but overall he looked lean and fit. He politely asked my parents about their trip out west, and displayed some knowledge of the culture they had pillaged for their decorative artifacts.

By Gawpassatan standards, and despite having been responsible for a vulgar religion, Ian Armstrong was a towering intellectual. The one official photograph ever taken of him at home on Black Hill showed him sitting authorially in front of a section of an impressive library, with a hefty, significant-looking book open in his hands. The library itself was not so unusual in the larger houses of our town; the open book might merely have been pretension. What separated Uncle Ian from his fellows on the Gawpassat hills was that he actually read his books, one after another. He even seemed to understand them, to the point that he held strong and often persuasive opinions about events or trends that he had not personally witnessed or seen on television. Most Gawpassatans, even if they had attended fancy schools and developed an exquisite sense of superiority, were too busy constructing perfect lives to have time to read. It was a joke I shared with Marcus that since graduating from college we had written more books than we had read.

It is certainly true that I looked up to Uncle Ian as a man, although I chalked up much of his charisma and accomplishments to the luck of having been born at exactly the right time: just in time to have had an opportunity almost to be killed in the Battle of the Bulge. Through no fault of their own, the subsequent generation of men had grown up more slowly; some would say we looked childish and undignified in our business suits and our polished shoes, in an era when going overseas referred not to civilization-saving combat but to expensive honeymoons in Greece. There were no more soldiers in Gawpassat. I had never, ever met a veteran of the armed forces who wasn't old enough to be my father or grandfather. We bred our modern soldiers elsewhere.

Our putative father-son relationship aside, I think I can say that I had always truly identified with Uncle Ian. That is one of the reasons why I may have been feeling down in the dumps that summer, when I came back home. I had just reached the age when wonderful things were supposed to have started happening to me. They had happened to Uncle Ian, all right: a flash of insight, a niche filled, a job well done – the rewards had been gigantic and quick in coming. His life had never been the same since his original idea took off. He had known fame and wealth and adulation. Things had happened to Uncle Ian, all right.

74

Uncle Ian put his arm around my shoulder and proudly pulled me close to him.

'Wonderful to see *this* boy,' he said, stressing the determiner as if comparing me to Melissa's boys; or perhaps it was a southern thing.

'Well, yes,' said my parents, in almost perfect unison. My father continued for both of them, 'We haven't really had a chance to catch up.'

I said, 'I'm very happy to be back. I really am.'

My uncle squeezed my shoulder, then let go of me. We were a happy, perfect family. My sister's children beamed, all of them. The sun had turned silver in the haze. Even Jean managed a sardonic upturn of one corner of her mouth.

My parents were palpably relieved to see Uncle Ian looking so well and so positive. Like everyone, they must have harboured a long-standing fear that the Great Man *wasn't really kidding*, that the Word was more than just a money-spinner to him. Even I had begun to worry, since my return to Gawpassat and its Word-Signing madness, that people like Melissa and her children would be delighted if my uncle died, thereby vindicating their faith. Now I thought I could see that they were merely showing him the respect a Great Man deserved after a long and successful career, and that they would wash their hands of the Word once the Date had come and gone without

181

incident. As for Uncle Ian's plans for me – his supposed son and heir – I could see no other course but to go along with his game without asking too many questions. Any contributions he wanted to make to my financial well-being – on the condition that my father not be made aware of the Great Man's primary delusion – were fine with me.

Benjamin made sure everyone had a drink, then we all sat down and behaved like rich, happy people. Jean hadn't yet said a word, but two or three times she lowered her dark glasses and gave me an important look. I loved Jean, but I sometimes thought she would risk scandalizing the whole world by marrying her own ex-uncle-in-law if it meant she could move into that Black Hill house. She had found out just slightly too late that rebellion really wouldn't get her anywhere in Gawpassat, not any more. I had recognized the symptoms almost the moment I saw her again, a brand-new set to her mouth and jaw that said she thought she had figured out what she wanted, hated herself for it, and was now too old to get it in any case. My sister, whom I had looked up to until things evened out in our early twenties, had turned into the kind of woman for whom the Gawpassat lexicon contained half-a-dozen unpleasant epithets. I believe Jean caught me thinking this, at our family reunion by the pool, because she flared a nostril at me.

'Raise your glasses to the return of the prodigal son,' said Uncle Ian, knowing that any *double entendre* would not be lost on me. Everyone gave me a more or less nervous look in the eye as they toasted my visit. The ice was broken when Melissa's youngest, a baby girl, crawled into the swimming pool and had to be dragged out by Uncle Ian's nimble bodyguards. In a nervous atmosphere the likes of which I had rarely experienced, my family tiptoed into conversation.

My mother wanted to hear about developments at the Institute during her absence.

My father asked if anyone had seen that amazing story on the news about the lizard in Indonesia whose saliva cured acne.

Melissa wondered whether anyone had any opinion on the presidential election, then only three months away.

After a dark silence caused by Melissa's unanswerable political question, the exchange resumed with an irreverent anecdote from Jean about a man she knew whose wife had left him because he had taken up the Word; Uncle Ian laughed, and everyone was able to breathe again.

More drinks were served, more items were ticked off people's lists of things to say, until a more than unusually unpleasant silence was filled by Uncle Ian's statement that he loved us all, dearly, and just wanted us to know it. We all grumbled uncomfortably, because the open expression of love for one's friends and relatives was one of the teachings of the Word that Gawpassatans found it hardest to take on board.

'I realize how curious you all must be,' Uncle Ian said at last, 'and I appreciate your delicate handling of the question of the Date.'

None of the others had ever heard him mention the Date by name, I'm quite sure. Uncle Ian's slightly over-long white hair flickered in the mildest of sea breezes that swept up the lawn and fluttered the lilac blossoms. We waited in silence for the Great Man to continue.

'I have had a very long time to contemplate it, and the Date, I think, has been good for me.' I glanced at my parents, who could not conceal their surprise at Uncle Ian's strange monotone, and a statement that sounded as if it came straight out of *The First Word*. 'I could not have lived the way I have without the Date. Time had a different meaning for me than for anyone else in the world. The Date was the most special gift I ever received in my life.'

Looking at my parents again, I guessed that they were somewhat insulted to be spoken to by their old friend in such a portentous and self-important way. This isn't a conversation, they must have been thinking, this is a *sermon*. My mother folded her arms and tapped her foot impatiently. My father smoothed an eyebrow. Benjamin noisily refilled Jean's drink. My nephew Matt yawned so hard his jaw cracked audibly.

'Listen to me, my dear friends. *The Last Word* is nearly complete.' He made no eye contact with anyone, not even me. He raised his chin, so that his prophet's eyes gleamed in the sunlight. 'The journey, started so long ago, is almost at its end.'

Goodness, I thought. How bold of Uncle Ian to try to fool my parents and siblings as well as everyone else in the world.

'I am going to be taken from you,' he said. 'I am going home.'

Anyone spying on us out of earshot would have taken our gathering as a typical Gawpassatan mansion-owner's Sunday afternoon excuse to get tight together, with an assortment of unnaturally polite and cooperative children in attendance. In fact, this tiny band of ex-relatives of Ian Armstrong's were in on a fairly believable bid for immortality. What would his religion come to be called? 'Armstrongianity' didn't quite have that ringing-down-the-ages feel to it. Perhaps *The Last Word* would suggest a workable name.

'I will be called tomorrow. I am going home,' Uncle Ian repeated.

'Don't go home yet,' said one of Melissa's girls, who looked five or six years old. 'You just got here.'

Uncle Ian lowered his gaze to look at the girl. 'You wonderful, you beautiful child,' he said.

Everyone was moved – except me and Jean. She shot me a look that said if I didn't spill everything I knew when this . . . *moment* was over, there'd be hell to pay.

Her expression changed considerably when Uncle Ian said, 'I will be taken from you tomorrow,' looking at me, extending a hand, 'and *Matthew* will be at my side.'

75

Uncle Ian once advised me on how to make a lot of money, which he considered a noble enterprise in life. We were out on the *Claire* – Uncle Ian, my parents and Jean and I – 'sailing along apropos of nowhere,' as my father would have put it.

I had taken the tiller, and was flanked by Uncle Ian and my father. It was a cool, early-spring day, and we all wore sweaters and jackets and wool hats. Jean and my mother laboured below, making lentil soup and slicing sausages.

My uncle may have drunk a few too many pre-daiquiri hot toddies that morning, because even before we had rounded Clark's Island he had been tactless and indiscreet on the subject of religion, though not necessarily his own. He had expounded favourably on his glorious predecessors in the monotheism stakes, but added, 'If I wanted religion I would invent my own; I wouldn't buy one from a stranger.'

Before we had a chance to question him on this obvious and rather self-defeating statement, Uncle Ian put a hand on my shoulder and switched into his fatherly advice mode.

'If you want to make a lot of money, my boy,' he began, but he was interrupted by my father.

'Now, Ian.' My father didn't know what his old friend was going to say, but he had never shared the Virginian's love of wealth for wealth's sake.

'I want to know,' I said. I was fifteen years old, and already fascinated by the power of money.

'Well, listen real close, then,' said Uncle Ian, ignoring my father's sigh. 'What you have to do is, you have to sell something someone *wants*.'

My father and I gave him sarcastic looks.

'Thanks a lot,' I said.

'Your wisdom,' said my father – for those were the days when it was possible to kid Ian Armstrong about his wisdom – 'has astonished us. Let's race back to port, clamber ashore and build empires.'

'There is more to what I say than meets the ear,' said Uncle Ian, sucking his drink through a straw. 'Selling something someone wants requires, to a certain extent, selflessness. You cannot sell what interests *you*, what *you* would want to buy. You have to imagine what it is *most* people think or know they want, and provide it. That's a lot harder than it sounds, unless you are building obvious things, like washing machines.'

185

'That sounds sort of . . . straightforward,' said my father, displaying an unusual archness.

'Ah, does it? I leave you with just one other thought, then. My simple theory leads to the logical conclusion that if you are not like most people, and yet you make what most people want, then you will not want your own product. Think about that.'

We never did think about that, not until much later, because I had managed to steer the beautiful *Claire* on to a sandbar.

76

I will never forget the way my family looked at me after Uncle Ian told them I would somehow be participating in his staged death. There had never been a clearer indication of the heir's likely identity. Their whole view of me reeled into perspective: family leader, idol to thousands, Gawpassat's wealthiest person, the man in the canary-yellow helicopter. I felt a rush of hubris very much like the best imaginable drug at the sight of my closest relatives suddenly thinking a great deal of me.

Who knows what kind of self-satisfied expression I allowed to leak into my features, but I remained silent. I let Uncle Ian's unexpected words speak for themselves. Jean lowered her dark glasses again, raised her eyebrows, cocked her head to one side and mouthed the question, '*What?*'

'Don't be saddened,' said Uncle Ian, although saddened was the last thing anyone was. They were aghast. 'Isn't life wonderful?'

'Yes,' said one of Melissa's boys, who was holding a plastic hand-grenade.

'You wonderful, you beautiful child,' said Uncle Ian, which made everyone even more nervous. I thought he was doing a super acting job; he really did look and sound like an ecstatic visionary. 'You will remember me, won't you?'

'Of course I will, sir. We all will,' said the boy, with an articulateness that caused my sister Melissa to radiate with pride. It sounded rehearsed, to me.

I wondered how proud of her uncle Melissa would have been if she could have seen him hunched over the console of his globe-girdling espionage equipment, invading the deepest privacy of poor old Agnes. Melissa had always been the most morally outraged member of our family. Everything shocked her, no matter how remote from her own universe. She couldn't believe that everyone in the world didn't behave as perfectly as she and her husband did – the men calm and productive, the women serene and fecund. The evening news on television, which she never missed despite having so large a brood to manage, turned her cheeks crimson with indignation or sympathy. She particularly hated Indian bus and ferry accidents, when hundreds or even thousands perished. It was clear to Melissa that the Indian buses and ferries were badly constructed or outmoded, that safety precautions were lacking to say the least, and that the authorities were allowing severe overcrowding. She would ask the rest of her family if we didn't agree with her, and receive a handful of exasperated nods in reply. Melissa was galled by terrorism. She could not abide famine. Whenever an aeroplane crashed she demanded an investigation, material stress tests, pilot evaluation, control-tower inspection. I suppose her point was that if the world could simply pull its socks up and be more like Gawpassat, from pole to pole, then there would be no more need for television news.

'That's enough about that, then,' said Uncle Ian, although I'm sure no-one looking at him at that moment had begun to catalogue the questions they wished to ask. 'The children must play. The rest of us will chat, like a family, the way we always have.'

The weirdly obedient children leapt up and resumed their games and their swimming. Uncle Ian gestured to his servants and bodyguards, instructing them to help the children set up their toys, to referee, to watch over the pool.

Uncle Ian reclined in his chair and clasped his hands behind his head. He looked relaxed, which had an infectious, calming effect on my family. Jean crunched an ice cube in her mouth and swirled her drink in her glass. Melissa for once ignored her children and concentrated on the Great Man. My mother fingered her pearls like worry beads and smiled into the distance. My father took off his shoes and socks, splayed his toes in the sunshine, then crossed his legs. No-one mentioned Agnes.

I wondered what my father made, deep down, of Ian Armstrong. I was quite certain he could have no objection to his friend's having amassed great wealth in a single, preposterous lifetime. His snobbery had limits, and he prided himself on having partnered parvenu tennis players, sailed with *arriviste* yachtsmen, contributed cultural artifacts to a public school. I know that he had a healthy, superior disdain for a society and culture that could give rise to a phenomenon like the Word, but he would not have blamed the fortunate beneficiary. No doubt he would have said he found Ian Armstrong 'amusing', the way floundering aristocrats in the past must have pretended to take pleasure in the revolutionary changes about them, hoping to derive entertainment from the decline of their own values.

I can remember only one occasion when my father lost his temper with his wife's then brother-in-law. It was at a family gathering around our pool, identical to the one on that day so close to the Date, except that Uncle Ian was still married to my Aunt Charlotte. Many a scotch and soda had been consumed. My older sisters had gone down to the rocks to 'look for seals', which probably meant Jean wanted a cigarette. Claire and I paddled around the swimming pool in a two-seater inflatable canoe. I remember the grown-ups' conversation because they were talking about the private life of one of our teachers, a recent convert to the Word and a person for whose death I had consciously prayed on numerous pre-exam occasions.

'He's queer,' said Uncle Ian, thinking Claire and I weren't able to overhear; we were able to do so, but we did not know the meaning of the word he had used.

'No, he's not,' said my father.

'Queer as the Tower of Pisa,' said Uncle Ian.

'Keep your voice down, Ian,' said my mother.

'Bent as a corkscrew.'

'*Ian.*'

That would have ended their exchange, had Claire not marched into school two days later and announced to the class, in front of the teacher in question, that Mister Armstrong said he was queer. The children thought that was an hilarious adjective, and some even claimed to know vaguely what it meant. This embarrassing episode made my father so angry that, according to my mother's later testimony, he drove up Black Hill that night and told the Great Man to watch his mouth in future, to keep his smutty thoughts to himself when there were children present.

'Well, he *is* queer,' said Uncle Ian.

I'm told that my father then launched into an unprecedented ten-minute lecture on the subject of what was and what was not proper conversational material in front of youngsters, adding that if family embarrassment were to be avoided, Uncle Ian ought to keep in mind 'the quasi-consanguinity of his interlocutors.'

Apparently Uncle Ian was left speechless.

77

By the pool, in front of his curious and admiring audience, Uncle Ian held forth on the subject of love. Love, he said, was something he wished he had known more of. He blamed himself, he said, and added that the time had come for him to unbosom his conscience of certain guilty feelings relating to his first wife, my Aunt Charlotte. Charlotte, he wanted to tell us all, was the first and only woman he had truly loved in his life. I found this a remarkably inconsiderate and tactless statement, if indeed he believed that the woman sitting five feet away from him was the mother of his two children. He also wanted us to know that he felt he had 'made his peace' with Charlotte before her death. He said that, if anything, he had suffered more than Charlotte from the separation and divorce he had demanded. He was sorry she had died. He had made her a very wealthy woman. Somewhere in Surrey there now existed – thanks to the Word, to Uncle Ian's generosity and to a notoriously punitive divorce-court judge – an outstanding public garden and the best institute of arachnology in Britain. Charlotte had always loved spiders.

I was twenty-seven years old when Aunt Charlotte died. I had visited her only once in England, what with Everest and law school and one thing or another. I will never forget how strange it was to see her then, because she was exactly like my mother in almost every way except that her beast of a husband had abandoned her. If ever there were an example of happiness not being something money could buy, Aunt Charlotte provided it. Permanently furious, vengeful, embarrassed, humiliated – Aunt Charlotte did not live out a happy life once Uncle Ian's pelf fell into her lap. She was paralysed by her fury. She never worked, she never made new friends, she simply hired experts to build a reasonable garden and an exemplary spider zoo.

Aunt Charlotte loved England, though, for negative reasons. When I visited she took me walking and driving around the countryside surrounding her stately home, explaining how unlike Gawpassat England was in every way. She referred to her years with Ian Armstrong as a 'fugue', and claimed that she regretted every moment of what she had been through. When I unwisely protested that those had probably been the best years of her life, whether she admitted it or not, she became unladylike. I confess that I approached my visit voyeuristically: I didn't know too many people who honestly thought that a large part of their youth had been utterly pointless and misspent. I wanted existential pointers from Aunt Charlotte; what I got instead was bile.

Living with Ian Armstrong, according to Aunt Charlotte, was like living with an especially beloved but dangerous sort of domesticated animal that might at any moment lunge for one's throat. She was careful to insist that he was never physically violent towards her, just exasperatingly unpredictable. She said she felt like a laboratory rat being tested for the limits of psychological endurance. When I pressed her for specific examples, she became frustratingly inarticulate. Amazed at my own rudeness, I told her she must be exaggerating, that plenty of women had more to put up with in their husbands than princely wealth and mild manic depression. Hearing this, Aunt Charlotte shuddered and said I was exactly like my uncle.

78

'This has been a splendid reunion,' said Uncle Ian, draining his third or fourth drink. 'I'm so happy to see all of you looking so well. Now, if nobody minds, and because I'm so awfully busy, I wonder if before I go I might just have a word in private with young Matthew here.' He pointed at me.

Now my relatives really were bowled over. My parents exhaled audibly. Melissa's eyes opened wide. Jean crunched an ice cube in her mouth. It looked for a minute as if they might have had enough, that they were sick of following Uncle Ian's orders. They wanted answers from their old friend, not obfuscation, and they wanted them now. Their indignation lasted only seconds, though; it dissolved into capitulation before our eyes – mine and Uncle Ian's, the Great Men. They stood up, shook Uncle Ian's hand with awkward solemnity, and trudged up the lawn towards the house and children. I felt another rush of power and privilege as Uncle Ian drew his chair closer to mine. I had a moment, as we waited for my nuclear family to move out of earshot, to imagine what it would be like for them to loathe and envy me for the rest of their lives.

Uncle Ian looked terrific. His face was so close to mine that I could smell the scotch on his breath. He looked like a man who had twenty years left in him. He pumped his eyebrows at me, then winked. He seemed to know exactly how I felt. We were conspirators. My family reached the screen doors of the verandah, gathered a few children around them, turned and looked back down the lawn at us – two figures full of mystery.

'You like this, don't you,' said my uncle.

'I don't know.'

'Sure you do. I can see that you do.'

It was the best time of day for summer in Gawpassat. The sun had sunk behind the house, casting a cool shadow on the lawn. A dozen sailboats out on Gawpassat Bay still shone in bright sunlight.

My uncle may have looked physically fit, but there was an important, rather worrying gleam in his eye. I thought I was probably in store for another dose of confessional monologue; consistent with its author's personality, the Word recommended unburdening oneself during moments of personal stress.

'Look how they're trying not to watch. It's almost embarrassing. I do love your parents very much, I tell you that honestly. But I'll tell you another thing, and I cannot dig deeper than this. The way your mother's husband is looking at me right now, that's something I've craved and cherished all my life. All my life. Do you know that when I came here to this beautiful place, when you were not imagined by creation, Elliot and Margaret Richmond seemed to me just exactly like what I wanted for myself. That's America, I thought. Rich people living in a perfect place. But do you know what? I must have done too good a job trying to be what I thought I was supposed to be, because – and I'll blow my own horn if I want to – because I am now the ideal. I am the apotheosis of this *entire society*.'

My uncle said this with one hand raised to the bay and a fascist orator's firmness of chin. His whole performance looked and sounded ridiculously rehearsed. 'I am the apotheosis of this *entire society*'? I was pretty sure I knew what 'apotheosis' meant, and it was all I could do not to interrupt him and express my disagreement.

'I am not talking about covetousness, or the act of possessing,' he said, losing me. 'I am talking about having become the embodiment of a great historical trend. Now, don't you look at me that way, Top.'

'Sorry, what way is that?'

'You were squinting at me. You just don't believe, do you –

you can't see what's right there in front of your eyes, a man who has superseded all that went before.'

I supposed my uncle meant that the Gawpassatan establishment had been forced to step aside to make room for the Great Man, whose fortune and social prestige were built on appealing unashamedly to the unwashed. Members of the establishment could get so *cross* when they saw hundreds of years of culture jettisoned for the sake of someone like Ian Armstrong's wallet and ego.

'If I understand you correctly, Uncle Ian, then I think I can honestly say I believe.'

With a gesture perceptible only to Benjamin, Uncle Ian ordered another drink. I didn't remember him being much more than a half-a-dozen-stiff-ones-a-day man, like most Gawpassatans, but now he had the look of a drinker with intent. He gulped his next scotch so hard his eyes teared, and it took him a minute to regain his voice.

'I am so . . . *gratified* to hear that,' he said. 'And I need you to believe one more thing, if only as a favour to an old man.' Uncle Ian cleared his throat, and seemed to have some difficulty looking me in the eye. 'I need you to believe, Matt, that you are my natural son. It would mean the world to me if you would think . . . ' Uncle Ian almost choked on those last words. He'd come all over misty. 'That you're my boy. That I'm your old man. It's just so that, you see, I could go out trusting in the future. It would mean everything to me, strange as it may seem to you.'

With my whole family watching from the top of the lawn, it would hardly have done for me to lean over and give Uncle Ian a big hug, which is what I felt was expected of me. It was a terrible moment. I realized that anything I said, any negative gut reaction I betrayed, could cost me at least the opportunity of making a fortune the easy way. I was embarrassed for my uncle, but I didn't dare reassure him one way or the other.

79

I found it most peculiar that Uncle Ian wanted me to believe that he was my biological father, when his own belief was quite sufficient for his self-delusion. I was quite sure, sitting there next to him at my second private audience in two days, that even if I did believe him it would change nothing in the way I felt about the man who had raised me. As for the life of tawdry deceit my mother may have lived out – well, no-one said life wasn't going to be full of one's mother's tawdry deceit.

Still, it was a strange sensation to imagine, however briefly, that I shared roughly half the Great Man's genes. It reminded me of Noel, Gawpassat's convicted rapist, who had been adopted shortly after his birth. Eugenicists would have had a field day with him. I will never forget how he was treated when his progressive father decided it was a good idea to come into school and explain to a classroom full of ten-year-olds that Noel's mother had some sort of congenital Fallopian-tube defect, and that our friend Noel had been born to another lady who didn't have enough money to take care of him. Noel, despite being one of the bigger, stronger boys, was persecuted remorselessly for at least three years, until some humanity entered our systems: girls told us to stop being mean to him or they wouldn't go out with us. I remember distinctly that we teased Noel not because of the biology of his situation – we didn't even understand that part – but because his father had been imprudent enough to mention to us that the likely reason Noel had been put up for adoption was that *his real mother was poor.*

When Noel was packed off to jail as a result of his taste-less offence, there were quite a few long faces among my contemporaries. Some of them must have thought they had driven Noel to the deed. I wouldn't go that far, but the whole sorry episode made me realize in a guilty way that the most brutal and annoying human behaviour – notably bigotry, cruelty and blind obedience to oppressive power – is essentially and literally childish. If it hadn't been for girls, and enough pocket money to go out with them, we would have banded together in violent gangs and roamed about destroying everything that was remotely good-looking or valuable. You can't say enough for prosperity and homogeneity when it comes to making people behave civilly towards one another.

80

'It won't be for long,' said my uncle.

'I beg your pardon?'

'You won't have to believe for long – that would be entirely up to you. I just need you to believe on the Date. I need you to spend the day with me. Spend the one day with me, being my boy. Do you understand what I'm asking?'

'I think I do, Uncle Ian. It's very unusual.'

'You can imagine that there will be a certain amount of attention paid to us. I'm told there isn't a free hotel room within fifty miles. People are sleeping in their cars, or on those filthy beaches down the way.'

'Is this really true? I'm sorry, I just didn't know. No-one said anything. I had no idea.'

'I have an escape planned. You know, for the bigger escape.'

Now that Uncle Ian had negotiated the most emotional segment of what he wished to say to me, he became animated. This led me to believe that whatever it was he had planned, it wasn't his death.

'You can just imagine,' he said, 'how the hills will be crawling with folks? There are so few people I can really trust, but arrangements have been made so that we will not be inconvenienced. No, everything will be fine. Everything will go ahead. These people, these people who revere me, who worship me, they will line the shore. They will stake out the Yacht Club. They will try to be one step ahead.'

I wanted to ask if he would be charging admission.

'What I need from you is so simple, Top. And I will be

195

so proud of you. On the morning of the Date, I will send a car for you. No-one needs to know about this.' Uncle Ian twitched half of his body in the direction of my parents. 'You bring a suitcase, whatever you normally travel with, and it will be . . .' Uncle Ian sighed, and looked me straight in the eye for the first time in many minutes. 'You see, it will be you coming home to Gawpassat to visit me.'

'I think I understand.'

'You'll do it?'

I wished then that I had been employed in a line of work that would have prepared me for making important snap decisions. In the normal course of my business associations, I was rarely called upon to answer questions more difficult than whether I did or did not have a particular day, week or month free. A glance at my diary always sufficed.

I wondered if Uncle Ian had any idea how badly I had so far squandered my education and other advantages; if so, he might have thought twice about even pretending to consider me his son and heir. I worried that he might have based his selection solely on the misplaced aura of grandeur that automatically attached itself to explorers and mountaineers.

I must have taken all of fifteen seconds to answer Uncle Ian's question – long enough to chastise myself for seeing any option in the matter. This was no time for a moral stand. My uncle had probably lost his mind, and he needed me to fulfil some sort of harmless fantasy. Without thinking for a moment that my answer might make me a rich man, I smiled and replied: 'Of course.'

As if reading Uncle Ian's thoughts, and his intention to leave, Benjamin, his bodyguards and the rest of the crew packed up their golf cart and left – left, that is, under the clatter and roar of Uncle Ian's canary-yellow helicopter, which lowered itself on to the centre of our lawn and scooped up the Great Man almost in mid-stride. He waved from the window at me and my family as his gaudy bird ascended to tree-top level, tipped its nose, and accelerated into its ten-second journey to the summit of Black Hill.

I stood alone by the swimming pool as my parents and sisters and nieces and nephews first walked, then jogged, then ran down the hill to be briefed by their newly glamorous relative. The children were the first to reach me. 'Uncle, uncle,' they chanted. They could only have known intuitively that anything out of the ordinary was afoot. Even Lizzie, the perfect advertisement for the Word, seemed to lose her composure in the excitement. She pulled at my wrist and hopped impatiently in place. Her parents and grandparents reached us seconds later and demanded, without the usual protocol, to know what Uncle Ian had said to me.

'Nothing much,' I said. 'We haven't spoken in ages, Uncle Ian and I. He just wanted to catch up with me. Care to do the same?'

81

'Hello, Laurie?'

'Hi there. What's up?'

'Nothing much. Or there might be, but I'm not supposed to say. Not even to you. I'm not supposed to say I'm not supposed to say, even. Still, I wanted to give you a hello before you went to bed.'

'I see.'

'Don't be angry.'

I really wanted to ask Laurie how she would feel about me if I became Heir to the Word, to Black Hill, to Uncle Ian's countless millions, to the adoration of the masses. It was not an easy question to formulate in the abstract. I had to assume Uncle Ian was listening, and that every other telephone extension in my house was pressed to the ear of one or other of my relatives. I recognized that it would be a rare girlfriend who would not at least keep an open mind about huge, unexpected wealth, but one of the reasons I thought I might be in love with Laurie was that she was out of the ordinary.

My parents had made a charming effort to keep their curiosity under control, going as far as to ask me questions about myself that were unrelated to the Date. Laurie was not quite so understanding. She pressed me for answers even when I insisted that there was little to tell, and that our conversation was being monitored all over Gawpassat.

'You're torturing me,' she said – which, coming from someone with her expertise in the matter, carried some weight.

My parents' house was dead quiet, though I knew it was occupied by at least a dozen people.

'How am I supposed to trust you,' asked Laurie, in an unpleasant voice, 'if you've been keeping all this Word and Date crap from me all this time?'

'You're just supposed to,' I said, rationally.

Laurie cursed.

'Don't ever talk to me that way,' I said.

She cursed again.

'Watch your step,' I said. 'Just watch your step.'

'I don't have to take that from you, Matthew.'

'Don't call me Matthew.'

'It's your name, you—'

'I'm hanging up now.'

'You wouldn't dare.'

'I'm hanging up now, Laurie, unless you apologize properly.'

'Apologize for *what*, you—'

'I'm hanging up.'

'What's come over you? What's going *on* over there?'

I put down the phone, expecting not to speak to Laurie for a while. The house came alive with the sounds of a family trying to behave normally.

82

Uncle Ian's *Fourth Word* had a great deal to say about the Great Man's pointers on a subject he called the 'forging of relationships'. This work comprised maddeningly obvious advice about concession and understanding, sympathy and selflessness: good stuff, but impracticable. I'm sure that the average believer in the Word found it a challenging few chapters of over-intellectualized psychology; I thought it was the maladroit common-sense guesswork of a man who had never 'forged' a 'relationship' in his life. Uncle Ian's most recent behaviour only confirmed to me how selfish a Great Man he really was, and how little he had actually enjoyed the fruits of his invention. It reminded me that I was still waiting to meet my first happy rich person.

Uncle Ian's divorce from Aunt Charlotte was brutal; it scarred everyone within singeing distance of their disagreements. Socially, Gawpassat reeled. Aunt Charlotte's exile was a foregone conclusion, and those who were slow to realign with her ex-husband were ostracized from Black Hill for the rest of their lives. Their split was said to have occurred because Aunt Charlotte was constitutionally incapable, as an English woman, to give proper social credit to her husband's achievements; that, at any rate, was my mother's initial view. As advertised by Uncle Ian, their irreconcilable differences amounted to nothing more than the usual boredom and frustration that, as my father used to say, 'modern married people use as excuses to break their holy vows with the airy indifference shown by matadors to charging bulls.'

I was too young to understand the tensions of Uncle Ian and Aunt Charlotte's breakup. Jean and Melissa told me it was as if a glacier had flowed down Black Hill. News coverage never helps in such situations, and the couple received their uncharitable share. Uncle Ian had by then almost stopped giving interviews, but one survives in which he answered charges of hypocrisy by claiming that God had told him he would be divorced not just once but twice. This probably helped to explain why my Auntie Intellectual would find out within hours that her marriage had ceased to exist.

Uncle Ian was helped during several lapses of morality by the fact that he had never been a preacher. He had never delivered lectures or sermons – and even in private he rarely made the slightest judgemental suggestion. His business was based on the most fundamental aspect of spiritual leadership: God told me, so I know; follow if you will. It is amazing how many people willingly did so.

There had been a tremendous boom in spirituality during my lifetime, which spokesmen for traditional religions tended to ignore in their bemoaning of low church attendance and the breakdown of society's values. People believed any damned thing at all, but luckily for the followers of the Word, Uncle Ian demanded nothing in return for his teachings other than money: he did not ask them to dress in uncomfortable or embarrassing clothing (except at Word-sanctioned weddings); he did not ask them to commit mass suicide; he did not ask them to spend their free time ringing doorbells and pamphleteering; he did not ask them to mope about, pulsating with guilt, at the least infringement of his 'lifestyle guidelines'.

It was my view that depending on what *The Last Word* had to say, and how powerfully it was expressed, the Word might have a future of sustainable profitability. It might even outlive the Great Man. I sincerely doubted that posterity meant any-thing to Uncle Ian, which is why I was certain the Date would amount only to a grand and very expensive publicity stunt. I confess I had begun to feel thrilled at the thought of my partici-pation. I did not enjoy keeping what information I had from my parents and sisters, but after everything Uncle Ian had done for all of us I thought it was the least I could do in return. I regretted having been so short with Laurie on the same subject, but even then I had begun to feel the importance of my station, the need to keep outsiders in their place, and the power of mystery.

83

I had my instructions. I allowed my family to fume with curiosity. I spent that evening alone in the library, reading *The Third Word* and an accompanying explanatory text by Dr Max Sohlman. The Word grew on me. If it had been better written, it might have made the international grade. I gravely packed my bag before going to bed, and put myself in an apocalyptic frame of mind.

In bed that night I read *The Sixth Word* for the first time, Uncle Ian's latest, four-year-old book. His style by then had been radically compressed to one-sentence paragraphs, each a 'Word Thought', most not meaningful to the conventionally-educated mind. 'Picture a frame,' one of them read. That was it: *Picture a frame*. I could see the play on words – just – but I had never been strong on profound interpretation. 'Record and play back your thirst,' was another. I guessed that the effect was supposed to be cumulative, and that I had missed some key thematic links along the way.

Shortly before midnight, the telephone rang downstairs. This was unheard of. It could only mean a wrong number or a death in the family. With typical self-centredness, I listed to myself the ways I could now be embarrassed: Uncle Ian calling with last-minute changes of plan, which would infuriate my parents; Laurie calling to tack a last word on to our tiff; Jean calling from Trainer's hoping somehow to blackmail me into telling her everything I knew.

Someone answered the telephone. I got up and walked out of my bedroom, down the hallway to the top of the stairs, to save anyone the trip to wake me: we did not shout, in my parents' house. My mother came to the bottom of the stairs and started to climb them.

'Is it for me?'

'Oh, *my*,' she said, clutching the banister with one hand, her throat with the other.

'I'm so sorry. I didn't mean to frighten you.'

'Yes, yes it's for you. It's Little Dave Periman.'

'What?'

'Shh. You can use the phone in our room. We're awake.'

'Thank you.'

I went down to the end of the hallway to the master bed-room, sat down in the chair my mother used to look at herself in the mirror in the morning, and picked up the telephone.

There were all sorts of clicks on the line, one of which sounded like my mother only pretending to disconnect.

'Dave?'

'Matty-boy?' Dave said, or some such rah-rah nickname of his own invention.

'Where are you?'

'We're in the car. We are supposed to be heading out on our honeymoon. Don't listen,' he said, apparently to his wife. 'Have you got your ears covered? Good. Matt?'

'Yes?'

'We were supposed to go on what they call Chopper Safari, in Tanzania. You know about that, I'm sure.'

'No, I hadn't heard of that.'

'It's first rate,' said Dave, to whom I hadn't spoken in ten years. 'Just like a real safari except that you never have to touch the ground. Scares the absolute fuck out of the wild animals.'

'I'll bet.'

'Beth would have loved it.'

'Would have?'

'Yeah, well, I've had to cancel. Maybe some other time.'

'Sure.'

'So, look, Matty-boy, I'm glad we're having this talk. You can listen now, babe.' Again, I assumed this last was directed at Beth Periman, née Rhodes.

'Dave, congratulations. I never said congratulations.'

'Thanks. I had no *idea* you were going to be in town, or you would have *been* there.'

'I'm sure it was a terrific wedding.'

'It's just getting started. We had to make our dramatic exit, though.'

'But no honeymoon, eh?'

'Nope. Not at this time. Which I sort of wanted to talk to you about. If that's OK.'

'What do you mean?'

'I mean, what with you and your uncle having your heart-to-hearts . . .'

'How can you *possibly* know about that, Dave?'

'You remember Gawpassat, Matt. Listen close and you can hear the squeak of the mattresses.'

'I see.'

'Anyhow, the point is, I'm sticking around. Beth doesn't mind. She knows how important this is. We're talking about the same thing, right?'

'I suppose so. You mean tomorrow.'

'Tomorrow, right. And what I want to say to you – the reason I am calling from my limo the moment after I leave the reception of my own first wedding to beautiful Beth,' there was the sound of a theatrical kiss, 'is so that you know I am *there* for you tomorrow. Do you hear me?'

'You're *there* for me.'

'Exactly. *Ciao*, babe.'

I replaced the receiver and looked up at my reflection in my mother's mirror. I looked good. That man I had just spoken to, Little Dave Periman, was without a doubt Gawpassat's most admired and successful young man. And yet he had cancelled his honeymoon, called me from his limousine, said he would be *there* for me on the Date. Everyone knew. It was no longer rumour. It was hours away, and it was fact. People like Little Dave – soon to be a Big Dave, when he had a Little Dave of his own – were already falling into line behind the Heir.

I resolved to tell Uncle Ian about this conversation. He would probably have a transcript on his desk in the morning anyway, but it was best to be open with the Great Man. He would understand my excitement. He would integrate the news into his overall plan for survival, whatever it was. He would be grateful for my honesty, and when the *real* Date came along he would remember how helpful I had tried to be.

What a scam, I thought. Uncle Ian had built in a sure-fire marketing ploy, thirty-five years or more in advance. How he must have gloated, high on Black Hill, as the years passed and he contemplated a twilight burst of fame and glory. Not only had he conquered his dream town, he had its most illustrious denizens salivating for more. The Periman family! My God.

84

Jean once cruelly told me that she thought I had climbed Mount Everest because of Dave Periman. How else, she argued, could I have competed with so thoroughly successful a man? I replied that to call Dave Periman 'successful' was like calling the Pacific Ocean 'wet'. The Perimans may not have lived in Gawpassat as long as the Richmonds (we founded the place, but one didn't dwell on that), but they made the town their own many generations before Ian Armstrong's invasion. When you grow up with a twit like Dave Periman, it's hard to see him the way the outside world does – that is to say, as an accomplished lawyer, banker, board member, philanthropist, art collector, baseball-team owner, and all-round Favourite Son.

There is one thing I know about Dave that makes me sick to think about. There are few things he could have done that would have made me respect him less. He could have been a rapist, like Noel, and I would have looked for reasons to try to be sympathetic. He could have been a murderer or a wicked landlord, and I might have found room in my own black heart to forgive him. What Dave Periman did, the summer between our junior and senior years, was to commit *insurance fraud*.

His Aunt Catherine had given him a valuable antique pocket watch, which she must have assumed he would put in a safe place and give to his own nephew one day. Dave immediately insured the watch for tens of thousands of dollars. I inspected the watch soon after it was given to him, and for once I could see why a small, impractical object might have material worth: the watch was beautiful. Dave told me the valuer had called it a 'gold, eight-day, quarter-striking, minute-repeating lever clock-watch.' Some British or European genius of horology had fashioned it at the beginning of the nineteenth century. By the looks of it, a master jeweller or two had helped out with the decoration. The watch had been preserved as if in a vacuum, and its movement whirred gorgeously within its gold casing. Dave told me that these watches were normally a steal, but this one had what the experts called *provenance*. It had belonged to two princes and a queen.

Out sailing one day, in the kind of salt spray antique watches cannot abide, Dave reached into his windbreaker and extracted the watch, opened it, and announced the time. I told him to put the watch away, he would damage it. 'Damage it?' asked Dave, with a giggle, tossing the watch over his shoulder into the ocean.

I felt myself trying to dive over the stern of the boat after the watch, but Dave, still laughing, held me back. When I regained my breath, I asked Dave why he hadn't simply sold the watch, rather than destroying it and committing that most awful of crimes, *insurance fraud*. 'Two reasons,' he replied, as if he committed *insurance fraud* every day of the week. 'First of all, it would be insulting to my Aunt Catherine if I were to sell a personal gift; this way there is no chance that she'll ever know that her watch isn't in my possession. And secondly, you can't get shit at auction these days – the insurance value is relatively huge.'

Dave sailed us back to Gawpassat; I sat next to him drinking coffee from a thermos, miserable and appalled. Dave didn't need that money, I thought, any more than Aunt Catherine had needed her beautiful watch in the first place. Dave's crude rationale was probably that a slick sports car could belong to him the following day without a single inconvenient meeting with his trust-fund manager. As we rounded Clark's Island, I asked him how he thought he would convince the insurance company that his watch had been stolen. Dave gave me a pitiful look. 'Stolen?' he said. 'No, Matt. Lost overboard. You saw what happened. God, how we scrambled along the gunwales trying to stop it. *Just* out of our reach, eh? Coming about!'

85

I slept well. I awoke and got out of bed at six o'clock; I reasoned that it might be insulting to squander what Uncle Ian had advertised as his last day alive. I dressed for international travel, lugged my grip downstairs, and drank a glass of orange juice in the kitchen. At six-thirty I walked outside into the humid morning and started down the drive. Francesco's limousine awaited me at the gate.

'I've got it,' I said, when Francesco opened his door to help me. 'Carry on.'

All was quiet on Lincoln Street. We wound our way down the dewy hillside in silence. A steaming cup of black coffee was clipped to a retractable table at my side. Our ride was so smooth that I was able to drink the coffee without spilling it. When we reached the main drag on the waterfront, I could see that it was not a normal Monday morning in Gawpassat. There were too many cars – too many obviously non-Gawpassatan cars – with steamed windows and people inside. There were foreign-looking strollers along the sea wall. Our two coffee shops, side by side in the centre of town, overflowed with customers. Everyone turned to watch me and Francesco purl by, and bystanders patted their pockets for cameras as if trying to draw revolvers.

We turned right, up Jefferson Street, where two members of the Gawpassatan police force manned a barricade and turned back the tourists. They waved us through without question. Francesco's posture, and his hands on the wheel, looked tense. I wasn't exactly relaxed myself: I reflected that the last three days had not been the most boring of my life (the most boring days of my life were on the big mountain). At one point we had to squeeze to the side of the road to let a yellow advanced-learning-for-kindergarten bus get by. It had twenty children aboard, or more. For some reason Gawpassat's brightest children were also the wealthiest; almost all of them lived on Black Hill.

Halfway up the hill we passed my niece, Lizzie, who stood erect in a lay-by wearing a full sea fisherman's oilskin, complete with sou'wester. At the gates of Uncle Ian's mansion, a gaggle of photographers had gathered. They parted, and flashed aimlessly at the one-way smoked windows that screened the passenger compartment of Francesco's car. Through the gates we went, to the front staircase of the Black Hill house. Francesco darted out to my aid, took my bag, and led me to the door. He rang the bell, put down my bag, and scurried back to his car. The door was opened by Benjamin as the limousine hummed back down the drive.

'Welcome home, sir,' said Benjamin. I suddenly remembered that Benjamin had gone to Princeton.

'Thanks, Benjie. Good to see you.'

'And you, sir. Please come this way. Did you have a pleasant journey?'

'Very pleasant, thanks. My old man up yet?'

'Yes he is, sir. He is reading the papers in the study.'

'Top!' It was Uncle Ian, halfway down the main staircase, wearing a dressing gown and waving a newspaper. 'Top, my boy!'

'Hey, Dad,' I said.

Uncle Ian continued down the stairs. 'Well, come on then, son. Come here and give your old Dad a hug.'

Benjamin disappeared with my bag as I went over to the bottom of the staircase, extended my arms, and received my uncle in a strong, warm, filial hug. He patted me on the back, said 'Ho ho ho,' held me at arm's length by the shoulders, dusted off one of my lapels with the back of his hand, chucked me in the jaw, then led me by the elbow into the immense, glassed-in room known as the Hall of Crystal.

'I just thought,' he said, 'that I would greet you with a Bloody Mary. Then you have to tell me *everything*.'

The Hall of Crystal had been added on to the Black Hill mansion when I was a teenager; its purpose was to be grand.

It contained grand objects, like mirrors; display cases full of rare silver forks; a billiards table that was so precious no-one was allowed to use it; a real, full-size 1932 Shilton Roadster; fountains spraying into pools full of valuable carp; and enough vulgar crystal posed here and there to give the room its name. People in town thought it was deliberate that at precisely two in the afternoon during the days surrounding the Fourth of July, blinding sunlight reflected off the massive French windows of the Hall of Crystal straight into the main dining room of the Yacht Club, then swept along the waterfront dazzling all who gathered in the town park for their holiday picnics. Uncle Ian said it was a coincidence.

The sacred Bloody Mary had already been prepared – in quantity, of course – and awaited us in a sweating silver ewer. Gawpassatans had been attached to the drink for generations, snobbishly and ridiculously so, and Uncle Ian had therefore thrown himself into the perfection of its recipe as if his whole social identity relied upon the result. Long ago he had divulged to me his expert sources: a novelist from out west; a publisher of beautifully illustrated war books from the city; a Gawpassatan who had given his life and fortune to yachting – all of them long dead of alcoholism, so that the secret rested with my uncle, presumably to be revealed only in *The Last Word*. Such was that particular drink's appeal in our neck of the woods, that Gawpassatans could score social points by remarking, if asked about the Great Man, that he seemed to make the best Bloody Mary ever tasted. This implied intimacy with Uncle Ian, as well as the refined palate for the great Bloody Mary that rich people reckoned was their birthright.

It was the time of morning when the Hall of Crystal came into its own. The rising orange sun, its outline only just perceptible through the haze, touched every tacky *objet* with its heat and colour: vases, miniature horses, boats and ballerinas, mirrors, candlesticks and unidentifiable globs of modern art – all were naturally illuminated as we sat down in ocean-scented furniture to begin our talk.

Beneath his open dressing gown, Uncle Ian wore the kind

of white, loose cotton shirt and trousers I would normally have
associated with a morose homosexual playwright exiled to the
south of France. He looked terrific, in other words, and his
deep tan was displayed to best advantage. His hair, still wet
from a shower or laps in the pool, was slicked back on his
head and curled once at the collar. He looked like someone
who had been divorced more than twice, which gave me the
idea for an appropriate conversational gambit.

'How's Agnes?' I asked abruptly, like an angry son who had
never forgiven his father's remarrying.

'*Agnes*,' said Uncle Ian, frowning humorously. 'Well, now,
you *do* cut to the quick, son.' I could see that I had said the right
thing. 'Agnes, you may not be devastated to know, has ceased
technically to be your stepmother.'

'Oh?'

'We came to a little arrangement over the weekend.'

'Good, well, no more about that, then.'

'Exactly. Now, a toast to your homecoming. Cheers, son.'

'Cheers, Dad. It's great to be back. Nothing has changed.'

'Time stands still when you're away.'

'Right.'

'Now tell me, where have you just come from? Israel? Was
that what I heard?'

'Correct. A silly little mission. An engineering company
needed a computer, and I was asked to escort the machine.
They bought it its own first-class seat.'

'What a strange thing to be asked to do. Where do you
actually *live*, by the way?'

'That's a tough one, Dad. I've kept my chattels to a minimum. I have an address in Milan, which is quite central.'

'I've never been to Milan.'

'You'd hate it, even to visit. You belong exactly here, Dad,
you always have.'

'You'll be seeing your mother, while you're in town?'

'Uhm. I guess so.'

'I don't know what it is about you two. You're all grown
up now. No reason to hold grudges.'

'Of course. You're right, as usual, Dad.'

I was enjoying this conversation. It felt natural. I realized, if I hadn't already, why a rich, lonely man like Uncle Ian might want to arrange such an encounter. He looked genuinely paternal – proud and moved and interested. My real father was so distant and formal that we had never kicked off our shoes, shared a pitcher of booze and *caught up* quite in this systematic way.

'So, Dad,' I said, holding up my glass of Bloody Mary. 'You haven't lost your touch.'

'To tell you the truth, I delegate the Bloody Mary-making these days. A touch of arthritis in the wrists. I can't juice all those lemons the way I used to. The recipe is in safe hands, you'll be glad to know.'

I nodded and sipped, and nodded again.

'It's going to be a beautiful day,' I said. 'A breeze at last, I think. That is, Francesco told me it's been awfully hot over the last couple of days.'

'Yes, well, that's good. I thought we might go for a sail, you and I. Unless you're too tired, want to rest up for the day.'

'Not at all. I drank two glasses of Drambuie on the plane and slept all the way here. I feel fine.'

'Grand,' said Uncle Ian, using a very Gawpassatan adjective.

I thought that if my performance were to be at all convincing, I ought to pose the most obvious question a son would have. I put down my drink, leaned over and put one finger gently on Uncle Ian's knee.

'I just have to ask,' I said, shyly, lowering my voice. 'It is . . . the Date today, isn't it?'

'It certainly is. Good of you to drop by for it, you dog.'

'That's why all the people downtown?'

'People. Oh? Really?'

'Swarms of them.'

'How embarrassing.'

'Flattering, more like. They've been waiting a long time.'

'Tell me about it, son.'

'I spoke to Little Dave Periman last night, by the way. He's cancelled his honeymoon in order to be here.'

'*Has* he? He's a good boy. The Perimans have been very good to the Word over the years.'

'I know they have.'

Now Uncle Ian looked thoughtful. He took a sip of his drink, then refilled both our glasses. He smacked his lips and squinted into the sunshine. The vulgar crystal glowed all around us. The Black Hill house, which must have contained at least a dozen staff, was so quiet I could hear the tick-tick of the alarm system resetting itself in the adjacent ballroom.

'Top, I've got to say something. We've been close, haven't we?'

'Sure we have.'

'We don't have a lot of – you know, a lot of *garbage* between us, do we?'

'Not that I'm aware of.'

'I'm so glad to hear you say it. But there is one thing, that one little difference of opinion.'

'Is there? I don't know what you mean.'

Uncle Ian laughed through his nose. 'Well, what I mean is,' he said, 'no-one could really accuse you of being the greatest, the number-one fan of the Word, could they?'

'I suppose not.'

'You do believe, don't you?'

I didn't pause long. 'Dad, there are different ways of be-lieving. I'm sure I believe roughly in the way – for example – the Perimans do. Don't worry. I think the Word has been terrific.'

'Has been?'

'*Is* terrific. There is no other religion I respect more in the whole world.'

'Well said.'

'Come on, don't get me wrong, Dad. I'm awfully . . . *close* to the Word, don't you think? I'm not your average believer.'

'But the Word is *good*, isn't it? Don't you really think so? I'd hate it if you didn't think so.'

'Of course it's good. Just look at you – just look at this,' I said, gesturing around us at the vulgar crystal.

'I'm so glad to hear you say that.'

There was a pleasant pause as the sun filled up the room.

'I wanted to ask you,' said my uncle, a few minutes later. 'How's that . . . friend of yours, that Marcus fellow.' Only ten years before, his ellipses would have been confidently filled by the word 'coloured'.

'An obscene success story. He'd be thrilled that you asked.'

'Well, I liked what you did together. I liked him. I liked your book, too.'

'Marcus wrote nearly all of it. I took most of the photographs. The expedition was my idea, but his enthusiasm and ability sort of overwhelmed the project. We don't communicate or correspond any longer.'

'That's a shame.'

'Yes.'

86

It wasn't really a shame. Marcus made me nervous. He made me feel selfish and irresponsible. He had such an annoying pedigree, what with all of that overcoming of hardship and racism and disadvantage. He went from strength to strength in his career and private life (he had of course married the rich, beautiful daughter of not just his boss but the Boss of Bosses who worked from a mansion much like my uncle's in an even wealthier town than Gawpassat, if such a place is imaginable). This was shaming. My experience with failure has taught me that paranoia is a predictable by-product of the condition: I began to think that Marcus was living his life the way he did for the sole purpose of making me feel low. When I heard that he had found time to hone a golf swing that was the envy of the country club that – to everyone's amazement and relief – actually admitted him, I thought that was the last straw. I knew I would never see him again, unless it was at a college reunion where he would look terrifically fit and young and rich, wearing one of those white scarves I hated, and I would hover around listening to my classmates asking him wide-eyed, ingratiating questions. *And* he had climbed Mount Everest.

The truth is I had to drag him up that mountain, psychologically speaking. He was sick as a dog most of the time, and held up our progress. I would never have reminded him of this later, but he *complained*. He missed his girlfriend. His lips split. His pack was unbalanced. His hands sweated. His beard itched. When I finally asked Marcus if he would do me a favour and *cut it out*, one would think I had insulted his masculinity. He sulked. He didn't do his share of the work. He said he didn't see how it was possible that we were ever going to reach the summit. He wondered aloud, repeatedly, if I thought the weather would suddenly turn nasty and that we would be killed. He had a terrible time sleeping, and, thinking this unfair, tried to keep me awake as well with stories about his young girlfriend's heavenly body.

He was better on the way down and out from the mountain. He knew a lot of songs that kept our legs moving. We met hundreds of other intrepid mountaineers, including two Canadian girls who refused to believe we had climbed the real thing. One of the most irksome conversations I ever had was with those girls. They succeeded in transforming our conquering of Mount Everest into a theoretical act – or worse, some sort of existential gesture we might have wanted to make for our personal enlightenment, rather than simply to impress girls. We succeeded in impressing them anyway, in other ways, but still their disbelief rankled. What use was all that effort and tedium if girls weren't going to believe us?

It would be unfair to mountaineering if I claimed not to have derived some personal pleasure in the experience of climbing Everest. There were unforgettable moments of satisfaction, of pain, of fear and of awe. Climbers are so hilariously exposed, on any big mountain, that there is little time for them to wonder about purpose or meaning. Just looking at the summit photograph of myself, I can feel the thinnest air on earth

213

stinging my face, and the feeling of unlimited energy in my body. The view was swell, too.

I cringe down to my shoes every time I remember my terrible mistake: I overexposed Marcus's photograph on the summit, so that his black face was lost in the shadows of his flapping parka hood.

87

'How's Laurie, Top? Still in the torture racket?'

'She's fine, thanks for asking. Yes, still torturing herself. I'm hoping to see her soon. We always seem to be flying in opposite directions.'

'Are you thinking of marrying her?' This was the sort of direct question my real father could never have brought himself to ask.

'I don't know if I am or not. I'm afraid to say Laurie might take some convincing.'

'Nonsense.'

'It's true. She thinks I'm sour and negative. Can you *believe* that?'

'Heaven forbid.'

'I don't want to be disloyal to her, but to tell you the truth I think she believes I ought to have a proper job. Can you *imagine*?'

'Preposterous. If I may quote from my own works, "An educated man need never do anything he dislikes." I was called élitist for thinking that. Elitist? Me? It just seems so obvious. It's a bad climate out there, Top, when people start frowning on you when you state the obvious. It used to be only the loony women who complained. Now it's everyone. If I were just starting out now, I think I'd have a hell of a time trying to get people to listen, through their ridiculous prejudices.'

'I'm sure you're right.'

'Anyway, you'll get your Laurie, if you want her.'

His confidence was unanswerable. He had an aura of wisdom

about him that was certainly one of the major causes of his success. His official photographs captured a look of profundity and trustworthiness, as well as a playful squint to his eyes that said his main lesson on life was simply that people ought to lie back and enjoy it.

One of the central teachings of the Word was that in order for people to live happy lives, they ought to start out with extremely low expectations. No-one seemed to mind hearing this from someone whose life, since his early thirties, had been one long adventure in wealth and celebrity. I suppose they kept in mind those legendary years chopping wood for his invalid parents, and gave the man credit for having overcome all the odds in making something of himself. I had never been convinced by his stories of childhood hardship, and I thought it was pompous of Uncle Ian and his ilk to patronize children by saying 'When I was your age, son, I had to *walk five miles through waist-high snow* to get to school.' It was something to look forward to that if I ever had children they would live in squalor compared with what I had experienced. 'When I was your age, my boy,' I'd say to my son, as he left the house at dawn to work in the frozen-fish packing factory before walking to his first class of the morning, 'I used to *drive my own sports car* to school.'

Uncle Ian put down his drink and crossed his legs. 'Yes,' he said, 'you'll get your Laurie. I'm only sorry I never had the pleasure of meeting her. Your mother says she's nice. And of course I've spied on her.'

'My mother thinks it's immoral to be divorced. She's never had a cordial word to say to Laurie, ever.'

'That is a quirk about your mother, to say the least. You have to admit it's odd that she would disdain divorce and at the same time . . . you know.'

'Yes. My thoughts exactly.'

'There's no explaining the human beast,' said my uncle, who had spent his career trying to do just that. 'Anyway, your Laurie – she's *thin*, I hope?'

'Thin, yes.'

'Excellent. A drinker?'

'She drinks.'

'Good.'

I was waiting for that earthy side of Uncle Ian's personality to assert itself.

'Fun in the sack, is she?'

'Sure.'

'Would she like living in Gawpassat, do you think?'

'I have no idea. She wouldn't be used to it, that's for sure.'

'Has she got any dough?'

'Not a *sou*.'

'Her ex chimes in with support, I suppose?'

'I'm afraid not. He's a musician. They don't speak any longer. They were far too young, and Laurie pretends it never happened. I don't ask her about him.'

'Divorce is an ugly blot on a girl. You can see what your mother means, really. Nevertheless, I think I can give you my blessing.'

'I beg your pardon?'

'I mean, you have my permission to marry her if you choose to. I thought you might like to have my permission.'

'Sorry, of course, Dad. It means a lot to me. Thanks.'

We smiled at each other. Uncle Ian picked up his glass and raised it towards me. I toasted him in silence, with a meaningful, loving pursing of my lips.

'Right,' said my uncle, as if changing the subject before he burst into tears. 'Let's have our sail. I haven't been out on the *Claire* for six weeks or more.'

88

The *Claire*, formerly the *Cerise*, was the most beautiful sailboat in Gawpassat. I wouldn't have given Uncle Ian a lot of credit for taste in other areas, so I had to assume that it was only a coincidence that he ended up buying a yacht that would have been a tourist attraction on its own merits, even if she hadn't been the flagship of the Great Man's little fleet. My uncle owned three boats that I knew of: a three-storey stink-pot of the kind normally favoured by arms-dealers and lottery winners, complete with indoor swimming pool and a thirty-seat cinema; an attractive sixty-odd-foot sloop with bare-kneed ten-man crew; and the *Claire*, a fabulously stylish mahogany, teak and brass number with an ingenious sailing system that allowed all thirty-six feet of her to be sailed almost effortlessly by a single, elderly hand.

The *Claire* had *provenance*. She was built in Finland in the twenties by a Swedish industrialist who sailed her home to the Stockholm archipelago, where he wished to be alone. He committed suicide aboard the then *Cerise* on his eightieth birthday, and she was sold to a Nazi. The Nazi kept her in Vichy, France, but was not alive to retrieve her after the war. She fell into the hands of an unscrupulous Marseillais with no respect for sailboats, but was saved when he sold her to a hotelier who would soon make enough money out of his Riviera hotels to be able to refurbish the *Cerise* completely and sell her at a profit to a Hollywood mogul. The disgusting mogul seduced girls aboard the *Cerise* throughout the 'fifties and early 'sixties. The intimate parties the *Cerise* knew must have been among the most innovative of the age. The mogul became at least the second man to die aboard the *Cerise*; probably the first to do so of natural causes. The *Cerise* promptly fell into the hands of an Italian actress who, when her career, marriage and affair all ended simultaneously around the time of her twenty-sixth birthday, sold the vessel to a *nouveau-riche* American oil man on his first visit to the south of France. He had the *Cerise* transported to the United States, where he intended to use her as the 'bar' of a floating restaurant somewhere in the Mississippi delta. She lasted only hours down south, because she was intercepted by a naval architect and yacht enthusiast who recognized her value and offered the oil man a sum even he considered worthwhile. The naval architect was a cousin of Big Dave Periman, and asked permission to moor the boat at the Gawpassat Yacht Club. Once Uncle Ian laid eyes on the

Cerise, her future ownership was a virtual *fait accompli*.

Uncle Ian was a sailor after my own heart: he believed in eating and drinking well aboard ship, in behaving exactly as one would in a private room of an exclusive club, except for having one's nostrils filled with invigorating sea air. He did not believe in the discomforts associated with optimum boat speed. He had nothing against dropping sails and drifting, except that the graceful lines of his yacht were best shown off to fellow sailors when heeling at a drink-threatening pitch. Aboard the *Claire*, as she became when my sister died, Uncle Ian and his guests took care of the cooking and bartending themselves; the boat was too small for intimate talk in front of staff, even for one as accustomed to servants as my uncle. Uncle Ian used to threaten to sail the *Claire* to Greece, for what reason I have no idea. He loved the boat, but he felt unworthy. I can remember one perfect day when Uncle Ian told me that if Claire hadn't died he would have given her the yacht as an eighteenth birthday present. 'She's the only one of you who ever really cared about sailing,' he said. 'I don't deserve this boat.'

89

We boarded Uncle Ian's canary-yellow helicopter, buckled ourselves into swivelling leather chairs, donned our head-phones. Uncle Ian had replaced his dressing gown with a blue windbreaker. He wore old-fashioned white canvas tennis shoes and no socks. We took off from the front lawn and hovered over the Black Hill mansion for several long minutes, as Uncle Ian appraised his property with wet eyes and two fingers pressed to his lips. Our pilot took us banking up and down, back and forth over all three hills, close to treetop level; it felt like a roller coaster ride. On one pass over Gray Hill I saw my parents standing on the lawn outside our house, coffee mugs in hand, waving. Finally we swooped down White Hill, over the vast lawns of the Institute of the Word, and shot over the Yacht Club and the crowds and cars lining the shore.

'This is the part I like,' I heard Uncle Ian say over the intercom, as we clattered along at sailboat level above flat seas. Uncle Ian pressed his face to the window and looked straight down at the water tearing by. Halfway out into the bay, we regained altitude and made for the black cloud of the city. We took a brief tour of its mighty buildings and monuments – commenting to each other that we felt a mixture of awe and revulsion at the sight – then our two-man crew headed us back out towards the water for the homeward run. A mile out of Gawpassat, our pilot slowed to a hovering standstill seven hundred feet over the water. He turned the craft sideways to give Uncle Ian a postcard view of his three hills. Music came over our headphones – I don't know anything about classical music, but it was somewhat stirring and sad at the same time.

After a suitable amount of time – long enough for Uncle Ian to soak up an aerial view of what had attracted him to our magical town in the first place – our pilot took us in on Gawpassat as if on an attack run. This would have been a familiar sight to Gawpassat locals, but the tourists must have been thrilled. We strained at our seat belts as the craft banked and slowed and descended smoothly on to a small grassy peninsula adjacent to the Yacht Club. The flagpole that normally flew the Stars and Stripes and the Yacht Club colours had been removed to permit our landing. I could see through the window that extra police forces had been called in for crowd control. They held back hundreds of people who waved signs and flags or held up placards reading 'The Date of the Word!' or 'The Last Word!' or 'The Word: Believe!'

Uncle Ian told me to stay where I was until the rotors stopped turning, because it was undignified to step out of a helicopter hunched and dishevelled. When all was quiet, he patted the pilots on the shoulder; they turned around and casually saluted him. He told me to give him a moment on the ground, then to follow. He opened the door himself, kicked out the steps, and climbed carefully down to the ground. A cheer went up. The flags and signs were waved more furiously. Uncle Ian raised a hand and smiled. It was an exclusively white crowd, many of them sunburned, all of them colourfully dressed, practically none of them slim enough to be used as an advertisement for the Word. Every other person held up a camera of some kind. The white lights of television crews were held high, illuminating the yellow helicopter and Uncle Ian's bright white clothes. This was the first time the Great Man had been confronted by his people since the early days of the Word, when he had to sign books in a bullet-proof booth. There was little evidence of security, for obvious reasons: an assassination attempt would have played right into Uncle Ian's hands.

I could hear the cheers of the crowd – monosyllabic, deep, rhythmic, probably '*Word, word, word* . . . ' There had never been that many people in Gawpassat at one time. Uncle Ian turned to beckon me down the steps, into view of the crowd. If I recall correctly, I began to get an erection.

90

Laurie and I had enjoyed a more tempestuous romantic involvement than either one of us had previously known. It was all my fault. Laurie knew exactly what she was doing: she was studying torture and torturers, it was as simple as that. She was practical, she was diligent and, though she hadn't read a word of the Word, she had low expectations. I, on the other hand, was best known as the Nephew of the Word, and I wandered around hoping for some mysterious force to liberate me from my chronic indecision. Laurie had a life; I had a holding pattern. It was as if I had guessed all along that Uncle Ian would favour me with some sort of high-profile employment at the Institute.

Still, I never dreamt that he would ever take me on a helicopter ride and show me off to his fans. His self-indulgent talk about being my father, his demand that I ought to pretend to be his son, and his taking a last ride around his fiefdom were just matters of theatrical gesture and publicity-seeking.

I decided that my uncle must have seen the Date approaching, found himself in almost perfect physical health, and decided to milk his rash prediction for all it was worth. As I stepped out of the helicopter on to the grass next to Uncle Ian and heard the muffled sound of a crowd whispering '*Who's that?*', I couldn't help thinking that Laurie ought to have been there to see me. That would show her.

'*Who's that?*' whispered the crowd, as the cameras flashed. '*Who's that?*' I reflexively smiled at them and waved timidly, like a publicity-shy celebrity embarrassed by his own fame. Many members of the crowd seemed to be laughing involuntarily, letting their happiness at seeing Uncle Ian on so important a day bubble to the surface. Most of Gawpassat was there too, and they quickly spread the news of who the young man was at Uncle Ian's side. I must have made quite a contrast, standing next to the Great Man – dressed in a seersucker suit with the jacket slung over my shoulder, tie loosened in the heat, shoes not quite American.

'*Who's that?*' said the crowd. Word spread, thanks to those rubber-necking Gawpassatans, so that seconds later I heard my name rolling through the throng: '*Matthew Richmond, Matthew Richmond . . .*' I searched the front row for friends and relations, but they all looked eerily identical to me – fleshy, ecstatic people with cameras slung around their necks and children on their shoulders. Uncle Ian led me by the elbow past the main crowd, over to an entrance to the Yacht Club that had been cordoned off from the masses. Waving all the while, we made our way out to the side of the restaurant where my sister and I had celebrated that famous birthday, and from there to the permanent mooring of the *Claire*.

She was as beautiful as a sailboat can be. A man I had never seen before helped us aboard. The engine was already running. The man leapt back on to the dock and cast off our lines. A minute later we were waving from the helm at hundreds of people leaning over the sea wall. We tacked several times around the harbour with Uncle Ian proudly manning the giant, ornately carved tiller.

'Look at this,' he said. 'Will you just look at this.'

For a recluse, he seemed to be getting a lot of pleasure out of his proximity to the people. He really was crying out for assassination, sailing close to the rocks below the wall, waving up at his followers, a big, handsome smile broken on his long, brown face. I had never felt anything like that combination of fear and excitement: the satisfaction of being on the receiving end of adulation can never be overestimated, nor the latent threat of the slavering populace at large.

'Ho *ho*!' shouted Uncle Ian, bringing the bow around into the channel between the dozens of moored yachts Gawpassatans sailed three times a year.

We could hear the cheers behind us as we set off out of the harbour. I clambered forward to raise the main as Uncle Ian cut the engine. I had to be careful. I felt clumsy in my street shoes, so I took them off. The *Claire* was so unique a solo vessel, and Uncle Ian had done so much to refine and modernize her since the last time I had been aboard, that I feared almost anything I did would be redundant. I was not surprised when an electric motor raised the mainsail for me, then the jib for good measure. I returned to the cockpit to the smell of coffee – automatically brewing below, of course.

A motley flotilla of lesser craft tried to follow us out of the harbour, but were cut off by the harbour master and two other motorized launches enlisted for the purpose. When Uncle Ian stood tall in the stern of the *Claire* and waved them off, I was amazed to see that everyone obeyed. In my day we would have come alongside and sprayed beer over all over the gorgeous teak deck.

Uncle Ian sat down when we reached the mouth of the harbour, and accepted the mug of coffee I had retrieved from below decks. As soon as we emerged from the shelter of the Gawpassat hills, the breeze freshened and carried us off at a reasonable rate towards Clark's Island. The *Claire* was a heavy boat, designed not for speed but for beauty and the personal convenience of one lonely, suicidal Swede.

'Quite a send-off, eh Dad?' I said. It is quite possible, given

222

the prevarication I was accustomed to in my work, that I managed not to sound self-conscious.

'By God, yes,' said my uncle, standing up again, astride the tiller. 'By God, yes. What a day. Did you see it all? Did you see it all?'

He had begun to repeat himself again, which I had come to think of as a bad sign. Still, I could see the sport in what he had set out to do – rallying a crowd, raising expectations. He had never lacked for imagination. As long as he didn't get drunk, he might be able to see everything through.

'Hey, Top, son, go below, will you? Find us that bottle of Armagnac? It'll go well with this coffee.'

'Sure.'

I did as he told me, pausing to whistle when I saw the contents of the liquor cabinet. I filled two glasses on the bevelled mahogany table, and brought them up into the open air.

'I do believe we're getting some air,' said my uncle. 'Look at this, Top. Can you believe it? I think I see a fair-weather cloud.'

We didn't get a lot of distinct clouds, in summer. Most people blamed the filthy city for our weather; others said it had always been that way.

'You're right. It's clearing up. If we're lucky it'll rain one of these weeks.'

'You noticed how dry it is? Good boy.'

The old *Claire* creaked a fair bit, despite the extensive work of Uncle Ian's men over a period of more than twenty years. She smelt of wax.

'I take it we're headed for the island?'

'That's right. There's something I want to show you.'

'Oh?'

'You'll see when we get there. It couldn't be more *vulgar*, as you would probably say.'

'I don't say *vulgar*, Dad. I'm not one of them.'

'Sure you're not. Anyway, listen, I bought Clark's.'

'You bought the island? Jesus, Dad.'

'What do you mean, Jesus? Remember to whom you are speaking, my boy. That island is *mine*.'

'I never even knew who owned it before.'

'No-one owned it, unless you count the government. I have struck a very beautiful and well-balanced deal with the authorities. It seems there are a couple of tragic birds they want to protect, and I have guaranteed the little darlings' safety. In exchange I get to build on a corner of the island. A *nice* corner of the island. With its own bird sanctuary, natch.'

'Natch.'

'Silly birds, by the way. On their last legs in any case, I'm sure. I have promised only to look after them in the manner to which they have become accustomed – that's to say, downwind from a megalopolis and four nuclear power plants, downstream from the world's biggest toilet, clinging to their last remaining habitat on earth with nothing to eat any more but – *coming about!*'

I covered my glass, ducked, and changed sides.

'This is amazing news,' I said. 'I mean, *Clark's Island*, for God's sake.'

'Please, Top. We don't like blasphemy aboard the *Claire*.'

'I'm sorry, but really. It's just such a beautiful place. There's that dock, and the forest, and the beach. I mean, the *beach*.'

'Fond memories, I suppose?'

'Well, of course, you know everything.'

I used to sail out to Clark's Island in Claire's tiny Bering dinghy, loaded down with girls and cheap wine.

'Why don't you tell me about it,' said Uncle Ian.

'I'm sure you can visualize the scene.'

'Indulge me.'

'OK, well. It was just so exciting to sail for a couple of hours, at night, having to make conversation. It was almost chivalrous, the way we had to talk all the way out there. And then that little beach, in the moonlight or what have you.'

'Or what have you.'

'All right. I sailed out there with a few girls. We used to drink wine in the moonlight, et cetera.'

'You dog. You were probably thirteen years old.'

'Well.'

'When I was that age—'

'You were walking five miles through waist-high snow to school.'

'Exactly. Tell me more.'

'It was exciting. I used to make up stories about how *I* owned Clark's Island, now that you mention it. The most thrilling thing, as I recall, was how the girls, by the time we'd talked and sailed all the way out there, would be just beside themselves with lust. If I may say so.'

'You may.'

'I guess since you're supposedly divorced again now, Dad, I can ask if you ever sailed a girl out to Clark's Island.'

'*Did* I.'

'I figured.'

'But let's not talk about that now, son. It was so long ago. We're having a great day, don't you think?'

'I think we are.'

91

We were having a great day. I liked being out on the water. Uncle Ian might have been crazy, but it was worth humouring him to get a slice of his expensive fantasy. I expected there to be plenty more to come before he revealed his true intentions. I wouldn't have put it past him to have a submarine waiting for him out at Clark's Island, so that he could descend into oblivion for a suitably tantalizing period of time. He looked so happy and sure of himself. I wasn't used to talking to men who were even older than my father, and Uncle Ian surprised me with his lucidity and good spirits.

He dropped sails and skilfully powered the boat to a stop alongside the Clark's Island dock, which was only just long enough to accommodate the *Claire*.

'Be a good boy and give me a hand ashore.'

I helped my uncle on to the dock by his elbow. He moved stiffly, while still managing to walk with the bearing of a man twenty years younger. He'd had quite a lot to drink already, but it didn't show.

'I'm going to take you on a brief tour. I'd very much like your approval of this project.'

We walked up a path that was new since my last visit, about a decade before. It had been neatly cut and paved with gravel, and log steps had been implanted across the gentle slope every few yards.

'If you see one of those silly little birds, don't make any loud noises,' he said, leading the way. 'They look like big mosquitoes with white wings and fanned tails. Better off extinct, but don't tell the ornithologists I said so. I've never been interested in skinny birds.'

Clark's Island was basically a single dome-shaped hill. On one side was the famous miniature beach, and on the other a tiny area of marshland where the protected birds clung to existence. The path took us to the top of the hill.

'This is what I wanted to show you,' said Uncle Ian, as we reached a man-made clearing near the summit.

There was work in progress. It was not a house, nor a cottage, but a monument. A narrow swathe of trees and undergrowth had been cleared from the hillside, leading in a straight line down to the water, facing the hills of Gawpassat.

'They've been taking their sweet time,' said Uncle Ian. 'I wanted it finished today. Still, it has been hot.'

Uncle Ian's workmen had levelled a patch of ground and erected a plinth. They had begun planting hedges and small trees along the sides of the cleared corridor. We walked around to the front of the monument, which was engraved with Uncle Ian's date of birth, and the Date. It was then that I noticed the statue, leaning against a portable toilet at the edge of the clearing. It was unmistakably an iron, life-sized statue of Ian Armstrong in heroic pose, right arm raised, index finger pointing into the distance.

The unspeakable tastelessness of the monument gave it a

kind of grandeur, when I tried to imagine the finished result. Uncle Ian's straight right arm and index finger would point directly at Black Hill. A grassy park and rose garden would surround the plinth. The path from the dock and the corridor down to the water had been built for the convenience of visiting pilgrims. What a scene it would be: those same brightly dressed people we had just seen crowding downtown Gawpassat, surrounding the monument, taking photographs, holding hands to pray, remembering for years and years the Founder of the Word who had made his name and his life *right over there* in the Black Hill mansion.

'I'm so impressed,' I said.

'That's good. I'm glad to hear it.' Uncle Ian puffed out his chest, taking a deep breath. 'Here,' he said. 'Help me up, will you?'

'I beg your pardon?'

'Come on, give me a boost, boy.'

We went over to the monument, and I hoisted Uncle Ian up on to the plinth like a jockey on to a horse. He rose slowly to his feet, and adopted the pose of his likeness over by the toilet. He raised his arm and pointed across the water at his house.

'I wrap myself in my virtue,' he said, sonorously. 'Did you hear me?'

'I heard you.'

'I heard you *what*?'

'I heard you, Dad?'

'Wonderful. And don't you forget what I said. Do you know, if you'd thought to bring a camera you could have made half a million dollars with a picture of me standing here like this?'

'Do you think so?'

'I *know* so. I'm getting huge in Britain, where they pay for that sort of thing.'

'I didn't know you were huge in Britain.'

'Novelty value, I'm afraid. Look-at-the-silly-American. Still, it's publicity.'

I was so relieved to hear Uncle Ian remark on the lighter side of the Date. Not that I'd ever really been worried, but now I was absolutely certain he wasn't going to do anything foolish.

'Now look,' he said. 'If you don't mind, I'd like to spend a couple of minutes here alone. You run on down to the boat and see if there isn't a plate or two of grub in the galley. Run along, now. I'll be able to get down from here just fine.'

92

While Uncle Ian privately wrapped himself in his virtue, I walked down to the beach and thought about specific examples from my past of love-making with teenaged girls. Sniffing wistfully, I returned to the *Claire* and located our lunch. I set what was another routine feast on a folding table in the sunshine, then sat down on the deck to eat a pickle and look back at the beach to remember more clearly.

I was incapable of pure nostalgia. I looked back dismissively, impatiently, like someone trying to shake a wasp from his sleeve. I was an unsympathetic character, I knew that; I got what I deserved. There were all sorts of decisions I could have made that would have insulated me from comparisons to people like Little Dave Periman. Still, spoilt rich kids have their own kinds of deprivation. Having a god for an uncle wasn't necessarily a help, and I didn't know if I appreciated this charade about being given one more chance to make something of myself. There he was on the hill, impersonating his own monument, taking everyone for a ride as usual, including me. I began to think that part of Uncle Ian's ploy was to make me feel as wretched as possible about my pitiful lack of accomplishment. When *he* was my age, etc., etc. It was pretty easy for an old guy like Uncle Ian to have lived an exceptional life, then to rub my face in it just because I was his closest male relative. He was capable of that sort of thing, he really was. He was capable of going to great lengths to make me feel awful.

It took several minutes for me to snap out of this self-centred train of thought. I ate another pickle, and wondered what was keeping Uncle Ian. I opened two bottles of wine. How long could he stand there in his conquering-emperor pose? Was he stranded on the plinth? Locked in the portable toilet? Or, I suddenly thought – because the mystery of the Word was so infectious, and Uncle Ian so enigmatic – had he actually killed himself in that grandiose position on the hill? I laughed off this thought and waited for five minutes more, sipping from a bottle of twenty-year-old burgundy that was probably reserved for special occasions even in Uncle Ian's cellar. I took another sip, and reminded myself that I ought to spend more money on good wine. Where was Uncle Ian?

'*Dad*?' I called out, for Clark's Island was small enough for my voice to carry to the top of the hill. '*Dad*?'

There was no answer. I took another sip from the bottle of delicious wine, then poured myself a glass. I ate a slice of exotic sausage, after dipping it in a pot of hot mustard. I would have heard Uncle Ian if he had called out to me. There was little in the way of noise except for the rustling of reeds, the lapping of water, and what my father used to call 'the agonized shrieks of crabs.'

My father had always had a strange way of expressing himself. If it wasn't the agonized shrieks of crabs, or the twining in brute passion, or the airy indifference shown by matadors to charging bulls, it was some other hyperbolic construction. Thanks to my father's influence, my sisters and I used to be known around Gawpassat as the 'Vocabs'. My father embarrassed us all one day at a high school baseball game, when he rose from his seat in the bleachers and pronounced the umpire's call 'an *abomination*!' Children can spend years living down that sort of thing.

'*Dad*?' I called out again. '*Dad*?'

I tried to remain calm. I removed my tie and finished my glass of wine. I worried that some of the food would go bad in the sun. A few more minutes passed, and my heart began to beat faster. I climbed on to the dock and stood on tip-toe to see if I could get a glimpse of Uncle Ian and his monument. I recalled what he had said about murder. Was I supposed to murder my uncle? I decided that if God caused me to pull a weapon I didn't know I had and blow away the Great Man, I would become a believer in the Word.

I had just made up my mind to climb the hill and take a look for him, when Uncle Ian strode out of the woods on the new gravel path. He had discarded his jacket and shoes.

'Sorry to keep you waiting, son. I guess I was feeling a tad solemn, for a moment there. It's very hard to say goodbye.'

'Of course it is.'

'Ah, wonderful,' he said, noticing the spread of food aboard the *Claire*. 'Just exactly what I asked for. I hope I have expressed to my people how much I appreciate their work.'

Apparently I had been casually snacking on Uncle Ian's specially ordered last meal.

The seas were calm enough for us to sail along and eat in comfort at the same time. In the spirit of the occasion, I emulated my uncle by drinking his precious wine with unseemly abandon. We didn't say much to each other while we ate and drank, which gave me time to reflect on the peculiar strength of family ties. I sat there aboard the *Claire* – on the Date with the Great Man – for the same reason most fathers willingly handed over whatever assets they managed to accumulate during their lifetimes to their beastly, ungrateful children. There were dozens of people who had given their careers to serving Uncle Ian and the Word, while I had ignored them both; and yet, who was it who shared Uncle Ian's putative Last Meal? It was I, the closest male relative, that's who, even though we were probably not blood relations and he hadn't been married to my Aunt Charlotte for a quarter of a century. I thought he had probably been driven to inventing his paternity partly to lend some coherence to posterity. He was obviously fond of me, and I assumed that meant he would live out his decline with peace of mind, and that I would end up running one of the more important departments of the Institute. I wondered if I would want to take on the job, whatever it was, and if Laurie could be persuaded to live in Gawpassat with a beneficiary of nepotism.

I would make demands, of course. I would want to live in the house where my father grew up – the museum of the Word could be moved out to Clark's Island next to the monument, if necessary. I would want Noel to be my chauffeur. I would want the words 'Attorney at Law' printed on my business cards. I would want unrestricted use of the *Claire*. I would demand that no mention ever be made of Uncle Ian's paternal fantasy – my father's feelings were to be spared at all costs. I would demand a sinecure for Jean in the Department of Substance Abuse, which might indirectly do her some good.

'What are you smiling about?' my uncle asked me.

'Was I smiling? Yes, I suppose I was. I'm happy to see you. We shouldn't have been out of touch for so long. Life is so busy these days, as well as being short.'

'You're so right. I've been busy all my life, it seems to me. If you want things to be done right, you have to do them yourself. I've probably been a monster to work for. Especially these last few years, with the big project on the boil. I don't suppose you'd like to be the first to hear about the contents of *The Last Word*? Fetch me that leather case in the galley. It ought to be in one of the cabinets along the floor.'

I went below and found the case, which reminded me of some of the more ostentatious briefcases carried by my colleagues during my five weeks of honest employ. It was fat enough to carry a severed head. When I came up on deck I saw that Uncle Ian had refilled our glasses. I cleared away our plates and other dishes, and put the case on the table. I was beginning to feel quite drunk, and by my count we still had six bottles of wine on board.

'This, my boy,' said Uncle Ian, clicking open the case to reveal at least two reams of closely typed manuscript, 'is *The Last Word*.'

93

For the next two hours or more, Uncle Ian drank wine and delivered a monologue about his philosophical, scientific, spiritual and economic discoveries. They were discoveries, not theories: they were presented as truths. He flicked through his massive manuscript as he spoke, and more than once I had to lunge out to catch a priceless page or two before they could be carried overboard by the breeze.

He was particularly excited about his revolutionary view of human evolution, to the basics of which the Word had always subscribed. 'It's so *obvious*,' Uncle Ian kept saying, as he drove home points about Darwinian principles of natural selection being 'hare-brained' and 'shallow'. 'Everyone will agree on this in ten to twenty years,' he asserted. 'All species evolve through *will*. It's so *obvious*. People can change themselves through will and desire and frustration, and those minute changes are transferred to and imprinted on their genes, then passed on. It's so *obvious*. Evolution occurs much more quickly than anyone ever dreamt. It's an *engine*, not an *accident*. Everyone will know this and believe this in ten or twenty years' time. All the scientific stuff is here.' He jabbed at a section of the manuscript. 'The human race's days are numbered,' he said cheerfully. 'I have recorded a Date for it, here.' He pointed out a precise date on one of the pages. I wasn't going to live that long, so I shrugged. 'I've had to hold back on the *causes* of our extinction, I cannot be definite on that one. Anyway, anyway . . . *women*. Women come in for some high praise . . . '

He went on this way, almost breathlessly, as we sailed in a random direction out to sea. His *Last Word* covered a range of topics from the grand (the age, size and future of the universe), to the mundane (real-estate investment, pension plans, handy savings hints). It went without saying that weight loss and firm buttocks would result from close reading of *The Last Word*. His writing style had been compressed beyond even the epigrammatic structure of his previous works, so that whole chapters had been reduced to a couple of sentences, or sometimes a single word: 'Victim', read Chapter Ten. Politics were dismissed as too mundane for the Wordian to worry about. Constant striving for self-improvement was taken for granted as a good thing. The making of lists was recommended above prayer and meditation as a route to worldly salvation. Each extra minute a person was engaged in physical exercise was time well spent. Women were told that it was a good idea to be in the third trimester of pregnancy before contemplating marriage. It was urged that the income of professional actors and actresses be regulated by the federal government.

Evidently Uncle Ian believed he had reached such an exalted level of spiritual credibility that no claims of divine dictation were necessary to compile and publish his catalogue of advice and revelation. I thought it looked like a big seller: compendious and encyclopedic at the same time, open-minded on all popular aspects of the paranormal, sprinkled with optimistic truisms, damning of perverts and slobs. Seven years had passed since the publication of *The Sixth Word* – seven years of expansion into other media and other countries – and the new book looked to me like the kind of summing-up that would provide his believers with a satisfying cohesion. When I said as much to my uncle, he punched me on the shoulder and smiled proudly. He filled our glasses to toast his masterpiece. I tossed back the wine, despite feeling woozy from hours of drinking. I tried to resist the next glass, but Uncle Ian forced it upon me. He was an old-school drinker, and it would have struck him as unmanly if I had refused.

'This will show them,' he said. 'By God it will.' He had worked himself up into a bit of a lather during his two-hour exegesis. He laughed madly as he locked the manuscript back in its case. 'By God it will.'

'What a lot of work you've done.'

Uncle Ian stood up in the stern of the *Claire*, arms akimbo, looking back at the dim coastline where distant Clark's Island and the hills of Gawpassat were only just visible through the haze. Gawpassat was now at least a four-hour sail away, and I wondered where we were headed. Even if we turned back immediately, we would not reach home until after sundown. Before lunch Uncle Ian had fixed the tiller, and had touched it only twice or three times since then to make small but apparently random adjustments to our course. The seas were slightly rougher now, which I thought might explain the onset of my mild nausea – that and the two bottles of wine I had drunk since the early-morning Bloody Mary and noon-time Armagnac. I stood up next to Uncle Ian and breathed deeply through my nostrils. My legs felt unsteady.

'My boy, I do believe this is the finest day I've spent in years. The simple pleasures, you know what I mean? Good food and drink, the wide-open sea, catching up with family. Don't you agree?'

'I certainly do.'

'Why, somehow it almost seems to make the whole thing worthwhile.'

'What whole thing?'

'The whole life and living thing.'

'Ah. I thought you'd made sense of that in your books.'

'Better than anyone, my boy. Better than anyone even *knows*, probably.' Uncle Ian did sound a bit drunk now. 'I don't have that arrogance of the young man any more, though. I mean to say, when I was your age I just powered on regardless, and maybe that's where the truth comes from. I couldn't write *The First Word* today. What was called for was a conclusion, and that takes the vision of a man who has lived, who has thought, who has contemplated the world. Con-tem-*plated* the world.'

'Right.'

'Thirty-five years now, all those years I've lived on this body of water,' he continued. Even Uncle Ian couldn't avoid the Gawpassatan landlubber's habit of talking about the sea as if he had risen at dawn every day to repair nets, taken to stormy seas, brought in a commercial catch. 'Thirty-five years,' he said. 'I don't believe there can be a more satisfied man than your old Dad. Except for those *rodents*, the reporters and whatnot. They make you, then they make you miserable.'

'I'm sure that's true.'

Now Uncle Ian reached out and took my hand. This was unbearably embarrassing. Men did not hold hands in Gawpassat – especially not fathers and sons. His hand felt dry and bony. We stood that way for what seemed like ten minutes, until Uncle Ian gave my hand a final squeeze and announced that it was time for a scotch and soda. I went below to collect the ingredients, feeling quite dizzy and weak. When I returned, Uncle Ian had taken his shirt off and reclined on the deck in the waning sunshine. I poured him a strong drink, and a weak one for myself. I put his drink on the deck next to him, and sat down in the shade of the mainsail. I thought Uncle Ian was asleep, until he reached out, without opening his eyes, and closed his hand on his glass. He raised his head just enough to be able to take a sip.

I began to feel worse, and wondered if I would be able to vomit over the side without my uncle's noticing. I tried to keep my eyes open. Someone had to make sure we didn't run into anything. There were two fishing boats well out to starboard, and half-a-dozen sailboats towards shore. I was surprised, given the sendoff we had received, that helicopters hadn't followed us out to sea. Uncle Ian seemed to have a way with privacy.

'Top?' he said. 'Are you awake?'

'Yes. I'm drowsy, though. It's been a long day.'

'Go to sleep. Don't worry about the *Claire*. She knows where she's going.'

'That wouldn't be a good idea.'

'I'll take care of everything, son. Go to sleep.'

'Maybe for just a few minutes. You'll wake me in half an hour?'

'Of course I will.'

'Thanks. I'm comfortable here.'

'Go below, if you like.'

'No, no. I like the fresh air. I guess I haven't quite got my sea legs.'

'As you wish. And as a special treat, I'll tell you a story.'

'Thanks.'

'Once upon a time,' said Uncle Ian, 'there was a little boy who lived in rural Virginia. His parents were unwell from the very first he could remember. He grew up fast, taking care of his parents and his sister, living in poverty, chopping wood for the stove that heated their cabin and cooked their meagre food. The little boy had no entertainment but the family Bible and the joys of learning. From his earliest days, he craved knowledge. Top? Are you awake, son?'

I could still hear him, but I could not reply. I heard my glass fall from my hand to the deck, unbroken.

'Top?'

I couldn't even mumble, or move my lips.

'I'll tell you the story some other time,' he said, and I was fast asleep.

94

I awoke slowly, painfully, from what were obviously the combined effects of drugs and alcohol; it felt like climbing a slippery vine, hand over hand. My eyelids were so heavy I was fully awake before I could open them. I was lying down, and I felt a blanket covering my body. My mouth was so dry that my tongue was stuck to the roof of my mouth. I pushed off the blanket and tried to prop myself up on my elbows. I was in total darkness, and when I reached up I felt the roof of the cabin and the narrow join of the bow. I was in the forwardmost berth of the *Claire*, and I could feel the movement of the boat on the water and hear the creaks of her rigging.

I managed to open my eyes, not that it made any difference. I crawled about trying to find the door, so disorientated that only the shape of the cabin told me which direction was aft. I located the latch, and let myself into the next cabin. I crawled through there to the next door, which led to the galley. I groped my way to the stairs, and climbed into the night. It was cold and damp; the stars and moon were obscured by clouds.

'Uncle Ian?' I said, into the darkness, forgetting that he was supposed to be my father for the day. Thanks to the aura of lights surrounding our big city, I could make out a black silhouette of coastline dead ahead: we had been turned around. 'Uncle Ian?'

It was just so dark. I thought I must have crawled past him in the master cabin. I went below in search of a flashlight. I found a box of matches on the gas stove. I struck one of the matches, which gave off enough light that I was able to scrounge around in the cupboards. I found a candle, which I lit with the match, then an antique lamp that I lit with the candle. I went back through the sleeping quarters, but Uncle Ian wasn't there. Back up to the deck I went, barking my shins and hitting my head.

'Uncle Ian? Dad?'

I still felt unsteady on my feet, so I had to move slowly about the deck of the *Claire*. The seas were heavier than they had been all day, and we were still so far out I feared that we might have sailed into shipping lanes. Like so many people, I had a long-standing horror of being sucked into the screws of a supertanker. When I had made sure that Uncle Ian was nowhere on deck, I went aft and steered the *Claire* towards what seemed the nearest point of shoreline. I searched below again, and saw by the clock above the map table that it was four o'clock in the morning. I tried to turn on the two-way radio, but it had been sabotaged. In any case I was no expert, and I doubted that I could have operated it even if I had been able to turn it on. I went back up to man the tiller and think.

'Uncle Ian? Dad?'

I looked up at the mast, as if he might have shinnied up there to get a better look at the upcoming sunrise. I checked all the lines, thinking he might have tried to emulate my sister's demise and was even then being towed behind. In doing so, I noticed that the wooden locker in the bow that normally housed the anchor was open and empty. Its chain was also gone, whereas I was almost certain that I had noticed it threaded through the hawsehole earlier in the day. I went below to try to repair the radio, fiddled with it and felt ill. The suicidal Swede who had expended so much effort in customizing his beloved *Cerise* had made her almost impossible to figure out in the dark. I resolved to practise lowering the sails once daylight came, so that I wouldn't crash into the dock in Gawpassat harbour. All sailors have their pride, even in tragic emergencies.

95

At sunrise, the *Claire* was emptier than ever. I was so accustomed to getting places quickly that it frustrated me to rock gently over the swells in near silence, the coastline growing appreciably nearer only every hour or so. I brewed coffee. I looked out for other boats to signal. I looked for flares, and found *The Last Word* still locked safely in its leather case. The detritus of our lunch was gone, glasses, bottles, platters and all. When I could make out where I was most likely to make landfall, I steered in the direction of Gawpassat – it would cost me only an extra twenty minutes, and I had a feeling there might be a few interested parties waiting for us at the Yacht Club. I practised lowering and raising the sails and turning on the engine.

I remembered that other time aboard the *Claire*, just before I sailed her on to the sandbar, when Uncle Ian had tried to explain his theory of making money. His point seemed to have been that in order to sell a product like the Word to the masses, the author himself could not be expected to believe. It was looking increasingly likely to me that Uncle Ian had believed, but I reminded myself that he worked in mysterious ways. Any number of solutions presented themselves as I neared the mouth of the harbour. I had been unconscious for nearly twelve hours. My uncle could have been plucked from the yacht by sea or by air without my knowing.

Down came the sails, on came the engine. I entered the mouth of the harbour, standing up, searching the sea wall. Most of the cars had gone, but not all. A few faces poked over the wall, and seconds after I entered the channel there were dozens more. Despite my long journey, I had not had time to focus on my predicament. I didn't know what to say. I couldn't decide if I ought to behave like a grief-stricken victim of an accident at sea, or the heir to a claptrap religion who had come home with the goods. On the spur of the moment, I opted for the latter.

Standing proudly in the stern, waving to the bleary faces of my followers, I guided the *Claire* neatly to her mooring. The same man who had helped us aboard twenty-four hours previously was there to fasten my lines to the dock. I went below to retrieve the case containing *The Last Word*, then marched along the dock to where a sizeable crowd had gathered. My photograph was taken hundreds of times as I waved off questions and autograph seekers. Francesco was there with the big limousine.

'Black Hill,' I said, sliding into the back seat and reaching for the telephone. I called the police and asked them to meet me at my uncle's mansion in five minutes, adding that they ought to put into effect whatever measures they normally resorted to when someone went missing at sea.

On the seat next to me was that day's edition of the *Gawpassat Gazette*. The front page naturally carried a headline pertaining to the Date, and a half-page photograph of me and my uncle aboard the *Claire*, leaving the harbour. Sure enough, the anchor chain was clearly visible, right where it was supposed to be. The beautiful lines of the *Claire* ploughed the water beneath us as we waved up at the crowd and the photographer.

The Black Hill mansion was busier than I had ever seen it: painters on ladders worked at the trim; Benjamin led two men and two women in what appeared to be the most thorough possible cleaning, carrying furniture, bed linen, towels, dishes, curtains – anything that could be removed – out to a pavilion that had been erected on the main lawn; two vans bearing the markings of an industrial cleaning company were parked in the drive near the front door. I asked the wide-eyed Francesco to tell the police to meet me down at the pool house as soon as they arrived.

239

I just had time to pour myself a cup of coffee and eat a small portion of fruit salad from the perpetually stocked buffet table before Gawpassat's finest appeared. I knew them both: Steve, my age and intellectually sub-normal; and Walter, his brother-in-law, our Chief. Steve was a friendly man who lived for shore patrol. Walter actually thought he was a real policeman. I handed each a cup of coffee and did my best to relax them. Anyone would have been daunted by their first visit to the Black Hill house.

I had been arrested by Walter several times in my life – arrested in the sense of stopped, but never further inconvenienced. In a town like Gawpassat, the police are servants of the community. It would be above their station to detain a prominent resident unless he had committed a crime against another Gawpassatan. Driving and drug offences were swept under the carpet. Still, I had never been treated with such solicitousness by a member of the authorities as I was on that day following Uncle Ian's disappearance. Steve was speechless with nerves, and Walter, usually quick on the draw with his notebook, repeatedly apologized to me and asked if there were anything he could do, right away, to make me a happier young man. Steve trembled and Walter grovelled, so much so that I began to realize that, at least in their paranoid eyes, I owned the police force.

'This must be a terrible, terrible shock,' said Walter.

'Please, have a seat. Yes. A shock.'

'You were very close to your uncle, weren't you, sir.' Walter called me 'sir'. The last words he had spoken to me, many years before, were more along the lines of 'Don't let it happen again, Matt.'

'Yes, very close.'

'And you were . . . chosen,' said Walter.

I adopted a semi-divine cast of expression, and did not answer. Walter began, haltingly, to interrogate me. He seemed to understand the basics of this, the greatest investigation of his career: Uncle Ian and I had sailed out of the harbour together, yet only one of us had returned; one of us was therefore missing, and, because of my presence before his very eyes, that missing person was Uncle Ian. It was clear to me from Walter's first few awkward, stuttering, primitive questions that his personal view was that Uncle Ian had ascended to Heaven. When he asked me if I had 'seen anything unusual', I knew he meant not blood, not footprints, not threads of clothing stuck to the *Claire*'s rigging; but waterspouts, particularly powerful rays of sunlight, sudden thunderclaps, or a deafening chorus of angels. When I told him a reasonably accurate version of the truth – leaving out my uncle's fatherhood fantasy, omitting my symptoms of having been drugged, forgetting to mention the missing anchor – Walter put a fist to his chest and sighed, as if I had revealed to him that a hand the size of an aircraft-carrier had pierced the clouds and plucked Uncle Ian from the deck between its thumb and index finger. Steve looked faint.

When I suggested that my Uncle might have taken his own life, Walter begged my pardon and said that was most unlikely and out of character. Even when I agreed, he interrupted and said that with all due respect he wasn't convinced, as a policeman and an avid follower of the Word, that the Great Man wouldn't make a reappearance in – oh, three days' time or so. I asked where in the Word it said that the first prophet would be resurrected *à la* Christ; Walter pointed out that the Word didn't say he *wouldn't* be resurrected, and that what he expected was a visitation on our television screens. He, for one, would be watching.

The interrogation, which was actually more of an argument about official doctrine once the simple facts had been established, was interrupted by the soft, clearing-of-throat entrance of Benjamin.

'I wonder, sir,' he said to me, without asking the whereabouts of his absent boss, 'if you would like to see your morning mail.'

'Mail, Benjamin? Yes, I suppose I would.'

'Bring it along, Karen,' he said over his shoulder, and a woman appeared pushing a cart in front of her – a cart brimming with envelopes and telegrams and facsimile transmissions

241

and telephone messages. 'Those from Heads of State are on top.'

'Fine, leave it here,' I said. Benjamin and Karen vanished.

'I think we have all we need,' said Walter, using his eyes to tell Steve to stand up. 'We'll be on our way. And best of luck to you.'

I stood up and returned their Word Signs. When they had gone, I practised being the Great Man. 'Aspirin,' I said in a normal voice, into the air. Twenty seconds later, Benjamin reappeared with two pills and a glass of water.

96

Jean was the first to answer the telephone at my parents' house, when I could finally get through. She was furious with me. She demanded to know what I had done with our uncle. She explicitly accused me of having plotted the whole gimmick with Uncle Ian, dating as far back as college and Everest. She asked if I had seen myself on television, alighting on the Gawpassat Yacht Club dock like some sort of drug baron under indictment. I asked to speak to my parents, but she wasn't done with me yet. She wanted to know when Uncle Ian was coming back. She called me a rat, five times, for not having let her in on the plan. She said I had a lot of nerve, showing up after all that time just to muscle in on the family concern. She implied that I must have drugged, hypnotized or blackmailed our uncle into choosing me to accompany him on his last sail. Her voice filled with sarcasm as she described her version of what must have gone on aboard the *Claire*, grown men giggling together about the wool they were going to pull over people's eyes, the games they were going to play with innocent Gawpassatan bystanders and *sisters*, so that old *Top* became *Heir*, abandoning all those who had supported him and wished him well and worried about him and . . .

'Jean?'

'*What.*'

'Could I speak to one of our parents, please?'

'Sure. *Ingrate.*'

She banged down the telephone, and her hysteria was replaced by the almost worryingly calm tones of my father.

'How are you?' he said, which was the only way he would ever begin a telephone conversation, even under the most unusual circumstances.

'I'm fine, Dad,' I said, which was the only way I would ever reply.

'I understand there has been something of a kerfuffle, downtown.'

'You could say that.'

'You're unhurt, I trust?'

'Absolutely.'

'I'm so relieved.'

'Yes. Well, you know. Uncle Ian has disappeared. You knew that?'

'I had heard, yes. Most odd.'

'Yes.'

'Will he turn up, do you think?'

'I doubt it very much.'

'Then this would be a tragedy, then?'

'I think so, yes. I think he killed himself.'

'I'm sorry you had to be involved. Ghastly.'

'I didn't see or hear a thing, Dad. I really didn't. One minute he was there, twelve hours later he was gone. I'll explain it all to you.'

'No need. You've alerted the authorities?'

'Yes, Dad. Don't worry.'

'There seems to be an unusually large number of people downtown. I was just the slightest bit curious myself, to tell you the truth, so I took a stroll this morning.'

'You were there? You saw?'

'I melded with the crowd.'

'You certainly did. I was dazed, though. I wasn't looking at anyone.'

'Will you be coming home, later today? You must have a

great deal to think about. I could ask your mother about dinner?'

'I'll be there, Dad.'

'Good, Top. I'm glad.'

I spoke to my mother, too. She sounded as composed as my father did, but had one exceptional thing to say. When I responded to her concern by saying that I felt strangely sanguine about the whole experience, she said, 'I hope Ian wasn't too *hard* on you.' It was just the sort of remark, said in just such a tone, that might have caused a sensitive or overly curious son to work it over in his mind for years to come, and let it bother him. I ignored it.

Melissa wanted a word. She wanted to say that she had been moved by my return on the *Claire*. She had felt heartbroken and yet . . . and yet somehow rejuvenated at the same time. She wanted me to know that Reed and the kids sent their regards and, yes, their love – especially Matthew, who had been so impressed with me and grateful to have had a man-to-man chat at last. She also wanted to tell me that she herself had always known how deep my conviction had been. She thought I was very brave. Oh, and by the way, she added, Laurie had called twice. She had seen everything on the news, way over in London. The Date had apparently been reported there as the sad final act of a deluded and comical life. Aunt Charlotte and her spider zoo had been mentioned in passing. Anyway, Laurie really wanted to have a word with me, and sounded excited. I replied that I wasn't surprised, given what had happened, that my girlfriend ought to sound excited. Melissa signed off by saying that she didn't know what I meant by the word 'girlfriend', but that I could probably do a lot better than a divorcée obsessed with torture.

97

In one of those coincidences that are so useful to those of us fortunate enough to be religious leaders, Gawpassat's heat wave broke on the first morning after my solo return from Uncle Ian's disappearance: it started with violent heat-lightning, followed by ozone and thunderstorms, then clearing into brilliant blue skies and autumn temperatures. This was taken as a Sign, and a Good One.

It puzzled me that everyone – the police, my parents, my sisters, the journalists who tried to get through to me – took it for granted that I had inherited the Great Man's mantle. The gesture of returning alone from his disappearance seemed to have sufficed. I returned to Gray Hill that same afternoon, presenting to my family the new, friendly face of the Word. I spoke to Laurie, who for some reason was eager to drop her London interviews so that she could be by my side 'at this difficult time'. I had left behind a Black Hill mansion still being sterilized for my occupancy. A special broadcast of Uncle Ian's television programme seemed to confirm my new status. I kept the black briefcase always at my side, waiting for the right moment to spring its contents on a credulous world. The first night, alone in my old bedroom sitting under the photograph of Uncle Ian shaking hands with the astronaut, I opened the case and looked at the title page of the Great Man's *magnum opus*. '*The Seventh Word*', it read, simply enough; it was dated with the Date. As I fell asleep, I wondered if that meant *The Last Word* was mine.

What I do know is that those first three days were ones of speculation in the media – even in my own *Gawpassat Gazette*. A biography of the heir was cobbled together and broadcast around the world. That treatment made me sympathize for all time with politicians: it turned out that the Heir to the Word was supposed to have behaved in a saint-like way, and I hadn't. I came across as a womanizer and a scoundrel, and the purity of my political beliefs was called into question. Marcus, who frankly never could keep his mouth shut, called me 'driven but misdirected,' but, probably because he realized there was a possibility that I was now richer even than he, 'one hell of a climber and a good friend'. People whose names I had forgotten remembered special moments in my company. The

Institute released a prepared curriculum vitae that called me 'a scholar and a gentleman', while the new manager of Trainer's, whom I had never met, allowed that I was 'a moderate drinker, somewhat aloof, but very popular.' There was much conjecture about the reasons Uncle Ian might have bestowed the favour of his empire on me, and most commentators concluded, as Jean had, that I had been in league with the Great Man for more than a decade. That was the heathen press, of course; the mass media were still convinced that Uncle Ian would be resurrected or, at the very least, that some sort of Sign would make itself evident and lay to rest the mystery of his disappearance.

Laurie wanted me to send her money for her flight to my side. I told her to take her time, to see through her tortuous interviews, and to expect me to wire her appropriate funds in two or three weeks' time. I told her I had far too much on my plate to allow for an emotional reunion, just at the moment. I could hear in her voice the strain of having not to sound too eager. I decided to make a careful study of the effects of sudden wealth on people's affection for me; it could be useful for future Word policy statements. I had a business to run, after all. I went through the motions of asking my parents if they thought it would be appropriate if I moved into the Black Hill mansion, since everyone, especially Benjamin, seemed to expect it of me. Uncle Ian's various wills had to be examined, I told them, indicating the black leather briefcase I had considered handcuffing to my wrist, but in the meantime the continuity of the Word had to be preserved. Not only did they think this was a good idea – they bundled me out of their Gray Hill house the same way my law-firm supremo had practically carried me to the elevator when I told him I was engaged to a Hong Kong heiress. Jean drank Bloody Marys and sulked.

98

I slept in a guest room of Uncle Ian's mansion, a fact that was leaked by one of the staff and interpreted to mean that the Great Man would soon return to reclaim his rightful position as Head Prophet. Journalists crowded around the front gates, and I was afraid to leave the grounds. I was briefed on security. I announced that only my closest relatives and Dr Sohlman would have visiting privileges, but only Dr Sohlman took me up on the offer.

Dr Sohlman showed up to resign. He said he had done all he could for the Word, and produced a contract even I could see guaranteed him a most generous severance pay, as well as a pension that would see him safely retired in his beloved Sweden. He wished me luck as he departed, and said, 'Tangerines. If you want to put off the inevitable – which isn't all that bad, trust me, I know, I know – eat plenty of tangerines. And any other citrus fruit, if you want, actually. So long, Mr Richmond.'

My staff worked around me, cleaning, cleaning. I quickly became accustomed to having everything done for me, with the result that I felt compelled to act responsibly for the sake of the business and its remaining employees. It was a great thrill to make executive decisions; I had not known many challenges in my life, and I felt invigorated by the necessity of having to take the initiative for the Word. My first edict, once the lawyers and other authorities had taken a look at *The Seventh Word* and established that I had a stronger claim than anyone to Uncle Ian's enterprise, was to install and enshrine my sister Melissa, her husband Reed, and their however-many children as the First Family of the Word. They were photographed *en masse*, and a press release announced them as the embodiment of Uncle Ian's creed, the model family. Little Lizzie solemnly handed over her title as head foot-soldier of the Word to Sally, the next of Melissa's girls in line. I told Sally to go stand on the sea wall for three hours, wearing a parka.

Jean was not at all happy with her appointment as First Secretary of the Word. She wanted at least to be known as Chief of Staff, and wondered if a cash settlement was out of the question. I had to explain to her that it would probably take years before the estate was settled to everyone's satisfaction.

Already a sect forming that claimed to have seen Uncle Ian limping through the streets of our big, ugly city, muttering about betrayal. This sort of thing, I pointed out, could affect the prompt execution of Uncle Ian's wills.

I felt grown up. Plenty of Uncle Ian's clothes fitted me perfectly well, so that I might be seen strolling the Black Hill grounds in my chalk-yellow exiled-playwright-in-the-South-of-France outfit, deep in thought. I spent long hours in Uncle Ian's main study, pretending to edit the uneditable *Seventh Word*. I tried my hand at espionage in Uncle Ian's situation room. I gave orders at first diffidently, soon with cold command.

The search for Uncle Ian had been abandoned after forty-eight hours. After seventy-two hours, in the absence of resurrection, the conspiracy theorists went to work. For every zealot who believed Uncle Ian had been taken from us by God, there was one person who had either personally seen, or knew someone who had seen the Great Man in the flesh. These sightings usually had him staggering around like an insane homeless person, often practically naked, whispering secrets of the universe under his breath. I decided to release *The Seventh Word* posthaste.

The severity of Uncle Ian's financial difficulties didn't sink in for several weeks. I drank pots of coffee and pored over the books with Alan Prudhomme, Barbara Armstrong's keen young replacement. Barbara herself had sided with those who believed her brother was still alive, and had elected to continue her world tour uninterrupted. No-one knew where she was. It quickly became apparent that the years Uncle Ian had spent writing his *Seventh Word*, a twelve-hundred-page suicide note, had seen a distinct collapse of his organization's legendary financial robustness. Auntie Intellectual had cost far more than Uncle Ian had ever let on, and their divorce was by no means as final as Uncle Ian might have wished by the time the Date arrived. The purchase of Clark's Island, and Uncle Ian's undertaking to preserve the lifestyle of those skinny little birds, had cost us a fortune. A hefty chunk of money was simply *missing*, as must so often be the case when religious leaders disappear without trace; this fuelled the rage of the conspiracy theorists, and kept a stream of solemn tax inspectors appearing at my electronic gates.

The helicopter had to go. The Institute had to be leased for conventions. Jobs were sacrificed. The Gawpassat economy suffered, as the stores specializing in the needs of Word employees were forced out of business. All of this happened so quickly, in such a frenzy of lawyering, that I hardly had a chance to get a grip on power before I found myself shackled to a precarious enterprise.

I instituted a new policy of openness, which was a failure. People didn't want openness, they wanted mystery. Everything seemed to be slipping away, until I let it be known that there was a *telephone number* encrypted somewhere in *The Seventh Word*, and that the lucky believers who cracked the code might very well reach the Great Man on the other end. This gave us some breathing room.

It helped matters that so many of my followers thought I was a monster – which in a way I was, but not for the reasons they thought. Uncle Ian had warned me that there would be accusations of murder, but he had neglected to tell me that the circumstances of his disappearance would make people's suspicions *permanent*. All it would take to rekindle the public's interest in the Word would be yet another biography, yet another investigative probe, yet another feature film claiming to have solved the mystery. I could let them come to me.

Uncle Ian had said, 'You will have your Laurie,' and so it proved. So much so that we had an almost immediate falling out on the subject of her motives for suddenly pretending to love me, and I had to let her go. I may have been momentarily lonely in her absence, but I was also very busy.

99

There is no better way to come to love a law degree than by employing it to save one's own bacon. Every species of creditor

– especially bankers and representatives of the tax authorities – beat a path to the Black Hill house. When I first poked into Uncle Ian's shambolic books, I experienced a giddy sense of relief that I had never worked directly for the Great Man: I might easily have landed in prison. I was also glad to see that some of my problems were of such a gigantic magnitude that I would never again want for diverting, highly challenging labour.

The 'irregularities' that fell into my lap could be organized into three neat categories: 1) debt; 2) debt; 3) debt. The Word owed the tax man. The Word owed the local government for Clark's Island. The Word owed a muddled network of banks at home and abroad. The Word owed Agnes.

Uncle Ian had been a terrible businessman, but his sister Barbara had been worse. In her mid–sixties, she had become enamoured of a financial tool so patently risky that only just about everyone had used it to raise capital. The Word needed capital the way a stomach wound needed gauze. Uncle Ian went around buying things like islands and aircraft, and Barbara went around borrowing rotten money to pay for it all.

I might have been able to wrestle the Word back to a semblance of health in practically no time, if any of Uncle Ian's private bank accounts had contained any cash whatsoever. This state of affairs was referred to as the Black Hole, and remains to be explained. I became accustomed to a particular banker's expression that must be universal, for I saw it on the faces of at least four different nationalities. It occurs just as the banker presses a button on a computer keyboard, or removes a document from a file. It is an arched-eyebrowed, pursed-lipped, cheek-sucking look of shocked puzzlement and self-exculpation that says, '*How* could anyone have allowed this to happen?' The more closely connected to the débâcle a banker is, the more vividly he displays that look of innocent outrage.

Agnes turned out still to have been Uncle Ian's wife on the Date, that much was obvious. She had held him off, renegotiated and stonewalled for a period of nearly three years from the first time he had tried to initiate proceedings. As a wholly legitimate widow, she was a considerable burden. Her legal bills were sick-making. She had bought three houses abroad. She had compiled a crude blackmail dossier that easily counterbalanced Uncle Ian's sophisticated espionage.

In that first, terrible year, even the *Claire* had to go. I sold her to Little Dave Periman, thus ensuring that she would continue to live the most interesting of sailboats' lives. Dave said he might have her sailed to California, and if he ever does I wish her well.

What saved the business in the short term was the nature of the Word itself. Publicity being everything, Uncle Ian's disappearance dredged up a whole new wave of Word devotees. He had predicted his own death thirty-five years in advance, and that amazed people. I cannot stop the tide of new believers electrified by these events, any more than I can stop the tax man from pruning my uncle's empire to the quick. 'He's dead, he's dead,' I publicly insist (for otherwise I could not be Heir), but it only encourages the true believers.

I cannot go anywhere without being pestered by journalists, autograph seekers and disciples. I know exactly what my uncle meant when he complained about the 'rodents' burrowing under the fence. I will never be able to trust anyone.

100

Telling this story has been made possible by the recent death of my father: he would have understood, but he would have worried. I never believed for a moment that Uncle Ian was my real father, but I doubt that Dad would have enjoyed reading published speculation about his beloved wife.

For the record, my mother denies ever having had an affair with Uncle Ian, but the beauty of these things is that one can never truly know. She thinks my writing *The Last Word* is unseemly and despicable. I try to explain to her that it is my job, and in some ways honourable. I owe it to the business. I argue that the Word is a sham, bankrupt in every sense of the term, and yet people keep coming back for more. That is because people like to be teased and titillated, and they flock to success. That was Uncle Ian's great discovery and skill.

I have learned from the Great Man's example. I let cryptic hints leak out of Black Hill every now and then. I disappear for a week or two at a time and return tanned and serene. These small gestures result in speculation, which results in coverage, which results in subscriptions and sales. The Word is slowly coming back. It is so easy, when one has the power. I can even do it here, in *The Last Word*: There is a special telephone on the window-sill of my Black Hill office; if it ever rings, I am supposed to look out the window across Gawpassat Bay at Clark's Island and say, 'Yes Dad, it's still there.'